The Birth Of The Jersey Devil

The Birth Of The Jersey Devil

Reece Hensley

Doug Hensley

CONTENTS

The 13th Child
The Birth Of The Jersey Devil
By
Reece Hensley

Table Of Contents

Chapter 20: Peace Restored

2

Author's Notes

In the heart of New Jersey's Pine Barrens lies a village haunted by a curse born centuries ago. When John, the village leader, and his companions confront the legendary Nightbringer, they believe they've triumphed over darkness. But as shadows stir once more, they face a new, ancient evil—the Eternal Night. With the fate of their home hanging in the balance, they must summon every ounce of courage and light to face this ultimate threat. In a gripping tale of sacrifice, resilience, and the enduring battle between light and darkness, "The Final Darkness" explores the depths of fear and the boundless power of hope in the face of the unknown.

3

Chapter 1: The Unwanted Pregnancy Prologue

The Pine Barrens of New Jersey, 1735. A thick, unsettling fog rolled through the dense forest, cloaking the trees in an eerie shroud. Shadows danced ominously, playing tricks on the eyes of those brave—or foolish—enough to venture into its depths. Whispers of ancient curses and dark legends filled the air, seeping into the minds of the superstitious and the fearful. In the heart of this haunting landscape stood a modest cabin, home to the Leeds family. Little did they know, their lives were about to be forever changed by a night of unparalleled terror.

Section 1: The Leeds Family

The Leeds family was well-known in the Pine Barrens, not for their wealth or

4

status, but for their sheer size. Deborah Leeds, the matriarch, had borne twelve children. Life was hard in the Barrens, and each new child meant another mouth to feed, another body to clothe. John Leeds, Deborah's husband, was a hardworking man, but the endless toil of maintaining their small farm took its toll on his spirit and health.

Deborah was a woman of formidable strength, both physically and mentally. She managed the household with a firm hand, ensuring that her children were disciplined and well-behaved. Yet, as strong as she was, the prospect of another pregnancy weighed heavily on her. She often found herself staring out of the small window of their cabin, watching the shadows of the forest with a growing sense of dread.

Section 2: The Unwelcome News

It was a chilly evening in late autumn when Deborah first suspected she might

5

be pregnant again. She had been feeling unusually tired and nauseous, familiar signs that she had come to recognize all too well. As the realization dawned on her, a deep, bone-chilling fear gripped her heart. She couldn't bear the thought of another child, another burden.

That night, as she lay in bed beside her snoring husband, her mind raced with dark thoughts. She thought about the twelve children already under her care, the relentless work, the sleepless nights. She felt a surge of frustration and despair. In a moment of weakness, she muttered a curse under her breath, condemning the unborn child to a fate worse than death.

Section 3: The Curse

The curse she uttered was not one of mere words. It carried the weight of her anguish, her fear, and her resentment. "Let this child be the devil," she whispered, her voice trembling with a

6

mixture of rage and sorrow. She immediately regretted her words, but it was too late. The curse had been spoken, and the dark forces of the Pine Barrens had heard her plea.

The following days were a blur of dread and denial. Deborah tried to convince herself that the curse was just a momentary lapse, that it held no real power. But deep down, she knew the Barrens were a place of old magic and dark secrets. Whispers of strange creatures and malevolent spirits were woven into the fabric of the land.

Section 4: The Dark Forest

As her pregnancy progressed, Deborah found herself increasingly drawn to the forest. It was as if an invisible force was pulling her into the shadows of the Barrens. She would wander the woods, listening to the rustling leaves and the distant cries of unseen animals. The forest seemed to be alive, pulsating with

7

a sinister energy.

One evening, as the sun dipped below the horizon, Deborah ventured deeper into the woods than she had ever gone before. The trees grew thicker and more twisted, their branches clawing at the sky like skeletal fingers. She stumbled upon an old, abandoned cabin, hidden away in a small clearing. It was a place she had never seen before, a place that seemed to emanate an aura of malevolence.

As she approached the cabin, a sense of foreboding washed over her. The air grew colder, and she felt a chill run down her spine. She hesitated at the threshold, her heart pounding in her chest. Despite her fear, something compelled her to enter.

Section 5: The Witch's Warning

Inside the cabin, the air was thick with the scent of decay. Cobwebs hung from the ceiling, and the floor was covered in

8

dust and debris. In the center of the room stood a figure, cloaked in shadow. As Deborah's eyes adjusted to the dim light, she realized it was an old woman, her face lined with age and her eyes burning with an unnatural fire.

"I've been expecting you," the woman said in a voice that was both ancient and ageless. "You carry a heavy burden, child."

Deborah felt a wave of fear and awe wash over her. She tried to speak, but her voice caught in her throat.

"You have cursed your own flesh and blood," the woman continued, her eyes piercing into Deborah's soul. "The curse you uttered in your moment of weakness has awakened dark forces. The child you carry is marked."

Tears streamed down Deborah's face as the weight of her actions settled upon her. "What can I do?" she whispered, her voice trembling with desperation.

9

The old woman shook her head. "The curse cannot be undone. But there may be a way to protect yourself and your family. You must be strong, for the darkness will come for you."

Section 6: The Descent into Madness

The days and nights that followed were filled with a growing sense of dread. Deborah's pregnancy progressed rapidly, and with it, her fear and anxiety intensified. She began to have vivid nightmares, filled with images of a monstrous creature stalking the woods, its eyes glowing with malevolence.

Her health deteriorated, and she became increasingly isolated from her family. Her children noticed the change in her, but they were too young to understand the depth of her despair. John tried to comfort her, but his efforts were in vain. Deborah was haunted by the knowledge of the curse and the impending birth of her thirteenth child.

10

Section 7: The Storm

As the day of the birth approached, the weather took a turn for the worse. A violent storm swept through the Pine Barrens, lashing the trees with fierce winds and torrential rain. The sky was dark and foreboding, reflecting the turmoil within Deborah's soul.

On the night of the birth, the storm reached its peak. The wind howled like a pack of wolves, and thunder rumbled ominously in the distance. Inside the cabin, the atmosphere was tense and fearful. The midwives arrived, their faces pale and drawn as they prepared for the delivery.

Deborah's labor was long and difficult. She screamed in agony as the storm raged outside, the sound of her cries mingling with the roar of the wind. The midwives worked tirelessly, their hands trembling as they tried to help her through the birth.

11

Section 8: The Birth of the Beast

At last, the child was born. For a brief moment, there was silence. The midwives held their breath, hoping that the baby would be healthy and normal. But their hopes were dashed as the child let out a blood-curdling scream.

The baby, at first glance, appeared to be a normal newborn. But as the minutes passed, a horrifying transformation began. The baby's skin turned a sickly shade of gray, and its eyes glowed with an eerie red light. Wings sprouted from its back, and its fingers elongated into sharp claws. The midwives watched in horror as the child morphed into a monstrous creature, unlike anything they had ever seen.

The creature let out a screech that echoed through the cabin, causing the midwives to recoil in terror. It flapped its wings and flew up the chimney, disappearing into the stormy night. Deborah lay on the bed, exhausted and

12

horrified, her mind reeling from the sight of her transformed child.

Section 9: The Aftermath

The midwives fled the cabin, spreading the tale of the monstrous birth throughout the village. The news spread like wildfire, and soon the entire community was gripped by fear and superstition. The legend of the Jersey Devil was born, and the Pine Barrens were forever changed.

Deborah was left to grapple with the guilt and horror of what she had unleashed. She became a recluse, shunned by the villagers who feared her and the curse she had invoked. John tried to support her, but he too was haunted by the events of that night.

As the weeks passed, reports of strange sightings and eerie occurrences in the Pine Barrens began to surface. Livestock were found mutilated, and strange noises echoed through the woods at night. The

13

villagers lived in constant fear, always looking over their shoulders for the creature that had come to be known as the Jersey Devil.

Section 10: The First Sighting

One cold winter night, a group of hunters ventured into the Pine Barrens in search of game. They were experienced woodsmen, familiar with the dangers of the forest. But nothing could have prepared them for what they encountered.

As they trudged through the snow, they heard a strange, unearthly sound. It was a high-pitched screech, like the cry of a wounded animal, but unlike anything they had ever heard before. They exchanged uneasy glances and pressed on, their guns at the ready.

Suddenly, one of the hunters let out a shout of alarm. The others turned to see a dark figure swooping down from the trees. It moved with incredible speed, its

14

wings beating furiously as it approached. The hunters fired their guns, but the creature was too quick. It let out a terrifying screech and attacked, its claws tearing through their flesh.

The survivors fled in terror, leaving their fallen comrades behind. They ran through the forest, their hearts pounding with fear. When they finally reached the village, they were barely coherent, their minds shattered by the

Chapter 2: The Birth

Section 1: The Storm Approaches

The Pine Barrens were shrouded in an unnatural stillness as the storm approached. The air was thick and heavy, laden with the scent of damp earth and decaying leaves. The animals sensed the impending tempest, their calls falling silent, leaving an eerie quiet.

Inside the Leeds' cabin, Deborah lay in

15

bed, her body racked with pain as labor began. Her twelve children huddled together in a corner, their wide eyes reflecting the flickering light of the fireplace. John paced the room, his face etched with worry and fatigue. The midwives, summoned from the village, prepared for what they hoped would be a normal delivery, but an unspoken dread hung in the air.

Section 2: The Labor Begins

The first contraction hit Deborah like a wave of agony, doubling her over. She gritted her teeth, stifling a scream as she clutched the bed sheets. The midwives moved quickly, their hands steady but their eyes betraying their fear. They had heard the rumors, the whispers of a cursed child, but they pushed those thoughts aside, focusing on their task.

John knelt by Deborah's side, wiping the sweat from her brow. "You're strong, Deborah. You can do this," he

16

murmured, his voice breaking with emotion.

Deborah's eyes met his, filled with a mix of pain and terror. "John, I'm scared. Something's wrong. I can feel it."

John squeezed her hand, trying to mask his own fear. "It's just a difficult labor, that's all. The midwives will help you."

But deep down, he knew there was something unnatural about this birth. The storm outside seemed to mirror the turmoil within their home, growing in intensity as Deborah's labor progressed.

Section 3: The Cabin in Chaos

As the hours dragged on, the storm intensified. Lightning split the sky, followed by deafening cracks of thunder that rattled the cabin's walls. The wind howled like a banshee, and rain lashed against the windows in relentless sheets. Inside, the atmosphere was tense, fraught with fear and anticipation.

17

Deborah's screams grew louder, her pain almost unbearable. The midwives exchanged worried glances, their faces pale in the dim light. "It's taking too long," one of them whispered. "Something's not right."

The children huddled closer together, their small faces contorted with fear. The eldest, a boy of fourteen, tried to comfort his siblings, but his own fear was palpable. "It's going to be okay," he lied, his voice trembling. "Mama's strong. She'll be alright."

John felt helpless, torn between comforting his children and supporting his wife. He prayed silently, begging for strength and protection, but the storm outside seemed to mock his pleas, growing ever more violent.

Section 4: The Moment of Birth

At the height of the storm, a piercing scream filled the cabin, louder and more desperate than any before. Deborah

18

arched her back, her body convulsing as the baby finally began to emerge. The midwives moved swiftly, their hands slick with blood and sweat.

"One more push, Deborah!" one of them urged. "You're almost there!"

Deborah summoned every ounce of strength left in her, pushing with a primal roar. The baby slid into the midwife's waiting hands, and for a brief moment, there was silence. The midwives breathed a collective sigh of relief as they held the newborn, their initial fear giving way to hope.

But their relief was short-lived. **Section 5: The Transformation**

The baby's first cry was unlike any they had ever heard. It started as a normal wail but quickly morphed into a guttural, animalistic screech. The midwives recoiled in horror as the baby began to change before their eyes.

19

The infant's skin darkened to a sickly, mottled gray. Its eyes, once a normal newborn blue, glowed an unnatural red. Small, leathery wings sprouted from its back, and its fingers elongated into sharp, claw-like appendages. The transformation was swift and terrifying, leaving no doubt that this was no ordinary child.

Deborah, weak and exhausted, could only watch in horror as the midwives screamed and backed away from the creature. "No...no, it can't be!" she cried, her voice breaking. "What have I done?"

John stood frozen, his mind struggling to comprehend the nightmare unfolding before him. The creature let out another ear-piercing screech, flapping its wings furiously. The children screamed and huddled closer together, their terror palpable.

Section 6: The Creature Escapes

In a frenzy of motion, the creature flew

20

up the chimney, its claws scraping against the brick. The wind outside howled even louder, as if in response to the creature's escape. John rushed to the fireplace, but it was too late. The monstrous child was gone, lost to the stormy night.

The midwives fled the cabin, their faces ashen with terror. "We must warn the village!" one of them shouted as they disappeared into the darkness. "The devil is loose in the Pine Barrens!"

Deborah collapsed back onto the bed, her body trembling with shock and exhaustion. John wrapped his arms around her, his own heart pounding with fear. "We'll get through this, Deborah," he whispered, though his words felt hollow. "We have to."

Section 7: The Aftermath

The storm began to subside as dawn approached, leaving behind a landscape ravaged by its fury. Inside the cabin, the

21

atmosphere was one of stunned silence and disbelief. The children, exhausted from fear and lack of sleep, had finally dozed off in a huddled mass. Deborah lay in bed, her eyes staring blankly at the ceiling, her mind unable to process the events of the night.

John moved mechanically, cleaning up the remnants of the birth with a heavy heart. He avoided looking at the blood-stained sheets, trying to block out the memory of the creature that had emerged from his wife's womb. His hands trembled as he worked, the full weight of their predicament pressing down on him.

Outside, the Pine Barrens were eerily quiet, the storm having driven away any remaining wildlife. The trees stood like silent sentinels, their branches heavy with rain. The once comforting sounds of nature were replaced by an oppressive stillness, as if the forest itself was holding its breath.

22

Section 8: The Village Reacts

Word of the monstrous birth spread quickly through the village. The midwives, pale and shaken, recounted the horrifying details to anyone who would listen. Fear and superstition took hold of the villagers, who had always harbored a healthy respect for the dark and mysterious Pine Barrens.

The village elders convened an emergency meeting in the town square. People gathered, their faces etched with worry and fear. The atmosphere was tense, whispers of curses and dark magic filling the air.

"We must take action," one elder declared, his voice grave. "This creature cannot be allowed to roam free. It is an abomination, a sign that we have angered the spirits of the forest."

"But what can we do?" another villager

asked, his voice trembling. "We are just

simple folk. How can we fight a creature

23

born of dark magic?"

The elders exchanged uneasy glances. "We must consult the old woman," one of them finally said. "She knows the ways of the forest. Perhaps she can help us."

Section 9: The Old Woman's Guidance

The villagers reluctantly approached the old woman's hut, deep in the heart of the Pine Barrens. She was a reclusive figure, known for her knowledge of herbs and folklore, but also feared for her rumored connections to the supernatural.

The old woman greeted them with a knowing look, as if she had been expecting their visit. "So, the curse has come to pass," she said in a voice that seemed to echo with the weight of centuries. "The creature you speak of is the result of dark forces, awakened by a mother's curse."

24

The villagers listened in stunned silence as she recounted the tale of Deborah Leeds and the curse she had uttered. "There is little that can be done to reverse the curse," she continued. "But there may be a way to protect yourselves and perhaps even banish the creature from these woods."

She handed them a small, leather-bound book filled with ancient symbols and rituals. "This contains the knowledge you seek," she said. "But be warned, the path ahead is fraught with danger. The creature is powerful and will not be easily subdued."

Section 10: A Plan is Formed

Armed with the old woman's guidance, the villagers returned to the town square to formulate a plan. The book detailed a complex ritual that required rare herbs, precise incantations, and the cooperation of the entire village.

"We must prepare," the elder said.

25

"Gather the herbs, memorize the incantations. This is our only chance to rid the Pine Barrens of this curse."

The villagers set to work, each tasked with a specific role. Some ventured into the forest to gather the necessary herbs, while others practiced the incantations. The children were kept indoors, their parents' faces grim with determination and fear.

John and Deborah were asked to participate in the ritual, their presence deemed crucial to its success. Though weak and still in shock, Deborah agreed, driven by a desperate need to right the wrong she had unwittingly caused.

Section 11: The Ritual

As night fell, the villagers gathered in a clearing deep within the Pine Barrens. A large bonfire was lit, casting flickering shadows on the faces of those assembled. The air was thick with tension, the forest silent and watchful.

26

The elder began the ritual, his voice steady but laced with urgency. The villagers chanted the incantations in unison, their voices rising and falling like the wind. Deborah and John stood at the center, their hands clasped tightly together.

The old woman's book guided them through each step, the symbols and words glowing with an eerie light. The atmosphere grew charged with energy, the air crackling with unseen forces. As the ritual reached its climax, the creature appeared, drawn by the power of the incantations.

Section 12: The Creature's Return

The Jersey Devil descended upon the clearing with a ferocious screech, its eyes blazing with fury. The villagers recoiled in fear, but held their ground, their voices unwavering. The creature circled the bonfire, its wings casting monstrous shadows on the trees.

27

John and Deborah faced the creature, their fear overshadowed by a fierce determination. The elder directed them to recite the final incantation, their voices trembling but strong. The air vibrated with power as the words echoed through the clearing.

The creature let out a deafening roar, its body writhing in pain as the ritual took hold. It flapped its wings violently, trying to escape, but the power of the ritual held it in place. The villagers watched in awe and terror as the creature was slowly drawn into the circle of fire.

Section 13: The Final Confrontation

The creature fought against the ritual's power, its claws slashing at the air. The villagers continued to chant, their voices growing louder and more insistent. John and Deborah, their hands still clasped, felt a surge of energy coursing through them.

With one final, desperate effort, the

28

creature broke free from the circle, its wings beating furiously. It let out a spine-chilling screech and lunged at Deborah, its claws outstretched. John stepped in front of her, raising his arm to shield her.

The creature's claws raked across John's arm, drawing blood. He cried out in pain but stood firm, his eyes locked on the creature. "You will not take her!" he shouted, his voice filled with defiance.

The villagers, galvanized by John's bravery, intensified their chanting. The elder raised his arms, calling upon the old woman's guidance to strengthen the ritual. The air shimmered with a blinding light, and the creature was once again pulled towards the circle of fire.

Section 14: The Banishment

The creature's screams grew more desperate as the ritual reached its peak. The villagers' voices rose to a fever pitch, the incantations echoing through

29

the forest. The light around the creature intensified, enveloping it in a blinding glow.

With a final, ear-splitting screech, the creature was consumed by the light. The villagers watched in awe as it was slowly drawn into the fire, its form dissolving into ash. The light dimmed, and the forest fell silent once more.

The villagers collapsed to the ground, exhausted but victorious. The elder approached John and Deborah, his face etched with relief. "It is done," he said, his voice trembling. "The creature is banished."

Section 15: The Aftermath

The village slowly began to recover from the ordeal. The Pine Barrens, once a place of fear and darkness, began to heal. The old woman's guidance had proven true, and the villagers' bravery had driven the Jersey Devil from their midst.

30

Deborah and John returned to their cabin, their bond stronger than ever. The events of that night had left deep scars, but also a renewed sense of hope. They vowed to rebuild their lives, to cherish their children and the peace they had fought so hard to restore.

Section 16: A New Beginning

As the seasons changed, the Pine Barrens began to flourish once more. The village, though still wary of the dark forces that lurked in the forest, found a renewed sense of community and strength. The legend of the Jersey Devil became a cautionary tale, a reminder of the power of curses and the resilience of the human spirit.

John and Deborah welcomed their thirteenth child, a baby boy, into the world. Though their hearts were still heavy with the memory of the curse, they found solace in the love and strength of their family. The boy grew

31

up strong and healthy, a testament to their enduring spirit.

Section 17: The Legend Lives On

The story of the Jersey Devil continued to be told around campfires and in hushed whispers, a reminder of the darkness that had once threatened their lives. But it was also a story of bravery, of a community that had come together to face a terrifying foe and had emerged stronger for it.

The old woman remained a guardian of the forest, her wisdom and knowledge a beacon for those who sought her guidance. The villagers, though respectful of the Pine Barrens, no longer lived in fear. They had faced the darkness and prevailed.

Section 18: The Pine Barrens Watchful Eye

As time passed, the Pine Barrens retained its mysterious allure. The forest,

32

with its ancient trees and hidden secrets, remained a place of wonder and caution. The villagers learned to live in harmony with the land, respecting its power and its beauty.

John and Deborah's family grew, their children learning the ways of the forest and the stories of their ancestors. They taught them to be cautious, but also to be brave, to respect the old magic of the Pine Barrens but not to fear it.

Section 19: The Legacy of the Curse

The legacy of the curse left a lasting impression on the village. It served as a reminder of the consequences of anger and despair, but also of the power of love and community. The villagers learned to face their fears together, to support one another in times of darkness.

The elder, now a respected leader, continued to guide the village with wisdom and compassion. He reminded

33

them of the importance of unity and resilience, of the strength that came from facing their fears together.

Section 20: The Dawn of a New Era

As the years passed, the Pine Barrens remained a place of mystery and wonder. The village thrived, its people living in harmony with the land. The legend of the Jersey Devil became a part of their history, a testament to their bravery and resilience.

John and Deborah, now elders themselves, watched their children and grandchildren grow, their hearts filled with pride and hope. The darkness that had once threatened their lives had been banished, and in its place, a new dawn had risen.

The Pine Barrens, with its watchful trees and whispering winds, remained a place of beauty and mystery. The villagers knew that they had faced the darkness and prevailed, and that their legacy

34

would live on for generations to come.

Chapter 3: The First Night

Section 1: Uneasy Silence

As the sun set over the Pine Barrens, a heavy silence fell upon the Leeds' cabin. The family huddled together, their fear palpable in the dim light of the single flickering candle. Deborah lay in bed, her body still weak from the ordeal, while John kept a watchful eye on the shadows outside.

The forest, usually alive with the sounds of nocturnal creatures, was eerily quiet. The absence of familiar noises only heightened their anxiety. The wind whispered through the trees, carrying with it an unsettling sense of foreboding. The children, wide-eyed and fearful, clung to one another, their hearts pounding in their chests.

35

Section 2: The Creature Returns

In the dead of night, a chilling screech pierced the silence. The sound was otherworldly, sending shivers down the spines of everyone in the cabin. John sprang to his feet, grabbing the hunting rifle he kept by the door. The children whimpered, their eyes wide with terror.

"Stay here," John instructed, his voice trembling. "I'll check outside."

Deborah reached out, her hand trembling. "John, be careful. Please."

John nodded, his jaw set in determination. He stepped out into the night, the cold air biting at his skin. The forest was cloaked in darkness, the moon hidden behind thick clouds. The screech came again, closer this time, and John's heart raced. He moved cautiously, the rifle held tightly in his hands.

Section 3: A Shadow in the Dark

As John ventured deeper into the forest,

36

the screeching grew louder, more insistent. He strained his eyes, searching for any sign of movement in the inky blackness. The trees loomed above him, their branches like skeletal fingers reaching out to ensnare him.

Suddenly, a rustling sound to his left made him whip around. He aimed the rifle, his hands shaking. "Who's there?" he called out, his voice echoing through the silent woods.

There was no response, only the eerie whisper of the wind. John took a cautious step forward, his eyes scanning the darkness. Then, out of the corner of his eye, he saw it – a shadowy figure darting between the trees. He raised the rifle, his finger hovering over the trigger, but the figure was too quick, vanishing into the night.

Section 4: The Creature's Attack

Before John could react, the creature launched itself at him from the darkness.

37

Its eyes glowed with an unholy light, and its wings beat the air with a ferocious intensity. John stumbled back, firing a shot blindly into the night. The sound of the gunshot echoed through the forest, but the creature was unfazed.

It let out a deafening screech, its claws raking across John's chest. He cried out in pain, falling to the ground as the creature circled above him. Blood seeped through his shirt, and his vision blurred as he struggled to stay conscious.

In a desperate attempt to protect his family, John aimed the rifle once more, firing another shot. This time, the bullet found its mark, striking the creature in the wing. It let out a furious cry, retreating into the darkness.

Section 5: The Aftermath

John lay on the ground, his breathing ragged. He clutched his chest, trying to stem the flow of blood. The forest was

38

silent once more, the creature having disappeared into the night. John forced himself to his feet, his vision swimming. He had to get back to his family.

He stumbled through the trees, each step sending waves of pain through his body. By the time he reached the cabin, he was barely conscious. Deborah and the children rushed to his side, their faces etched with fear.

"John! What happened?" Deborah cried, her hands trembling as she pressed a cloth to his wound.

"It... it attacked me," John gasped. "We need to be on our guard. It's still out there."

Section 6: Vigilance

The family spent the rest of the night in a state of heightened alert. John's wound was bandaged as best as they could manage, but the pain was excruciating. Deborah stayed by his side, her eyes

39

never leaving the windows, her ears straining for any sound.

The children, though exhausted, kept watch with their mother. The fear of the creature returning kept them awake, their small bodies trembling with terror. Each creak of the cabin, each rustle of the wind, made their hearts race.

The hours dragged on, each minute feeling like an eternity. The candle flickered, casting eerie shadows on the walls. The family huddled together, finding solace in each other's presence. The night seemed endless, the darkness oppressive.

Section 7: The Elders' Warnings

With the first light of dawn, the family's ordeal was far from over. John's injury needed proper attention, and the threat of the creature loomed large. Deborah made the difficult decision to seek help from the village elders.

40

As the morning sun began to pierce through the trees, Deborah and John's eldest son, Thomas, set out for the village. The journey through the Pine Barrens was fraught with danger, but he moved with determination, driven by the need to protect his family.

The village was in a state of unrest, the rumors of the creature spreading like wildfire. When Thomas arrived, the elders convened an emergency meeting, their faces grim.

"The creature must be dealt with," the head elder declared. "We cannot allow it to terrorize our village."

Thomas relayed the events of the previous night, his voice shaking with fear and anger. The elders listened intently, their faces growing more serious with each word.

"This is no ordinary creature," one of them said. "It is born of dark magic, and it will not be easily defeated."

41

Section 8: Preparing for Battle

The villagers mobilized, gathering weapons and supplies for the hunt. The elders shared ancient knowledge, teaching the villagers how to protect themselves against dark forces. Talismans were crafted, wards were placed around homes, and prayers were recited.

Thomas returned to the cabin with a group of villagers, their faces set with determination. They inspected the scene of the attack, their eyes scanning the forest for any sign of the creature.

John, though weakened by his injuries, insisted on joining the hunt. "This is my fight," he said, his voice firm despite the pain. "I won't let that thing harm my family again."

Deborah, though fearful for her husband, knew there was no dissuading him. She kissed him goodbye, her heart heavy with worry. "Be careful," she whispered,

42

her eyes filled with tears. "Come back to us."

Section 9: The Hunt Begins

The villagers set out into the forest, their torches casting flickering light in the dimness of the Pine Barrens. The air was thick with tension, each step echoing with the weight of their mission. The forest seemed to close in around them, the trees whispering secrets and warnings.

The group moved cautiously, their eyes scanning the shadows for any sign of the creature. The memory of its attack on John was fresh in their minds, and they were determined to end its reign of terror.

Hours passed with no sign of the creature. The forest was eerily quiet, the usual sounds of wildlife conspicuously absent. The villagers' nerves were on edge, each rustle of leaves or snap of a twig sending shivers down their spines.

43

Section 10: The Creature's Lair

As dusk approached, the villagers stumbled upon a clearing deep in the forest. In the center stood an ancient, gnarled tree, its twisted branches reaching out like skeletal fingers. The ground around the tree was littered with bones and remnants of past victims, a testament to the creature's brutality.

"This must be its lair," John said, his voice barely above a whisper. "We need to be ready."

The villagers spread out, forming a perimeter around the clearing. They prepared their weapons, the tension mounting with each passing moment. The air grew colder, and an unnatural silence fell over the forest.

Suddenly, a blood-curdling screech echoed through the trees. The villagers tensed, their eyes darting around the clearing. The creature appeared from the shadows, its eyes glowing with

44

malevolent intent. **Section 11: The Battle**

The creature attacked with a ferocity that took the villagers by surprise. It swooped down, its claws slashing through the air. The villagers fought back with everything they had, their torches and weapons clashing against the creature's dark form.

John, despite his injuries, fought with a renewed determination. He dodged the creature's attacks, using the knowledge the elders had shared to avoid its deadly claws. The villagers worked together, their combined efforts slowly wearing the creature down.

The battle was intense, the clearing filled with the sounds of screams and the clash of metal. The creature fought back viciously, its eyes glowing with unholy fire. The villagers pressed on, their resolve unwavering.

45

Section 12: A Desperate Plan

As the battle raged on, it became clear that the creature was more powerful than they had anticipated. The villagers began to lose hope, their strength waning under the relentless assault. John, his body aching and bleeding, realized they needed a new plan.

"We need to trap it," he shouted over the noise of the battle. "Use the fire to drive it into the tree!"

The villagers quickly regrouped, their torches forming a ring of fire around the clearing. They worked together, driving the creature towards the ancient tree. The creature screeched in fury, its movements growing more frantic as it realized their plan.

With one final push, the villagers managed to corner the creature against the tree. The fire blazed around them, the heat intense. The creature thrashed and screeched, its eyes filled with rage

46

and fear.

Section 13: The Creature's Demise

The villagers held their ground, their torches burning brightly. The creature, now trapped, lashed out in desperation. John stepped forward, his eyes locked on the creature's glowing gaze. He raised his torch, the flames casting a fierce light.

"For my family," he whispered, plunging the torch into the creature's chest.

The creature let out a final, agonizing screech, its body convulsing as the fire consumed it. The villagers watched in awe and terror as the creature writhed in pain, its form dissolving into ash. The fire roared, and then, just as suddenly, it was over. The creature was gone, leaving only a pile of smoldering ashes in its wake.

47

Section 14: The Aftermath

The villagers stood in stunned silence, the reality of their victory slowly sinking in. The forest was quiet once more, the oppressive darkness lifting. The ancient tree stood as a silent witness to their triumph, its twisted branches now holding no menace.

John collapsed to the ground, his body wracked with pain and exhaustion. The villagers rushed to his side, their faces filled with relief and gratitude. They had faced the darkness and emerged victorious, but the cost had been high.

Deborah and the children, waiting anxiously at the cabin, saw the torches returning and ran to meet the villagers. When she saw John, her heart swelled with relief and pride. They embraced, tears streaming down their faces.

Section 15: Healing and Reflection The days that followed were filled with

48

healing and reflection. The village, though scarred by the ordeal, found a renewed sense of community and strength. They mourned their losses but celebrated their victory, knowing they had faced a great evil and prevailed.

John's wounds, though severe, began to heal under Deborah's care. The family grew closer, their bond strengthened by the trials they had endured. The village elders shared their wisdom, helping the community to understand and respect the forces that had been at play.

The legend of the Jersey Devil became a part of their history, a reminder of the darkness that had once threatened their lives. The villagers honored those who had fought and those who had fallen, their bravery a testament to the power of unity and resilience.

Section 16: A New Dawn

As the seasons changed, the Pine Barrens began to flourish once more.

49

The village, though still wary of the dark forces that lurked in the forest, found a renewed sense of peace and hope. The land that had once been shrouded in fear now held the promise of new beginnings.

John and Deborah's thirteenth child grew strong and healthy, a symbol of their family's enduring spirit. The village, though forever changed by their ordeal, emerged stronger and more united. They had faced the darkness and prevailed, their legacy one of bravery and resilience.

Section 17: The Watchful Forest

The Pine Barrens retained its mysterious allure, a place of beauty and caution. The villagers learned to live in harmony with the land, respecting its power and its secrets. The ancient trees, once witnesses to great evil, now stood as guardians of the village's peace.

The forest, though still home to many

50

mysteries, no longer held the same terror. The villagers, guided by the wisdom of the elders and their own experiences, learned to navigate its shadows with respect and care. The Pine Barrens remained a place of wonder, a testament to the enduring spirit of those who called it home.

Section 18: Passing Down the Story

The story of the Jersey Devil was passed down through generations, a cautionary tale and a symbol of hope. The villagers taught their children to respect the old magic of the forest, to understand the power of curses and the strength of community.

John and Deborah, now elders themselves, watched with pride as their children and grandchildren learned the ways of the forest. They shared their experiences, their bravery, and their wisdom, ensuring that the legacy of their victory would never be forgotten.

51

Section 19: A Legacy of Courage

The legacy of the curse left a lasting impression on the village. It served as a reminder of the consequences of anger and despair, but also of the power of love and unity. The villagers learned to face their fears together, to support one another in times of darkness.

The village elder, now a revered leader, continued to guide the community with wisdom and compassion. He reminded them of the importance of unity and resilience, of the strength that came from facing their fears together.

Section 20: The Eternal Vigil

As the years passed, the Pine Barrens remained a place of mystery and wonder. The village thrived, its people living in harmony with the land. The legend of the Jersey Devil became a part of their history, a testament to their bravery and resilience.

52

John and Deborah, having faced unimaginable darkness, found peace in the light of their family and community. Their story, a tale of courage and hope, was a beacon for future generations.

The Pine Barrens, with its watchful trees and whispering winds, remained a place of beauty and mystery. The villagers knew that they had faced the darkness and prevailed, their legacy living on for generations to come. The forest, ever watchful, stood as a silent guardian of their triumph and their enduring spirit.

Chapter 4: The Curse Unveiled

Section 1: Unearthed Secrets

The village had barely begun to recover from the recent encounter with the Jersey Devil. The night had left deep scars, not just on the body but on the minds of those who had faced the creature. As the days passed, John and

53

Deborah found themselves haunted by lingering questions about the origin of the curse that had plagued their family.

One evening, as the sun dipped below the horizon, casting long shadows through the forest, John and Deborah made their way to the village elder's home. The elder, a man of immense wisdom and years, greeted them with a somber expression, as if he had anticipated their visit.

"We need to know more about the curse," John began, his voice filled with a desperate urgency. "Where did it come from? How can we be sure it's truly gone?"

The elder nodded slowly and gestured for them to sit by the fire. "The curse is an old one, rooted in the darkest parts of our history. It is time you learned the full story."

54

Section 2: The Origin of the Curse

The elder began to recount a tale that stretched back centuries, to a time when the Pine Barrens was home to a thriving, if isolated, community. According to legend, a woman named Lydia Leeds had lived in the forest with her husband and twelve children. Stricken with despair over her thirteenth pregnancy, she had cursed the unborn child in a fit of rage and hopelessness.

"That child," the elder said, his voice low and ominous, "was born normal but soon transformed into the creature we now know as the Jersey Devil. It was a manifestation of Lydia's curse, a physical embodiment of her anguish and anger."

John and Deborah listened in silence, the weight of the story sinking in. They had known of the creature's origins in vague terms, but hearing the specifics, and understanding the depth of the curse, was profoundly unsettling.

55

Section 3: Signs of the Curse

As the elder continued, he revealed that the curse did not end with the creature's creation. It had woven itself into the very fabric of the Leeds family line, rearing its head in various forms over the generations. Signs of the curse included strange phenomena and unexplainable events that plagued the family members throughout the years.

"Have you noticed anything unusual?" the elder asked, his gaze piercing.

John and Deborah exchanged worried glances. There had been odd occurrences: objects moving on their own, shadows flitting through the corners of their vision, and a pervasive sense of being watched. They recounted these experiences to the elder, their voices trembling with the memory.

"These are signs that the curse is still active," the elder confirmed. "The creature may be banished, but the curse's

56

influence remains."

Section 4: The Witch's Prophecy

The elder then spoke of a prophecy linked to the curse, one that had been passed down through the generations. According to the prophecy, the curse could only be lifted by confronting the source of Lydia Leeds' anguish and finding a way to atone for her suffering.

"A witch who lived deep within the Pine Barrens foretold this," the elder explained. "She was a seer, able to see into the hearts of men and the threads of fate that bind us all. Her words were cryptic but clear: 'The curse shall break when the anguish of the mother is laid to rest.'"

John and Deborah felt a chill run down their spines. They realized that their battle was far from over. To truly rid themselves of the curse, they would need to delve deeper into the past and uncover the truth of Lydia Leeds'

57

suffering.

Section 5: The Journey Begins

Determined to free their family from the curse once and for all, John and Deborah set out on a journey to find the witch's hut, deep within the Pine Barrens. They prepared for the expedition with the help of the villagers, gathering supplies and weapons to defend themselves against any lingering dark forces.

Their children, though young, understood the gravity of their parents' mission. The village rallied around the Leeds family, offering support and protection while John and Deborah embarked on their perilous quest.

The forest seemed more menacing than ever as they ventured deeper into its heart. The trees, twisted and gnarled, appeared to watch their every move. The air was thick with an eerie stillness, broken only by the occasional rustle of unseen creatures.

58

Section 6: Night Terrors

On the first night of their journey, John and Deborah set up camp in a small clearing. The flickering firelight cast long, dancing shadows on the trees. Despite their exhaustion, sleep did not come easily. The darkness seemed alive, pressing in on them from all sides.

In the middle of the night, Deborah awoke with a start, a cold sweat dripping down her back. She had dreamt of Lydia Leeds, her face twisted with rage and sorrow, her eyes burning with a desperate plea for help. Deborah could still hear the echoes of Lydia's cries ringing in her ears.

John, too, was plagued by nightmares. He saw visions of the Jersey Devil, its eyes glowing with malevolent intent, its claws reaching out for him and his family. He woke with a start, his heart pounding in his chest.

The forest around them was silent, save

59

for the occasional rustle of leaves. The night seemed endless, each minute stretching into an eternity. The darkness felt oppressive, as if it were closing in on them, smothering their hope.

Section 7: The Witch's Hut

After days of treacherous travel, John and Deborah finally reached the witch's hut. It was a dilapidated structure, half-hidden by the encroaching forest. Vines and moss covered the weathered wood, and an eerie silence hung in the air.

They approached cautiously, their senses on high alert. The hut exuded a sense of foreboding, as if it were a living entity that did not welcome their presence. Taking a deep breath, John pushed open the creaking door, and they stepped inside.

The interior was dark and musty, filled with the remnants of a life long gone. Cobwebs draped the corners, and the air was thick with the smell of decay. In the

60

center of the room stood a weathered table, covered in dust and old, crumbling books.

As they explored the hut, they found a small, intricately carved box hidden under a loose floorboard. Inside the box was a collection of old letters, their ink faded but still legible. They realized these letters were from Lydia Leeds herself, written in the days leading up to the birth of her thirteenth child.

Section 8: Lydia's Anguish

Reading through the letters, John and Deborah discovered the depth of Lydia's despair. She had been isolated, living in fear of her husband's wrath and the judgment of the villagers. Each letter was a cry for help, a desperate plea for someone to understand her pain and suffering.

One letter, in particular, stood out. In it, Lydia wrote about the moment she cursed her unborn child, her words filled

61

with regret and sorrow. "I did not mean for this to happen," she wrote. "I was lost in my own anguish, and now my child suffers for it."

The letters painted a picture of a woman pushed to the brink, her spirit broken by years of hardship and neglect. John and Deborah felt a deep sense of sorrow and empathy for Lydia, understanding for the first time the true extent of her suffering.

Section 9: The Ritual of Atonement

As they continued to search the hut, they found an old, leather-bound book that seemed to contain instructions for a ritual of atonement. The ritual, according to the book, could lift the curse by addressing Lydia's anguish and offering a means of reconciliation.

The ritual required several rare ingredients, many of which could only be found deep within the Pine Barrens. John and Deborah knew that obtaining these ingredients would be no easy task,

62

but they were determined to see it through.

They left the hut with a renewed sense of purpose, ready to face whatever challenges lay ahead. The forest seemed to come alive around them, the shadows deepening and the air growing colder. They pressed on, their resolve unwavering.

Section 10: Gathering the Ingredients

The first ingredient on their list was a rare herb known as "Witch's Heart," said to grow only in the darkest, most secluded parts of the forest. John and Deborah navigated through treacherous terrain, the forest becoming increasingly hostile the deeper they ventured.

They encountered numerous obstacles, from treacherous bogs to dense thickets that seemed to close in around them. The air was filled with the sounds of unseen creatures, and the oppressive darkness made it difficult to see.

63

After hours of searching, they finally found a small patch of Witch's Heart growing at the base of a twisted tree.

The herb glowed faintly in the dim light, its leaves a deep, blood-red color. They carefully harvested the herb, their hands trembling with a mix of fear and excitement.

Section 11: The Guardian

Their next task was to find a rare crystal known as the "Tear of the Forest." According to the book, the crystal was guarded by an ancient spirit that resided in a hidden cave deep within the Pine Barrens. John and Deborah followed the directions, their journey fraught with danger.

As they neared the cave, the forest grew eerily quiet. The entrance was obscured by thick vines and moss, and an overwhelming sense of dread washed over them. Taking a deep breath, they pushed through the undergrowth and

64

entered the cave.

Inside, the air was cold and damp, the walls covered in strange, glowing symbols. They ventured deeper, the light from their torches casting eerie shadows. Suddenly, a low growl echoed through the cave, and they realized they were not alone.

A figure emerged from the darkness, its eyes glowing with an otherworldly light. The guardian of the crystal was a towering, spectral figure, its form shifting and changing as it moved. It let out a bone-chilling wail, sending shivers down their spines.

Section 12: The Battle for the Tear

John and Deborah knew they had to confront the guardian to obtain the Tear of the Forest. The spectral figure lunged at them, its form passing through the walls of the cave as if it were made of smoke. They fought back with all their might, using the knowledge they had

65

gained from the village elders.

The battle was intense, the cave echoing with the sounds of their struggle. The guardian's attacks were swift and relentless, its ethereal form difficult to combat. John and Deborah worked together, their movements synchronized as they dodged and struck back.

Finally, with a desperate lunge, John managed to strike the guardian with a silver dagger blessed by the village elders. The guardian let out a final, haunting wail before dissolving into mist, leaving behind a small, glowing crystal.

The Tear of the Forest pulsed with a soft, blue light. John and Deborah carefully picked it up, their bodies trembling with exhaustion and relief. They had succeeded, but the cost had been high.

Section 13: The Final Ingredient The last ingredient they needed was the

66

"Blood of the Innocent," a euphemism for the essence of purity and hope. According to the book, this ingredient could only be obtained from the heart of the forest, where the ancient spirits of the land resided.

John and Deborah made their way to the heart of the Pine Barrens, the journey growing increasingly perilous. The forest seemed to sense their purpose, the shadows growing darker and the air colder. They pressed on, driven by their determination to lift the curse.

In the heart of the forest, they found a clearing bathed in an ethereal light. In the center of the clearing stood an ancient tree, its branches reaching towards the sky. The air was filled with a sense of peace and tranquility, a stark contrast to the rest of the forest.

As they approached the tree, they felt a presence watching them. The spirits of the land, ancient and wise, revealed themselves in the form of shimmering

67

lights. John and Deborah explained their quest, their voices filled with reverence and humility.

Section 14: The Blessing of the Spirits

The spirits listened to their plea, their forms shifting and swirling around the ancient tree. After a moment of silence, they granted their blessing, offering a vial of pure, glowing liquid – the essence of purity and hope.

John and Deborah accepted the vial with gratitude, their hearts filled with hope. They had obtained all the ingredients needed for the ritual of atonement. Now, they had to return to the witch's hut and perform the ritual.

Section 15: The Ritual Begins

Returning to the witch's hut, John and Deborah prepared for the ritual with a mix of anticipation and dread. The air was thick with tension as they laid out the ingredients on the weathered table.

68

The ancient book lay open, its pages filled with instructions written in an archaic script.

They began the ritual, following the steps meticulously. They combined the Witch's Heart, the Tear of the Forest, and the essence of purity, chanting the incantations written in the book. The air around them crackled with energy, the light in the hut growing dim.

As they performed the ritual, they felt a presence growing stronger. The spirit of Lydia Leeds seemed to materialize before them, her form faint but unmistakable. Her eyes were filled with sorrow, her expression one of anguish and regret.

Section 16: Confronting the Past

Lydia's spirit spoke, her voice echoing through the hut. "Why have you summoned me?"

John and Deborah explained their

69

purpose, their voices trembling with emotion. They spoke of their desire to lift the curse, to bring peace to Lydia's tormented soul and free their family from the darkness that had plagued them for generations.

Lydia listened, her eyes softening with understanding. She revealed the true depth of her suffering, the years of isolation and fear that had driven her to curse her unborn child. Her regret was palpable, her desire for redemption clear.

Section 17: The Moment of Atonement

As the ritual reached its climax, John and Deborah felt a surge of energy. The air around them shimmered, and the spirit of Lydia Leeds began to fade, her form dissolving into the light. The hut was filled with a sense of peace, the oppressive darkness lifting.

The curse, bound by Lydia's anguish and regret, began to unravel. The shadows

70

that had haunted the Leeds family for generations dissipated, replaced by a sense of hope and renewal. The forest, once menacing and dark, seemed to breathe a sigh of relief.

Section 18: The Aftermath

With the ritual complete, John and Deborah returned to their village, their hearts lighter. The villagers greeted them with relief and joy, their faces filled with gratitude. The curse had been lifted, and the village could finally begin to heal.

John's injuries, though severe, began to mend more quickly. The oppressive weight that had hung over the Leeds family was gone, replaced by a sense of peace. The village, though still wary of the dark forces that lurked in the forest, found a renewed sense of unity and hope.

Section 19: Healing and Reflection The days that followed were filled with

71

healing and reflection. The villagers, having faced a great evil, emerged stronger and more united. They honored those who had fought and those who had fallen, their bravery a testament to the power of community and resilience.

John and Deborah shared their experiences with the villagers, their story serving as a reminder of the importance of understanding and compassion. The legend of the Jersey Devil became a part of their history, a symbol of the darkness they had overcome.

Section 20: A New Beginning

As the seasons changed, the Pine Barrens began to flourish once more. The village, though forever changed by their ordeal, found a renewed sense of peace and hope. The land that had once been shrouded in fear now held the promise of new beginnings.

John and Deborah's thirteenth child

72

grew strong and healthy, a symbol of their family's enduring spirit. The village, guided by the wisdom of the elders and the lessons of the past, embraced the future with open hearts.

The Pine Barrens, with its watchful trees and whispering winds, remained a place of beauty and mystery. The villagers, now wiser and more united, lived in harmony with the land, respecting its power and its secrets.

The legacy of the curse, a tale of sorrow and redemption, lived on in the hearts and minds of the villagers. The story of the Jersey Devil, once a source of fear, became a testament to their courage and resilience. The forest, ever watchful, stood as a silent guardian of their triumph and their enduring spirit.

73

Chapter 5: Echoes of the Past
Section 1: The Silent Return

John and Deborah returned to their cabin, their faces lined with exhaustion and relief. The villagers greeted them with a mixture of awe and respect, knowing the sacrifices they had made to lift the curse. The forest seemed calmer, as if acknowledging their victory. However, an unsettling feeling lingered in the air, like the echo of a scream that refused to fade away.

As they settled back into their routine, John couldn't shake the feeling that something still lurked in the shadows. The nights were eerily silent, the usual sounds of the forest replaced by an oppressive stillness. It was as if the Pine Barrens itself was holding its breath, waiting for something to happen.

Section 2: Strange Happenings The first signs of trouble came in the

74

form of small, inexplicable events. Objects in the cabin would move on their own, shifting positions overnight. Strange symbols appeared in the dirt outside their home, symbols that John recognized from the witch's hut. The air grew colder, and the shadows seemed to deepen, even in the daylight.

Deborah found herself plagued by nightmares. In her dreams, she saw the forest alive with shadows, the trees whispering in a language she couldn't understand. Lydia Leeds' spirit appeared to her, not as the tormented soul seeking redemption, but as a vengeful specter, her eyes burning with anger.

John, too, felt the weight of an unseen presence. He often found himself staring into the forest, feeling as if he was being watched. The sense of unease grew stronger with each passing day, making it difficult for him to focus on his work or sleep soundly at night.

75

Section 3: The First Attack

One night, the peaceful quiet of the village was shattered by a blood-curdling scream. John and Deborah rushed outside to find a villager, one of their closest friends, lying in the dirt, his body covered in deep, ragged wounds. He was barely alive, his eyes wide with terror.

"It was the Devil," he gasped, his voice barely a whisper. "It's not gone. It's still here."

The village was thrown into chaos. Fear spread like wildfire, and whispers of the Jersey Devil's return filled the air. The elder, who had guided John and Deborah through the ritual, looked more troubled than ever. He called a meeting, urging the villagers to remain calm and to stay indoors at night.

John and Deborah were devastated. They had risked everything to lift the curse, and now it seemed as though their

76

efforts had been in vain. The Jersey Devil was back, and it was more vengeful than ever.

Section 4: The Elders' Warning

The village elder pulled John and Deborah aside after the meeting. His eyes were dark with worry, and his voice was filled with a grave urgency. "The curse was never truly lifted," he said. "The ritual appeased Lydia's spirit, but it did not banish the creature itself. The Devil is a manifestation of pure rage and darkness. It cannot be destroyed so easily."

John felt a cold chill settle over him. "What do we do now?" he asked, his voice hoarse with fear.

"The creature feeds on fear and despair," the elder explained. "We must find a way to weaken it, to drive it back into the darkness from which it came. The forest holds many secrets, and there may be other ways to fight it. We need to

77

seek out the oldest and most hidden knowledge."

Section 5: The Forbidden Knowledge

The elder led them to a hidden section of the village archives, a place few knew existed. The air was thick with dust, and the shelves were lined with ancient tomes and scrolls. These were the records of the village's darkest times, accounts of battles with the supernatural and the unknown.

They pored over the texts, searching for anything that could help them. They found references to an ancient artifact, a relic that was said to have the power to banish dark spirits. The artifact, known as the "Heart of the Forest," was hidden somewhere within the Pine Barrens, protected by powerful enchantments.

"The Heart of the Forest," the elder said, his voice trembling with a mix of hope and fear. "If we can find it, we may have a chance to banish the Jersey Devil for

78

good."

Section 6: The Search Begins

Armed with this new knowledge, John and Deborah prepared to venture back into the forest. They knew the journey would be dangerous, but they had no choice. The Jersey Devil was growing bolder, its attacks becoming more frequent and violent. The village could not withstand its wrath for much longer.

The villagers rallied around them, providing supplies and weapons. Their faces were etched with determination and fear, knowing that their fate rested on John and Deborah's shoulders. The couple bid their children a tearful goodbye, promising to return and end the nightmare once and for all.

As they entered the forest, the trees seemed to close in around them, their branches twisting like skeletal fingers. The air was thick with an oppressive darkness, and the sounds of the forest

79

were unnaturally muted. They pressed on, their hearts heavy with the weight of their mission.

Section 7: The Trials of the Forest

The Pine Barrens was a labyrinth of twisting paths and hidden dangers. John and Deborah encountered numerous obstacles, from treacherous swamps to tangled thickets that seemed to have a life of their own. They fought off wild animals and avoided deadly traps set by the forest itself.

Each night, they were plagued by nightmares. The Jersey Devil haunted their dreams, its eyes glowing with malevolence. They woke up in cold sweats, their bodies trembling with fear. The forest seemed to mock them, its whispers growing louder and more insistent.

Despite the hardships, they pressed on, driven by the desperate need to save their village and their family. They

80

followed the clues in the ancient texts, navigating the forest with a mix of caution and determination. The further they went, the more they felt the presence of something powerful and ancient watching over them.

Section 8: The Guardian of the Heart

After days of grueling travel, they finally reached a hidden glade, bathed in an eerie, otherworldly light. In the center of the glade stood a massive tree, its trunk twisted and gnarled. At the base of the tree lay a stone altar, and upon it rested the Heart of the Forest.

The artifact was a small, intricately carved wooden heart, glowing with a soft, pulsating light. As they approached, a figure emerged from the shadows. The guardian of the Heart was a spectral being, its form shifting and ethereal. Its eyes glowed with a piercing blue light, and its voice echoed through the glade.

"Who dares to seek the Heart of the

81

Forest?" the guardian intoned, its voice filled with an ancient power.

John and Deborah explained their mission, their voices trembling with a mix of fear and determination. The guardian listened, its eyes narrowing as it considered their words.

"The Heart is a powerful artifact," the guardian said. "It can banish the darkness, but it requires a great sacrifice. Are you willing to pay the price?"

Section 9: The Price of Power

John and Deborah hesitated, knowing that the guardian's words were not to be taken lightly. The price of power was often steep, and they feared what it might entail. But they had come too far to turn back now.

"We are willing," John said, his voice resolute. "Whatever it takes, we will do it."

The guardian nodded, its eyes glowing

82

with approval. "Very well. The Heart requires a life force to activate its power. One of you must offer your essence to the artifact. It is the only way."

John and Deborah exchanged a pained look. They knew the choice was inevitable, but it didn't make it any easier. Deborah stepped forward, her eyes filled with determination and love.

"I will do it," she said, her voice steady. "For our family, for our village. I will give my essence to the Heart."

Section 10: The Ritual of Sacrifice

The guardian led them to the altar, its movements graceful and fluid. Deborah lay down on the stone, her heart pounding with fear and resolve. John stood beside her, his hand gripping hers tightly. The guardian began the ritual, chanting in an ancient language that resonated through the glade.

As the chant grew louder, the Heart of

83

the Forest began to glow brighter. Tendrils of light reached out from the artifact, wrapping around Deborah's body. She felt a searing pain as her essence was drawn into the Heart, her life force merging with its power.

John watched in horror and awe as the ritual continued. Deborah's body glowed with an ethereal light, her face serene despite the pain. The guardian's chant reached a crescendo, and the Heart pulsed with a blinding light.

In that moment, Deborah's essence fused with the Heart, imbuing it with the power to banish the Jersey Devil. Her body went limp, and John caught her in his arms, his heart breaking with grief and love.

Section 11: The Power of the Heart

With the ritual complete, the Heart of the Forest glowed with a newfound intensity. The guardian nodded, its eyes filled with a mixture of sadness and

84

respect. "The power of the Heart is now yours," it said. "Use it wisely, and you may banish the darkness that plagues your land."

John, his heart heavy with sorrow, took the Heart and vowed to fulfill Deborah's sacrifice. He left the glade, the guardian's eyes following him as he disappeared into the forest. The journey back to the village was long and arduous, the weight of his loss pressing down on him with each step.

Section 12: The Final Confrontation

When John returned to the village, the air was thick with fear and anticipation. The villagers gathered around him, their faces filled with hope and dread. John held up the Heart of the Forest, its glow a beacon of hope in the darkness.

"The Jersey Devil will come for us," John said, his voice strong despite his grief. "But we have the power to banish it. We must stand together and face it as

85

one."

The villagers, inspired by John's determination, prepared for the final confrontation. They fortified the village, setting traps and gathering weapons. As night fell, they waited with bated breath, knowing that the Jersey Devil would soon make its move.

The creature's arrival was heralded by an eerie silence, the air growing colder and the shadows deepening. The villagers stood their ground, their hearts pounding with fear and resolve. The Jersey Devil emerged from the darkness, its eyes glowing with malevolence.

John stepped forward, holding the Heart of the Forest high. The artifact pulsed with light, its power radiating through the village. The Jersey Devil let out a roar of rage, its form shifting and writhing as it approached.

86

Section 13: The Battle for the Village

The battle was fierce and terrifying. The Jersey Devil attacked with relentless fury, its claws slashing through the air and its eyes burning with hatred. The villagers fought back with all their might, their weapons gleaming in the light of the Heart.

John focused on the artifact, channeling its power to drive back the creature. The Heart's light grew brighter, casting out the shadows and weakening the Jersey Devil's form. The creature howled in pain, its body flickering as it struggled against the Heart's power.

Despite their fear, the villagers fought bravely, their determination unwavering. They knew that this was their only chance to banish the creature and save their village. They struck at the Jersey Devil with a ferocity born of desperation and hope.

87

Section 14: The Sacrifice Fulfilled

As the battle raged on, John felt Deborah's presence beside him, her essence guiding him and lending him strength. He knew that her sacrifice had given them the power to banish the darkness, and he was determined to see it through.

With a final, desperate effort, John channeled the full power of the Heart of the Forest. The artifact blazed with light, its energy enveloping the Jersey Devil and forcing it back. The creature let out a final, ear-piercing scream as it was consumed by the light, its form dissolving into nothingness.

The village fell silent, the air thick with the aftermath of the battle. The Jersey Devil was gone, banished by the power of the Heart and Deborah's sacrifice. The villagers stood in stunned silence, their hearts filled with a mixture of relief and sorrow.

88

Section 15: The Aftermath

With the Jersey Devil banished, the village began to heal. The oppressive darkness that had hung over the Pine Barrens lifted, replaced by a sense of peace and renewal. The villagers honored Deborah's sacrifice, her bravery and love a testament to the strength of their community.

John, though heartbroken by his loss, found solace in the knowledge that Deborah's sacrifice had saved their family and their village. He dedicated himself to preserving her memory and ensuring that the village remained safe from the darkness that had once plagued them.

The Heart of the Forest was returned to its sacred glade, its power a guardian against future threats. The villagers continued to honor the ancient knowledge and traditions, knowing that they held the key to their survival and prosperity.

89

Section 16: Healing and Reflection

In the months that followed, the village thrived. The land, once shrouded in fear, began to flourish, its beauty and vitality restored. The villagers worked together to rebuild and strengthen their community, their bonds forged in the fires of their shared ordeal.

John and his children found a new sense of peace, their hearts filled with the love and memory of Deborah. They knew that her spirit would always be with them, guiding and protecting them. The village, though forever changed by their experiences, emerged stronger and more united.

Section 17: The Legacy of the Curse

The story of the Jersey Devil and the curse of the Leeds family became a part of the village's history, a reminder of the darkness they had overcome. The legend was passed down through generations, a tale of bravery, sacrifice, and

90

redemption.

The villagers, now wiser and more vigilant, remained ever watchful of the forest and its secrets. They knew that the Pine Barrens held both beauty and danger, and they respected its power and mystery.

Section 18: A New Dawn

As time passed, the village continued to thrive, its people living in harmony with the land. The Pine Barrens, once a place of fear and darkness, became a symbol of resilience and hope. The villagers embraced their history, knowing that their strength and unity had saved them from the brink of despair.

John, now an elder himself, shared the story of Deborah and the Heart of the Forest with the younger generations. He taught them the importance of courage, sacrifice, and the power of love. The village, guided by these values, faced the future with hope and determination.

91

Section 19: The Spirit of the Forest

The Pine Barrens, ever watchful, stood as a silent guardian of the village's triumph. The forest, with its ancient trees and whispering winds, held the memories of the past and the promise of the future. The villagers, now attuned to the forest's rhythms, lived in harmony with its natural beauty and power.

The spirit of Deborah, ever present, watched over her family and village. Her sacrifice had brought peace and light to the Pine Barrens, and her legacy would endure through the ages. The villagers, guided by her memory, honored the land and its secrets, knowing that they held the key to their survival and prosperity.

Section 20: The Eternal Watch

As the years passed, the village continued to thrive, its people living in harmony with the land and each other. The story of the Jersey Devil and the curse of the Leeds family became a

92

cherished part of their history, a testament to their courage and resilience.

The Pine Barrens, with its ancient trees and whispering winds, remained a place of beauty and mystery. The villagers, now wiser and more united, lived in peace and harmony, their hearts filled with hope and gratitude.

The legacy of the curse, a tale of sorrow and redemption, lived on in the hearts and minds of the villagers. The story of the Jersey Devil, once a source of fear, became a symbol of their strength and unity. The forest, ever watchful, stood as a silent guardian of their triumph and their enduring spirit.

Chapter 6: The Whispers of Darkness

Section 1: Lingering Shadows

In the aftermath of the battle with the Jersey Devil, the village was shrouded in an uneasy calm. The air was thick with

93

the scent of smoke and fear, and the villagers moved about with a wary tension. Despite the creature's banishment, a sense of unease lingered in the air, like the echo of a nightmare that refused to fade away.

John felt the weight of Deborah's absence like a physical ache in his chest. Every corner of their cabin seemed haunted by memories of her, and he struggled to find solace in the quiet moments of solitude. The nights were the hardest, filled with restless dreams and whispered voices that seemed to echo from the darkness outside.

Section 2: The Return of the Shadows

As the days passed, strange occurrences began to plague the village once more. Animals went missing, their tracks leading into the forest but never returning. Villagers reported seeing shadowy figures lurking in the trees, their eyes glowing with an otherworldly

94

light. The air grew colder, and the once-familiar sounds of the forest were replaced by an eerie silence.

Whispers spread among the villagers, fueled by fear and uncertainty. Some believed that the Jersey Devil had returned, its banishment only temporary. Others whispered of darker forces at work, ancient spirits awakened by the battle and seeking vengeance upon the living.

John knew that something was terribly wrong. The peace they had fought so hard to achieve was unraveling before his eyes, and he feared that the darkness they had faced was far from defeated. He resolved to uncover the truth, no matter the cost.

Section 3: A Desperate Search

John sought out the village elder, hoping to find answers to the growing darkness that threatened to engulf them once more. The elder's face was drawn with

95

worry, his eyes clouded with a sense of foreboding.

"The Jersey Devil may be gone," the elder said, his voice grave, "but its presence has awakened something far more ancient and sinister. The forest holds many secrets, and I fear that we have only scratched the surface of its true power."

John listened intently, his heart heavy with dread. He knew that they were facing a threat unlike anything they had encountered before, and he vowed to do whatever it took to protect his family and his village.

"We must find the source of this darkness," John said, his voice firm. "We cannot allow it to consume us."

The elder nodded in agreement, his expression grim. "We will need to venture into the heart of the forest, to confront the darkness at its source. But be warned, John. The journey will be

96

perilous, and the dangers we face may be greater than anything we have ever known."

Section 4: Into the Abyss

Armed with determination and desperation, John and a small group of villagers set out into the heart of the Pine Barrens. The forest seemed to close in around them, its branches reaching out like grasping fingers. The air was thick with an oppressive darkness, and the ground seemed to tremble beneath their feet.

They pressed on, their hearts pounding with fear and anticipation. The forest seemed to come alive around them, its shadows twisting and shifting with unnatural movements. Strange symbols appeared on the trees, glowing with an eerie light that sent shivers down their spines.

As they ventured deeper into the forest, the air grew colder, and the darkness

97

seemed to deepen. They heard strange whispers echoing through the trees, voices that spoke in a language they could not understand. The ground beneath them seemed to shift and writhe, as if the very earth itself was alive with malevolent intent.

Section 5: The Ancient Ruins

After days of grueling travel, they stumbled upon a clearing in the forest, bathed in an ethereal light. In the center of the clearing stood a circle of ancient stone ruins, their weathered faces covered in strange symbols and carvings.

The air was thick with a sense of ancient power, and the hairs on the back of John's neck stood on end. He could feel the weight of centuries pressing down upon him, as if the very fabric of reality was unraveling before his eyes.

"This place reeks of dark magic," one of the villagers whispered, his voice

98

trembling with fear. "We should turn back while we still can."

But John knew that they had come too far to turn back now. Whatever darkness lurked within these ruins, they had to confront it head-on if they were to have any hope of saving their village.

Chapter 7

Section 6: The Guardian of the Ruins

As they approached the ruins, a figure emerged from the shadows, its form shrouded in darkness. Its eyes gleamed with a malevolent light, and its voice echoed through the clearing like a whisper on the wind.

"Who dares to disturb the ancient guardians of this forest?" the figure intoned, its voice dripping with malice.

John stepped forward, his heart pounding with fear and resolve. "We seek answers," he said, his voice steady

99

despite the tremble in his limbs. "We seek to understand the darkness that plagues our village, and to put an end to it once and for all."

The figure regarded him with a mix of amusement and contempt. "You are fools to think that you can challenge the darkness that lurks within these ruins," it said, its voice echoing with a chilling finality. "But if you are determined to proceed, know that the price of your folly may be greater than you can imagine."

Section 7: The Trial of Shadows

The figure vanished into the darkness, leaving John and the villagers to confront the ancient ruins alone. They entered cautiously, their senses on high alert for any sign of danger. The air was thick with an oppressive stillness, and the silence seemed to press down upon them like a weight.

As they ventured deeper into the ruins,

100

they encountered strange traps and obstacles, designed to test their resolve and their strength. They fought off swarms of shadowy creatures that seemed to materialize out of thin air, their claws and fangs glinting in the dim light.

With each passing moment, the darkness seemed to close in around them, threatening to swallow them whole. But they pressed on, driven by the desperate need to uncover the truth and to save their village from the growing menace.

Section 8: The Chamber of Shadows

At last, they reached the heart of the ruins, a chamber bathed in an otherworldly glow. In the center of the chamber stood a pedestal, upon which rested a small, glowing orb. The orb pulsed with a faint light, its surface swirling with shadows and whispers.

"This must be the source of the darkness," one of the villagers said, his

101

voice hushed with awe.

John approached the pedestal cautiously, his heart pounding with anticipation. He reached out to touch the orb, his fingers trembling with fear and uncertainty.

But before he could make contact, a voice echoed through the chamber, freezing him in his tracks.

"Who dares to disturb the ancient guardians of this forest?"

Section 9: The Guardian's Challenge

A figure emerged from the shadows, its form shrouded in darkness. Its eyes gleamed with a malevolent light, and its voice echoed through the chamber like a whisper on the wind.

"We are the guardians of this forest," the figure intoned, its voice dripping with malice. "And we will own you.

John stood his ground, his heart pounding with fear and determination. "We mean no harm," he said, his voice

102

steady despite the tremble in his limbs. "We seek to understand the darkness that plagues our village, and to put an end to it once and for all."

The figure regarded him with a mix of amusement and contempt. "You are foolish to think that you can challenge the darkness that lurks within these ruins," it said, its voice echoing with a chilling finality. "But if you are determined to proceed, know that the price of your folly may be greater than you can imagine."

John exchanged a glance with the villagers, their faces pale with fear but their resolve unwavering. They knew that they had come too far to turn back now, and they were prepared to face whatever darkness awaited them within the ruins.

"We understand the risks," John said, his voice firm. "But we cannot allow the darkness to consume our village. We will do whatever it takes to protect our

103

home and our loved ones."

The figure regarded them for a moment, its eyes narrowing with suspicion. Then, with a gesture of its hand, it vanished into the shadows, leaving John and the villagers to confront the darkness alone.

Section 10: The Trials of the Ruins

As they ventured deeper into the chamber, they encountered strange traps and obstacles, designed to test their resolve and their strength. They fought off swarms of shadowy creatures that seemed to materialize out of thin air, their claws and fangs glinting in the dim light.

With each passing moment, the darkness seemed to close in around them, threatening to swallow them whole. But they pressed on, driven by the desperate need to uncover the truth and to save their village from the growing menace.

They encountered puzzles and riddles,

104

each more fiendish than the last, designed to challenge their minds and their wits. They faced illusions and hallucinations, their senses assaulted by visions of their deepest fears and darkest desires.

But through it all, they remained steadfast, their determination unwavering in the face of overwhelming darkness. They knew that they were fighting for more than just their own lives—they were fighting for the future of their village, and for the light that still flickered within their hearts.

Section 11: Confronting the Darkness

At last, they reached the heart of the ruins, a chamber bathed in an otherworldly glow. In the center of the chamber stood a pedestal, upon which rested a small, glowing orb. The orb pulsed with a faint light, its surface swirling with shadows and whispers.

"This must be the source of the

105

darkness," one of the villagers said, his voice hushed with awe.

John approached the pedestal cautiously, his heart pounding with anticipation. He reached out to touch the orb, his fingers trembling with fear and uncertainty.

But before he could make contact, a voice echoed through the chamber, freezing him in his tracks.

"Who dares to disturb the ancient guardians of this forest?"

Section 12: The Guardian's Challenge

A figure emerged from the shadows, its form shrouded in darkness. Its eyes gleamed with a malevolent light, and its voice echoed through the chamber like a whisper on the wind.

"We are the guardians of this forest," the figure intoned, its voice dripping with malice. "And we will not allow you to defile our sacred sanctuary."

John stood his ground, his heart

106

pounding with fear and determination. "We mean no harm," he said, his voice steady despite the tremble in his limbs.

"We seek to understand the darkness that plagues our village, and to put an end to it once and for all."

The figure regarded him with a mix of amusement and contempt. "You are foolish to think that you can challenge the darkness that lurks within these ruins," it said, its voice echoing with a chilling finality. "But if you are determined to proceed, know that the price of your folly may be greater than you can imagine."

John exchanged a glance with the villagers, their faces pale with fear but their resolve unwavering. They knew that they had come too far to turn back now, and they were prepared to face whatever darkness awaited them within the ruins.

"We understand the risks," John said, his voice firm. "But we cannot allow the

107

darkness to consume our village. We will do whatever it takes to protect our home and our loved ones."

The figure regarded them for a moment, its eyes narrowing with suspicion. Then, with a gesture of its hand, it vanished into the shadows, leaving John and the villagers to confront the darkness alone.

Section 13: The Heart of Darkness

As they approached the pedestal, the orb seemed to pulse with a dark energy, its light flickering and wavering like a dying flame. John reached out to touch it, his fingers trembling with fear and uncertainty.

But as soon as his hand made contact with the orb, a wave of darkness washed over him, engulfing him in its suffocating embrace. Visions flashed before his eyes—images of death and destruction, of despair and madness.

He heard the voices of the ancient

108

guardians, whispering in his mind like a serpent's hiss. They spoke of power and corruption, of the temptations of darkness and the folly of mortals who dared to challenge their authority.

John felt himself being pulled deeper into the abyss, his mind and soul consumed by the darkness that surrounded him. He fought against it with all his strength, clinging to the light that still burned within him like a flickering candle in the night.

Section 14: The Battle Within

With a desperate effort, John summoned all his courage and willpower, pushing back against the darkness that threatened to overwhelm him. He called upon the memories of his loved ones, of Deborah and their children, of the village that he had sworn to protect.

Slowly, agonizingly, he felt the darkness begin to recede, like a tide retreating from the shore. He reached out with his

109

mind and heart, reaching for the light that still burned within him, drawing strength from its warmth and purity.

At last, with a final surge of determination, John broke free from the darkness that had ensnared him, his spirit soaring like a bird released from its cage. He stood before the pedestal, his eyes blazing with defiance and resolve.

Section 15: The Power Within

With a steady hand, John reached out and touched the orb once more, his fingers tingling with a strange energy. As soon as his hand made contact, the orb began to glow with a brilliant light, its surface shimmering with a kaleidoscope

The Dance of Shadows Section 1: A Fractured Reality

As John touched the orb, a surge of power coursed through him, sending

110

shockwaves of energy rippling through the chamber. The air crackled with electricity, and the shadows seemed to twist and contort as if alive. With a blinding flash, the darkness was expelled, replaced by a blinding light that filled the chamber.

When John's vision cleared, he found himself standing in a realm unlike any he had ever seen before. The world around him seemed to flicker and shift, as if caught between dimensions. Strange symbols danced in the air, their meaning incomprehensible to mortal eyes.

Beside him, the villagers stood in awe and terror, their faces pale with fear. They clung to each other, seeking comfort in the face of the unknown. John knew that they had entered a realm of ancient magic and dark power, and that they would need all their strength and courage to survive.

111

Section 2: The Guardians' Trial

As they ventured deeper into the realm, they encountered strange trials and challenges, each more fiendish than the last. They faced illusions and hallucinations, their senses assaulted by visions of their deepest fears and darkest desires. They battled creatures of shadow and flame, their forms shifting and changing with each blow.

But through it all, they remained steadfast, their determination unwavering in the face of overwhelming darkness. They knew that they were fighting for more than just their own lives—they were fighting for the future of their village, and for the light that still flickered within their hearts.

Section 3: The Chamber of Echoes

At last, they reached the heart of the realm, a chamber bathed in an otherworldly glow. In the center of the chamber stood a pedestal, upon which

112

rested a small, glowing orb. The orb pulsed with a faint light, its surface swirling with shadows and whispers.

"This must be the source of the darkness," one of the villagers said, his voice hushed with awe.

John approached the pedestal cautiously, his heart pounding with anticipation. He reached out to touch the orb, his fingers trembling with fear and uncertainty.

But before he could make contact, a voice echoed through the chamber, freezing him in his tracks.

"Who dares to disturb the ancient guardians of this realm?"

Section 4: The Guardians' Challenge

A figure emerged from the shadows, its form shrouded in darkness. Its eyes gleamed with a malevolent light, and its voice echoed through the chamber like a whisper on the wind.

"We are the guardians of this realm," the

113

figure intoned, its voice dripping with malice. "And we will not allow you to defile our sacred sanctuary."

John stood his ground, his heart pounding with fear and determination. "We mean no harm," he said, his voice steady despite the tremble in his limbs. "We seek to understand the darkness that plagues our village, and to put an end to it once and for all."

The figure regarded him with a mix of amusement and contempt. "You are foolish to think that you can challenge the darkness that lurks within these ruins," it said, its voice echoing with a chilling finality. "But if you are determined to proceed, know that the price of your folly may be greater than you can imagine."

John exchanged a glance with the villagers, their faces pale with fear but their resolve unwavering. They knew that they had come too far to turn back now, and they were prepared to face

114

whatever darkness awaited them within the ruins.

"We understand the risks," John said, his voice firm. "But we cannot allow the darkness to consume our village. We will do whatever it takes to protect our home and our loved ones."

The figure regarded them for a moment, its eyes narrowing with suspicion. Then, with a gesture of its hand, it vanished into the shadows, leaving John and the villagers to confront the darkness alone.

Section 5: The Trials of the Ruins

As they ventured deeper into the chamber, they encountered strange traps and obstacles, designed to test their resolve and their strength.

They fought off swarms of shadowy creatures that seemed to material-ize out of thin air, their claws and fangs glinting in the dim light.

With each passing moment, the darkness

115

seemed to close in around them, threatening to swallow them whole. But they pressed on, driven by the desperate need to uncover the truth and to save their village from the growing menace.

They encountered puzzles and riddles, each more fiendish than the last, designed to challenge their minds and their wits. They faced illusions and hallucinations, their senses assaulted by visions of their deepest fears and darkest desires.

But through it all, they remained steadfast, their determination un-wavering in the face of overwhelming darkness. They knew that they were fighting for more than just their own lives—they were fighting for the future of their village, and for the light that still flickered within their hearts.

Section 6: Confronting the Darkness

At last, they reached the heart of the ruins, a chamber bathed in an

116

otherworldly glow. In the center of the chamber stood a pedestal, upon which rested a small, glowing orb. The orb pulsed with a faint light, its surface swirling with shadows and whispers.

"This must be the source of the darkness," one of the villagers said, his voice hushed with awe.

John approached the pedestal cautiously, his heart pounding with anticipation. He reached out to touch the orb, his fingers trembling with fear and uncertainty.

But before he could make contact, a voice echoed through the chamber, freezing him in his tracks.

"Who dares to disturb the ancient guardians of this forest?"

Section 7: The Guardian's Challenge

A figure emerged from the shadows, its form shrouded in darkness. Its eyes gleamed with a malevolent light, and its voice echoed through the chamber like a

117

whisper on the wind.

"We are the guardians of this forest," the figure intoned, its voice dripping with malice. "And we will not allow you to defile our sacred sanctuary."

John stood his ground, his heart pounding with fear and determination. "We mean no harm," he said, his voice steady despite the tremble in his limbs. "We seek to understand the darkness that plagues our village, and to put an end to it once and for all."

The figure regarded him with a mix of amusement and contempt. "You are foolish to think that you can challenge the darkness that lurks within these ruins," it said, its voice echoing with a chilling finality. "But if you are determined to proceed, know that the price of your folly may be greater than you can imagine."

John exchanged a glance with the villagers, their faces pale with fear but

118

their resolve unwavering. They knew that they had come too far to turn back now, and they were prepared to face whatever darkness awaited them within the ruins.

Chapter 8: The Labyrinth of Nightmares

Section 1: Echoes of Despair

As the figure's words faded into the darkness, John and the villagers stood frozen in apprehension. The air seemed to thicken around them, suffused with an oppressive weight that pressed down upon their chests. The chamber pulsed with an eerie glow, casting long shadows that danced across the ancient ruins.

John's mind raced with uncertainty, his thoughts consumed by the gravity of their situation. He knew that they had ventured into the heart of darkness, where the line between reality and

119

nightmare blurred into obscurity. With a deep breath, he steeled himself for the trials that lay ahead.

"We cannot falter," John declared, his voice resonating with determination. "Whatever lies within these ruins, we face it together, as one."

The villagers nodded in agreement, their expressions a mixture of fear and resolve. With a shared sense of purpose, they stepped forward, prepared to confront the shadows that lurked within the labyrinth of nightmares.

Section 2: The Veil of Illusions

As they ventured deeper into the ruins, they found themselves ensnared in a labyrinth of illusions and deceptions. The walls seemed to shift and warp, twisting their perceptions of reality with each passing moment. Familiar landmarks vanished into the darkness, replaced by mirages that taunted their senses.

120

John's heart raced as he struggled to discern truth from falsehood, his mind assailed by visions of his deepest fears and regrets. He saw Deborah's face in the shadows, her eyes filled with reproach and sorrow. He heard the laughter of their children echoing through the darkness, a cruel reminder of the life he had lost.

But through the haze of illusions, John clung to the light that burned within him, a beacon of hope amidst the encroaching darkness. With each step, he pushed forward, determined to unravel the mysteries of the ruins and banish the shadows that threatened to consume them all.

Section 3: The Whispers of Madness

As they pressed on, the air grew thick with the whispers of unseen voices, their words a cacophony of madness and despair. John felt the weight of their words pressing down upon him,

121

threatening to drown him in a sea of doubt and uncertainty.

"Weakness," the voices taunted, their words like daggers in his mind. "Failure. Despair."

But John refused to succumb to the darkness, his willpower a shield against the onslaught of madness. With each whispered insult, he pushed back, his determination unwavering in the face of adversity.

"We are stronger than you know," John declared, his voice ringing out with defiance. "We will not be swayed by your lies."

The villagers rallied behind him, their voices joining in a chorus of determination and defiance. Together, they pushed forward, their spirits unbroken despite the darkness that surrounded them.

122

Section 4: The Trial of Shadows

At last, they reached the heart of the ruins, a chamber bathed in an otherworldly glow. In the center of the chamber stood a pedestal, upon which rested a small, glowing orb. The orb pulsed with a faint light, its surface swirling with shadows and whispers.

"This must be the source of the darkness," one of the villagers said, his voice hushed with awe.

John approached the pedestal cautiously, his heart pounding with anticipation. He reached out to touch the orb, his fingers trembling with fear and uncertainty.

But before he could make contact, a voice echoed through the chamber, freezing him in his tracks.

"Who dares to disturb the ancient guardians of this forest?"

Section 5: The Guardian's Challenge

A figure emerged from the shadows, its

123

form shrouded in darkness. Its eyes gleamed with a malevolent light, and its voice echoed through the chamber like a whisper on the wind.

"We are the guardians of this forest," the figure intoned, its voice dripping with malice. "And we will not allow you to defile our sacred sanctuary."

John stood his ground, his heart pounding with fear and determination. "We mean no harm," he said, his voice steady despite the tremble in his limbs. "We seek to understand the darkness that plagues our village, and to put an end to it once and for all."

The figure regarded him with a mix of amusement and contempt. "You are foolish to think that you can challenge the darkness that lurks within these ruins," it said, its voice echoing with a chilling finality. "But if you are determined to proceed, know that the price of your folly may be greater than you can imagine."

124

John exchanged a glance with the villagers, their faces pale with fear but their resolve unwavering. They knew that they had come too far to turn back now, and they were prepared to face whatever darkness awaited them within the ruins.

"We understand the risks," John said, his voice firm. "But we cannot allow the darkness to consume our village. We will do whatever it takes to protect our home and our loved ones."

The figure regarded them for a moment, its eyes narrowing with suspicion. Then, with a gesture of its hand, it vanished into the shadows, leaving John and the villagers to confront the darkness alone.

Section 6: The Trials of the Ruins

As they ventured deeper into the chamber, they encountered strange traps and obstacles, designed to test their resolve and their strength. They fought off swarms of shadowy creatures that

125

seemed to materialize out of thin air, their claws and fangs glinting in the dim light.

With each passing moment, the darkness seemed to close in around them, threatening to swallow them whole. But they pressed on, driven by the desperate need to uncover the truth and to save their village from the growing menace.

They encountered puzzles and riddles, each more fiendish than the last, designed to challenge their minds and their wits. They faced illusions and hallucinations, their senses assaulted by visions of their deepest fears and darkest desires.

But through it all, they remained steadfast, their determination unwavering in the face of overwhelming darkness. They knew that they were fighting for more than just their own lives—they were fighting for the future of their village, and for the light that still flickered within their hearts.

126

Section 7: Confronting the Darkness

At last, they reached the heart of the ruins, a chamber bathed in an otherworldly glow. In the center of the chamber stood a pedestal, upon which rested a small, glowing orb. The orb pulsed with a faint light, its surface swirling with shadows and whispers.

"This must be the source of the darkness," one of the villagers said, his voice hushed with awe.

John approached the pedestal cautiously, his heart pounding with anticipation. He reached out to touch the orb, his fingers trembling with fear and uncertainty.

But before he could make contact, a voice echoed through the chamber, freezing him in his tracks.

"Who dares to disturb the ancient guardians of this forest?"

Section 8: The Guardian's Challenge

A figure emerged from the shadows, its

127

form shrouded in darkness. Its eyes gleamed with a malevolent light, and its voice echoed through the chamber like a whisper on the wind.

"We are the guardians of this forest," the figure intoned, its voice dripping with malice. "And we will not allow you to defile our sacred sanctuary."

John stood his ground, his heart pounding with fear and determination. "We mean no harm," he said, his voice steady despite the tremble in his limbs. "We seek to understand the darkness that plagues our village, and to put an end to it once and for all."

The figure regarded him with a mix of amusement and contempt. "You are foolish to think that you can challenge the darkness that lurks within these ruins," it said, its voice echoing with a chilling finality. "But if you are determined to proceed, know that the price of your folly may be greater than you can imagine."

128

John exchanged a glance with the villagers, their faces pale with fear but their resolve unwavering. They knew that they had come too far to turn back now, and they were prepared to face whatever darkness awaited them within the ruins.

"We understand the risks," John said, his voice firm. "But we cannot allow the darkness to consume our village. We will do whatever it takes to protect our home and our loved ones."

The figure regarded them for a moment, its eyes narrowing with suspicion. Then, with a gesture of its hand, it vanished into the shadows, leaving John and the villagers to confront the darkness alone.

Section 9: The Labyrinth's Trials

As they ventured deeper into the ruins, they encountered a series of trials designed to test their courage and resilience. They traversed treacherous pathways that seemed to shift and

129

change with each step, leading them deeper into the heart of darkness. They faced monstrous creatures that lurked in the shadows, their eyes gleaming with hunger and malice.

With each trial they faced, the darkness seemed to grow stronger, its presence looming over them like a suffocating fog. But John and the villagers refused to yield, their determination unyielding in the face of adversity. They pressed on, driven by the desperate need to uncover the truth and to save their village from the growing menace.

Section 10: The Chamber of Shadows

At last, they reached the heart of the ruins, a chamber bathed in an otherworldly glow. In the center of the chamber stood a pedestal, upon which rested a small, glowing orb. The orb pulsed with a faint light, its surface swirling with shadows and whispers.

"This must be the source of the

130

darkness," one of the villagers said, his voice hushed with awe.

John approached the pedestal cautiously, his heart pounding with anticipation. He reached out to touch the orb, his fingers trembling with fear and uncertainty.

But before he could make contact, a voice echoed through the chamber, freezing him in his tracks.

"Who dares to disturb the ancient guardians of this forest?"

Section 11: The Guardian's Challenge

A figure emerged from the shadows, its form shrouded in darkness. Its eyes gleamed with a malevolent light, and its voice echoed through the chamber like a whisper on the wind.

"We are the guardians of this forest," the figure intoned, its voice dripping with malice. "And we will not allow you to defile our sacred sanctuary."

John stood his ground, his heart

131

pounding with fear and determination. "We mean no harm," he said, his voice steady despite the tremble in his limbs.

"We seek to understand the darkness that plagues our village, and to put an end to it once and for all."

The figure regarded him with a mix of amusement and contempt. "You are foolish to think that you can challenge the darkness that lurks within these ruins," it said, its voice echoing with a chilling finality. "But if you are determined to proceed, know that the price of your folly may be greater than you can imagine."

John exchanged a glance with the villagers, their faces pale with fear but their resolve unwavering. They knew that they had come too far to turn back now, and they were prepared to face whatever darkness awaited them within the ruins.

"We understand the risks," John said, his voice firm. "But we cannot allow the

132

darkness to consume our village. We will do whatever it takes to protect our home and our loved ones."

The figure regarded them for a moment, its eyes narrowing with suspicion. Then, with a gesture of its hand, it vanished into the shadows, leaving John and the villagers to confront the darkness alone.

Section 12: The Trials of the Ruins

As they ventured deeper into the chamber, they encountered strange traps and obstacles, designed to test their resolve and their strength. They fought off swarms of shadowy creatures that seemed to materialize out of thin air, their claws and fangs glinting in the dim light.

With each passing moment, the darkness seemed to close in around them, threatening to swallow them whole. But they pressed on, driven by the desperate need to uncover the truth and to save their village from the growing menace.

133

They encountered puzzles and riddles, each more fiendish than the last, designed to challenge their minds and their wits. They faced illusions and hallucinations, their senses assaulted by visions of their deepest fears and darkest desires.

But through it all, they remained steadfast, their determination unwavering in the face of overwhelming darkness. They knew that they were fighting for more than just their own lives—they were fighting for the future of their village, and for the light that still flickered within their hearts.

Section 13: Confronting the Darkness

At last, they reached the heart of the ruins, a chamber bathed in an otherworldly glow. In the center of the chamber stood a pedestal, upon which rested a small, glowing orb. The orb pulsed with a faint light, its surface swirling with shadows and whispers.

134

"This must be the source of the darkness," one of the villagers said, his voice hushed with awe.

John approached the pedestal cautiously, his heart pounding with anticipation. He reached out to touch the orb, his fingers trembling with fear and uncertainty.

But before he could make contact, a voice echoed through the chamber, freezing him in his tracks.

"Who dares to disturb the ancient guardians of this forest?"

Chapter 9: The Abyss of Torment

Section 1: The Veil of Shadows

As John's fingers hovered inches away from the pulsating orb, the air around them seemed to thicken, suffused with a palpable sense of malevolence. The whispers of unseen entities echoed through the chamber, their words a

135

sinister chorus of doubt and despair.

"You are not worthy," they hissed, their voices like daggers in John's mind. "You will fail. Surrender to the darkness."

But John refused to yield, his resolve unshaken by the onslaught of darkness. With a determined grit, he pushed forward, his hand trembling as it reached out to make contact with the orb.

Suddenly, the chamber erupted into chaos, shadows writhing and twisting as if alive. The ground beneath them trembled, cracks spider-webbing across the stone floor like veins of darkness.

Section 2: The Guardian's Wrath

From the depths of the shadows, the figure emerged once more, its form contorted with rage. Its eyes blazed with an otherworldly fire, and its voice boomed through the chamber like thunder.

"Your defiance will not go unpunished,"

136

it roared, its words reverberating off the walls of the ruins. "You dare to challenge the darkness that has consumed this realm? Then prepare to face the consequences."

With a wave of its hand, the figure unleashed a torrent of dark energy, sending John and the villagers tumbling backward. They struggled to regain their footing as the darkness closed in around them, threatening to engulf them in its suffocating embrace.

But John refused to surrender, his spirit unyielding in the face of adversity. With a fierce cry, he raised his sword high, ready to face whatever horrors awaited them in the depths of the abyss.

Section 3: The Descent into Madness

With a collective resolve, John and the villagers plunged deeper into the ruins, their path shrouded in darkness. The air grew thick with the stench of decay, and the walls seemed to pulse with a

137

sickening energy.

They traversed treacherous passageways lined with jagged spikes and gaping chasms, each step bringing them closer to the heart of the abyss. Shadows danced on the walls, twisting and contorting into grotesque shapes that seemed to leer at them with malevolent intent.

But John pressed on, his determination unwavering in the face of the horrors that surrounded them. He knew that they were close to uncovering the truth behind the darkness that plagued their village, and he would not rest until they had banished it from their midst.

Section 4: The Chamber of Torment

At last, they reached the heart of the abyss, a chamber bathed in an eerie crimson light. In the center of the chamber stood a towering monolith, its surface etched with ancient runes and symbols. Dark energy crackled around

138

it, casting long shadows that seemed to reach out with grasping hands.

"This must be the source of the darkness," one of the villagers whispered, his voice trembling with fear.

John nodded grimly, his eyes fixed on the monolith before them. He knew that they had come too far to turn back now, and he would not allow the darkness to consume them.

With a determined stride, he approached the monolith, his sword at the ready. He could feel the energy pulsing from it, a malevolent force that threatened to overwhelm him.

But he would not falter. He raised his sword high and struck the monolith with all his might, unleashing a wave of light that banished the darkness from the chamber.

Section 5: The Guardian's Last Stand As the darkness receded, the figure

139

emerged from the shadows once more, its form twisted and contorted with rage. It bellowed with fury, its voice a cacophony of hatred and despair.

"You dare to defy me?" it roared, its eyes blazing with otherworldly fire. "You will pay for your insolence with your lives."

But John stood firm, his sword raised high in defiance. He would not allow the guardian to harm his village, no matter the cost.

With a mighty roar, he charged forward, his sword slicing through the darkness with ease. The guardian recoiled, its form flickering and fading as if unable to withstand the onslaught of light.

With a final blow, John struck the guardian down, banishing it from the realm once and for all. The chamber trembled with the force of the blow, and then fell silent, the darkness dissipating like morning mist.

140

Section 6: The Return to Light

As the darkness receded, John and the villagers emerged from the ruins, their hearts lightened by their victory. The sun shone brightly overhead, its warmth a welcome reprieve from the chill of the abyss.

They returned to their village, their spirits lifted by the knowledge that they had vanquished the darkness that had plagued them for so long. The townsfolk greeted them with cheers and applause, their faces alight with hope and gratitude.

John smiled as he looked out at the village he had sworn to protect. Though the scars of their ordeal would linger, he knew that they would rebuild, stronger than ever before.

And as he watched the sun set on the horizon, casting its golden light across the land, John knew that the darkness had been banished, and that light would

141

always prevail in the end.

Chapter 10: The Haunting Whispers

Section 1: Lingering Shadows

Despite the apparent victory over the darkness in the ruins, an eerie sense of unease settled over the village like a shroud. The air seemed heavier, laden with a palpable tension that refused to dissipate. Whispers of unseen specters and lingering shadows haunted the minds of the villagers, casting doubt on their newfound sense of security.

John, ever vigilant, sensed that their ordeal was far from over. He could feel the lingering presence of malevolent forces, their whispers echoing in the depths of his mind like a sinister melody. Determined to uncover the truth behind the lingering darkness, he gathered a group of brave volunteers to delve deeper into the mysteries that plagued

142

their village.

Section 2: The Withering Fields

Their investigation led them to the outskirts of the village, where the once lush fields now lay barren and desolate. The crops withered and died, their twisted forms a grim testament to the encroaching darkness that threatened to consume everything in its path.

As they ventured further into the fields, they encountered strange phenomena that defied explanation. Unearthly wails echoed through the air, sending shivers down their spines. Shadows danced on the horizon, their forms shifting and contorting with unnatural fluidity.

John's heart sank as he surveyed the devastation before him. It was clear that the darkness had not been vanquished— it had merely retreated, biding its time until it could strike once more.

143

Section 3: The Specter's Call

Suddenly, a piercing cry split the air, freezing John and his companions in their tracks. They turned as one, their eyes widening in horror as a figure emerged from the shadows. Its form was hazy and indistinct, its features obscured by a veil of darkness.

"Who dares to trespass in my domain?" the figure intoned, its voice a chilling whisper that sent shivers down their spines.

John stepped forward, his voice steady despite the tremble in his limbs. "We mean no harm," he said, his words ringing out with conviction. "We seek to understand the darkness that plagues our village, and to put an end to it once and for all."

The figure regarded him with a mix of amusement and contempt. "You think you can defeat me?" it said, its voice dripping with malice. "You are but ants

144

crawling in the shadows, powerless to stop the inevitable."

But John refused to be cowed by the specter's taunts. With a defiant glare, he raised his sword high, ready to face whatever horrors awaited them in the depths of the fields.

Section 4: The Haunted Grove

Their journey led them deeper into the heart of the fields, where a dense grove of gnarled trees loomed on the horizon. The air grew thick with an oppressive weight, and the trees seemed to leer down at them with twisted branches and grasping roots.

As they ventured further into the grove, they encountered strange apparitions that flitted through the shadows like wraiths. Their eyes gleamed with an otherworldly light, and their whispers filled the air with a cacophony of madness and despair.

145

John and his companions pressed on, their resolve unyielding in the face of the horrors that surrounded them. They knew that they were close to uncovering the truth behind the darkness that plagued their village, and they would not rest until they had banished it from their midst.

Section 5: The Guardian's Curse

At last, they reached the heart of the grove, where a towering figure stood silhouetted against the moonlit sky. Its form was twisted and contorted, its eyes burning with a malevolent light.

"We are the guardians of this land," the figure intoned, its voice echoing through the grove like a funeral dirge. "And we will not allow you to defile our sacred sanctuary."

John stepped forward, his sword raised high in defiance. "We seek only to rid our village of the darkness that plagues it," he said, his voice ringing out with

146

determination. "We mean no harm to you or your domain."

But the guardian would not be swayed. With a gesture of its hand, it unleashed a wave of dark energy, sending John and his companions tumbling backward.

Section 6: The Curse of the Guardian

As they struggled to regain their footing, the guardian advanced, its form wreathed in shadows. With each step, its presence seemed to grow stronger, its malevolent aura suffusing the grove with an oppressive darkness.

John knew that they were outmatched, their weapons powerless against the guardian's otherworldly strength. But he refused to surrender, his spirit unyielding in the face of adversity.

With a mighty roar, he charged forward, his sword flashing in the moonlight. But the guardian was ready, its form shifting and twisting to evade his blows.

147

As the battle raged on, John felt a creeping sense of dread wash over him. The guardian seemed invincible, its power beyond comprehension. And with each passing moment, the darkness seemed to close in around them, threatening to consume them all.

Section 7: The Guardian's Revelation

But just as all hope seemed lost, a voice echoed through the grove, cutting through the darkness like a ray of light. It was the voice of the guardian, its tone tinged with sadness and regret.

"We are not your enemy," the guardian said, its words a whisper on the wind. "We are but prisoners of the darkness that consumes us, cursed to wander these lands for eternity."

John's heart ached with sympathy as he looked upon the guardian's twisted form. He knew that they had been wrong to judge it so harshly, that it was not the enemy they had believed it to be.

148

"We seek to free you from your curse," John said, his voice filled with determination. "To banish the darkness that binds you and your brethren to this realm."

The guardian regarded him with a mix of surprise and gratitude. "You would do this for us?" it asked, its voice filled with disbelief.

John nodded solemnly. "We seek only to bring peace to our village," he said. "And if that means facing the darkness head-on, then so be it."

With a wave of its hand, the guardian released a burst of light that enveloped the grove, banishing the darkness and freeing the guardians from their cursed prison.

Section 8: The Return of Light

As the darkness receded, John and his companions emerged from the grove, their hearts lightened by their victory.

149

The fields began to flourish once more, their crops sprouting anew from the fertile soil.

The villagers greeted them with cheers and applause, their faces alight with hope and gratitude. John smiled as he looked out at the village he had sworn to protect. Though the scars of their ordeal would linger, he knew that they would rebuild, stronger than ever before.

And as he watched the sun rise on the horizon, casting its golden light across the land, John knew that the darkness had been banished once and for all, and that light would always prevail in the end.

Chapter 11: The Cursed Woods

Section 1: Whispering Shadows

Despite the recent victories against the darkness, a new sense of unease settled upon the village like a heavy fog.

150

Strange occurrences began to plague the outskirts of the settlement, rumors spreading of a malevolent force lurking within the nearby woods.

John, ever vigilant, could not ignore the whispers of fear that echoed through the village. Gathering a group of brave volunteers, he resolved to confront the darkness that threatened to engulf their home once more.

Section 2: The Forbidden Forest

Their journey led them deep into the heart of the forest, where ancient trees loomed overhead like silent sentinels. The air grew thick with an oppressive weight, and the shadows seemed to dance with a sinister life of their own.

As they ventured further into the forest, they encountered strange phenomena that defied explanation. Unearthly wails echoed through the trees, sending shivers down their spines. Eyes gleamed in the darkness, watching their every

151

move with a malevolent intent.

John's heart sank as he surveyed the twisted landscape before him. It was clear that they had entered a realm of darkness unlike anything they had encountered before, and he knew that they were in grave danger.

Section 3: The Haunted Clearing

Their journey led them to a clearing bathed in an eerie moonlight, where a sense of foreboding hung heavy in the air. Strange symbols adorned the trees, their meaning lost to the ages. A chill wind whispered through the undergrowth, carrying with it the faint scent of decay.

As they approached the center of the clearing, they encountered a figure cloaked in shadows. Its eyes gleamed with an otherworldly light, and its voice echoed through the night like a mournful lament.

152

"Who dares to disturb the peace of the forest?" the figure intoned, its voice filled with a sense of ancient sorrow.

John stepped forward, his voice steady despite the tremble in his limbs. "We seek only to understand the darkness that plagues our village," he said, his words ringing out with conviction. "We mean no harm to you or your domain."

But the figure would not be swayed. With a gesture of its hand, it unleashed a wave of dark energy, sending John and his companions tumbling backward.

Section 4: The Curse of the Forest

As they struggled to regain their footing, the figure advanced, its form wreathed in shadows. With each step, its presence seemed to grow stronger, its malevolent aura suffusing the clearing with an oppressive darkness.

John knew that they were outmatched, their weapons powerless against the

153

figure's otherworldly strength. But he refused to surrender, his spirit unyielding in the face of adversity.

With a mighty roar, he charged forward, his sword flashing in the moonlight. But the figure was ready, its form shifting and twisting to evade his blows.

As the battle raged on, John felt a creeping sense of dread wash over him. The figure seemed invincible, its power beyond comprehension.

And with each passing moment, the darkness seemed to close in around them, threatening to consume them all.

Section 5: The Guardian's Revelation

But just as all hope seemed lost, a voice echoed through the clearing, cutting through the darkness like a ray of light. It was the voice of the figure, its tone tinged with sadness and regret.

"We are not your enemy," the figure said, its words a whisper on the wind.

154

"We are but prisoners of the darkness that consumes us, cursed to wander these lands for eternity."

John's heart ached with sympathy as he looked upon the figure's twisted form. He knew that they had been wrong to judge it so harshly, that it was not the enemy they had believed it to be.

"We seek to free you from your curse," John said, his voice filled with determination. "To banish the darkness that binds you and your brethren to this realm."

The figure regarded him with a mix of surprise and gratitude. "You would do this for us?" it asked, its voice filled with disbelief.

John nodded solemnly. "We seek only to bring peace to our village," he said. "And if that means facing the darkness head-on, then so be it."

With a wave of its hand, the figure released a burst of light that enveloped

155

the clearing, banishing the darkness and freeing the guardians from their cursed prison.

Chapter 12: The Cursed Crypts

Section 1: Foreboding Silence

Despite the recent victories against the darkness, an ominous pall hung over the village like a shroud. Strange omens began to appear, unsettling the villagers and sowing seeds of fear and doubt. John, undeterred by the encroaching dread, resolved to uncover the source of the lingering malevolence.

Gathering a group of stalwart volunteers, he embarked on a perilous journey into the depths of the nearby crypts, where ancient secrets lay buried beneath layers of stone and shadow.

156

Section 2: Into the Abyss

The entrance to the crypts loomed before them, a gaping maw of darkness that seemed to swallow the feeble light that dared to penetrate its depths. As they ventured deeper into the earth, the air grew thick with a suffocating weight, and the darkness pressed in on them from all sides.

John led the way, his heart heavy with the weight of responsibility. He knew that they were treading on treacherous ground, where unseen dangers lurked in the shadows, waiting to ensnare the unwary.

But he refused to falter, his resolve unyielding in the face of adversity. With each step, he pushed forward, determined to uncover the truth hidden beneath the surface of the earth.

Section 3: Echoes of the Past

As they delved deeper into the crypts,

157

the air grew colder, and the darkness seemed to deepen. Strange whispers echoed through the corridors, their voices indistinct but filled with a sense of malevolence. Shadows danced on the walls, twisting and contorting into grotesque shapes that seemed to leer at them with malicious intent.

John and his companions pressed on, their spirits undaunted by the encroaching darkness. They knew that they were on the brink of discovering something terrible, something that threatened to tear their world apart.

But they would not be deterred. They had come too far to turn back now.

Section 4: The Chamber of Torment

At last, they reached the heart of the crypts, where a vast chamber stretched out before them. Ancient sarcophagi lined the walls, their stone lids adorned with intricate carvings depicting scenes of death and decay. A chill wind

158

whispered through the air, carrying with it the faint scent of decay and ancient malevolence.

In the center of the chamber stood a pedestal, upon which rested a small, glowing orb. The orb pulsed with a faint light, its surface swirling with shadows and whispers.

"This must be the source of the darkness," one of the volunteers said, his voice hushed with awe.

John approached the pedestal cautiously, his heart pounding with anticipation. He reached out to touch the orb, his fingers trembling with fear and uncertainty.

But before he could make contact, a deep, guttural growl reverberated through the chamber, freezing John and his companions in their tracks.

Section 5: The Guardian's Challenge

Out of the shadows emerged a towering figure, its form twisted and contorted

159

into a grotesque mockery of humanity. Its eyes burned with a malevolent fire, and its lips curled into a sinister grin.

"You dare to disturb the sanctity of this place?" the figure hissed, its voice echoing with the weight of centuries. "You trespass upon sacred ground, ignorant of the darkness that dwells within."

John squared his shoulders, his resolve unwavering despite the fear that gnawed at his insides. "We seek only to rid our village of the darkness that plagues it," he declared, his voice steady with determination. "We mean no harm to you or your domain."

The figure laughed, a sound that sent shivers down the spines of all who heard it. "You are but insects, scurrying in the shadows," it sneered. "You cannot hope to comprehend the true nature of the darkness that lurks within these crypts."

With a wave of its hand, the figure

160

unleashed a wave of dark energy, sending John and his companions sprawling to the ground. Shadows writhed and twisted around them, threatening to engulf them in their suffocating embrace.

But John refused to yield. With a fierce cry, he raised his sword high, ready to face whatever horrors awaited them in the depths of the crypts.

Section 6: The Abyssal Confrontation

As the battle raged on, John and his companions fought with a desperation born of necessity. They clashed with shadowy apparitions and twisted abominations, their weapons flashing in the dim light of the crypts.

But the darkness seemed endless, its depths unfathomable to mortal minds. With each passing moment, it seemed to grow stronger, its malevolent presence threatening to overwhelm them.

161

John gritted his teeth, his muscles straining with the effort of each blow. He knew that they were facing an enemy unlike any they had encountered before, and that their very souls were at stake.

But still, he fought on, driven by the desperate need to protect his village and his loved ones. He would not allow the darkness to consume them, not while he still drew breath.

Section 7: The Revelation of the Ancients

As the battle reached its crescendo, a voice echoed through the chamber, cutting through the darkness like a ray of light. It was the voice of the figure, its tone tinged with sorrow and regret.

"We are not your enemy," the figure said, its words a whisper on the wind. "We are but guardians of this realm, cursed to wander these crypts for all eternity."

162

John's heart ached with sympathy as he looked upon the figure's twisted form. He knew that they had been wrong to judge it so harshly, that it was not the enemy they had believed it to be.

"We seek to free you from your curse," John said, his voice filled with determination. "To banish the darkness that binds you and your brethren to this realm."

The figure regarded him with a mix of surprise and gratitude. "You would do this for us?" it asked, its voice filled with disbelief.

John nodded solemnly. "We seek only to bring peace to our village," he said. "And if that means facing the darkness head-on, then so be it."

With a wave of its hand, the figure released a burst of light that enveloped the chamber, banishing the darkness and freeing the guardians from their cursed prison.

163

Section 8: The Return of Light

As the darkness receded, John and his companions emerged from the crypts, their hearts lightened by their victory. The village greeted them with cheers and applause, their faces alight with hope and gratitude.

John smiled as he looked out at the village he had sworn to protect. Though the scars of their ordeal would linger, he knew that they would rebuild, stronger than ever before.

And as he watched the sun rise on the horizon, casting its golden light across the land, John knew that the darkness had been banished once and for all, and that light would always prevail in the end.

Chapter 13: The Return of the Devil

Section 1: Unsettling Calm

Despite the recent triumph over the

164

darkness in the crypts, an uneasy calm settled over the village. The air felt heavy, charged with a sense of foreboding that set the villagers on edge. They whispered among themselves, fearing that their victory was but a temporary reprieve from the malevolent forces that haunted their lives.

John, ever vigilant, sensed the lingering tension. He had learned to trust his instincts, and they told him that something dark and powerful still lurked in the shadows. Determined to protect his village, he gathered his closest allies to discuss the unsettling calm.

"We can't ignore the signs," John said, his voice grave. "There's something else out there, something worse than what we've faced before."

His companions nodded in agreement, their expressions grim. They knew that their battle was far from over.

165

Section 2: The Omen

As the villagers went about their daily routines, a series of strange and inexplicable events began to unfold. Animals went missing, their frantic cries echoing through the night. The once clear skies turned dark and stormy, casting an ominous shadow over the village. And then, one fateful evening, a blood-curdling scream pierced the air.

John and his companions rushed to the source of the scream, their hearts pounding with fear and anticipation. They found a young woman, her face pale and eyes wide with terror, standing at the edge of the forest.

"It's back," she whispered, her voice trembling. "The Devil... it's back."

A chill ran down John's spine as he looked into the depths of the forest. He knew that they were dealing with something far more sinister than they had ever encountered before.

166

Section 3: The Hunt Begins

Determined to confront the threat head-on, John and his companions prepared for a perilous journey into the heart of the forest. They armed themselves with weapons and provisions, knowing that they would need all the strength and courage they could muster.

The forest was a place of darkness and dread, its twisted trees and overgrown underbrush casting eerie shadows in the dim light. As they ventured deeper, the air grew colder, and the silence was broken only by the rustling of leaves and the distant howl of a wolf.

John led the way, his senses alert to every sound and movement. He knew that they were being watched, and he could feel the malevolent presence growing stronger with each step they took.

167

Section 4: The Abandoned Cabin

After hours of trekking through the dense forest, they stumbled upon an old, abandoned cabin. Its wooden walls were weathered and covered in moss, and the windows were shattered, giving it an eerie, haunted appearance.

"This place gives me the creeps," one of John's companions muttered, his voice barely above a whisper.

John nodded, his eyes scanning the area for any signs of danger. "Stay alert," he warned. "We don't know what we're dealing with yet."

As they cautiously approached the cabin, they noticed strange symbols carved into the door and walls. The symbols were unlike anything they had seen before, their meaning shrouded in mystery.

Pushing the door open, they entered the cabin, their weapons at the ready. Inside, they found remnants of a long-forgotten past—old furniture, dusty books, and the

168

remains of what appeared to be a ritualistic altar.

"What is this place?" another companion asked, his voice filled with unease.

John's eyes were drawn to a large, leather-bound book on the altar. He carefully opened it, revealing pages filled with cryptic writings and drawings of grotesque creatures.

"It's a journal," he said, his voice hushed. "A record of someone who lived here... someone who knew about the darkness in these woods."

Section 5: The Journal

As John read through the journal, a chilling story began to unfold. The journal belonged to a man named Ezekiel, who had once lived in the cabin and dedicated his life to studying the dark forces that inhabited the forest.

Ezekiel's writings spoke of a creature known as the Jersey Devil, a monstrous

169

being born of a curse and bound to the forest. He described its horrifying appearance—bat-like wings, a horse's head, and glowing red eyes that burned with a malevolent fire.

"The Jersey Devil is no mere legend," Ezekiel wrote. "It is a creature of pure evil, a harbinger of death and destruction. It feeds on fear and despair, and it will stop at nothing to claim its victims."

John's heart sank as he realized the gravity of their situation. The Jersey Devil was real, and it was hunting them.

Section 6: The First Attack

As they continued to read through the journal, a sudden noise outside the cabin made them freeze in their tracks. The sound of heavy footsteps and the rustling of leaves grew louder, and an overwhelming sense of dread filled the air.

170

"Prepare yourselves," John said, his voice steady but filled with urgency.

The door to the cabin burst open, and the Jersey Devil emerged from the shadows, its terrifying form illuminated by the moonlight. Its eyes glowed with a malevolent fire, and its mouth opened in a chilling roar.

John and his companions fought valiantly, their weapons clashing against the creature's hide. But the Jersey Devil was unlike any foe they had faced before —its strength was immense, and its movements were swift and deadly.

One by one, John's companions fell, their screams echoing through the night. John fought with all his might, but he knew that they were outmatched.

With a final, desperate cry, he plunged his sword into the creature's side, and the Jersey Devil let out a deafening roar of pain. But instead of retreating, it lashed out with renewed fury, sending

171

John crashing to the ground.

Section 7: The Aftermath

When John awoke, he found himself alone in the cabin, his body bruised and battered. The Jersey Devil was gone, leaving behind a trail of destruction and death.

With a heavy heart, he gathered the bodies of his fallen companions and carried them back to the village. The villagers watched in silence as he returned, their faces filled with grief and fear.

"We've lost too many," John said, his voice breaking. "But we can't give up. We have to find a way to stop this creature once and for all."

The village elders convened a council, and John shared what he had learned from Ezekiel's journal. They discussed possible strategies and sought the wisdom of ancient texts, hoping to find a

172

way to defeat the Jersey Devil.

Section 8: The Ritual

As they delved deeper into their research, they discovered an ancient ritual that could potentially banish the Jersey Devil from their world. The ritual required a rare and powerful artifact, known as the Eye of Shadows, which was said to be hidden deep within the forest.

John and a select group of volunteers prepared for their final journey. They knew that this would be their last chance to rid their village of the Jersey Devil, and they steeled themselves for the dangerous path ahead.

With the knowledge of the ritual and the determination to save their village, they set out into the forest once more, ready to face whatever horrors awaited them.

173

Section 9: The Eye of Shadows

Their journey led them to a hidden cave, its entrance concealed by overgrown vines and ancient stone. Inside, they found a series of treacherous passages and traps, designed to protect the Eye of Shadows from those who would misuse its power.

With careful precision, they navigated the cave's dangers, their hearts pounding with each step. At last, they reached a chamber bathed in an eerie light, where the Eye of Shadows rested upon a pedestal.

The artifact was a large, crystalline orb, its surface swirling with dark energy. As John approached it, he felt a surge of power, and he knew that this was the key to their salvation.

Carefully, he retrieved the Eye of Shadows, and they made their way back to the village, their spirits bolstered by the hope of victory.

174

Section 10: The Final Battle

With the Eye of Shadows in their possession, they prepared for the final battle against the Jersey Devil. The villagers gathered in the town square, their faces filled with determination and resolve.

As night fell, the air grew thick with tension, and a sense of impending doom settled over the village. They knew that the Jersey Devil would come for them, and they were ready.

The creature emerged from the shadows, its eyes burning with hatred and fury. It let out a chilling roar, and the villagers stood their ground, ready to face their fears.

John held the Eye of Shadows aloft, its dark energy pulsing with power. He began to recite the ancient incantation, his voice steady and strong.

The Jersey Devil lunged at them, its claws outstretched, but a barrier of light

175

surrounded the villagers, repelling the creature's attack. As John continued the ritual, the light grew brighter, and the Jersey Devil let out a howl of pain.

With a final, desperate effort, John completed the incantation, and the Eye of Shadows released a burst of energy that engulfed the Jersey Devil. The creature writhed in agony, its form disintegrating into shadows and smoke.

The villagers watched in awe as the Jersey Devil was banished, its malevolent presence eradicated from their world. A sense of peace and relief washed over them, and they knew that they had triumphed.

Section 11: A New Dawn

As the first light of dawn broke over the horizon, the villagers gathered to celebrate their victory. They mourned the loss of those who had fallen, but they knew that their sacrifice had not been in vain.

176

John stood at the edge of the forest, his heart filled with a mix of sorrow and hope. He knew that the darkness would always be a part of their world, but he also knew that they had the strength to face it.

With the Jersey Devil defeated and the Eye of Shadows safely hidden away, the village could finally begin to heal. They would rebuild, stronger and more united than ever before.

And as they watched the sun rise, casting its golden light across the land, they knew that they had emerged from the darkness, victorious and unbroken.

Chapter 14: Shadows of the Past

Section 1: Echoes of the Fallen

The village began its slow recovery from the horrors of the past. Life resumed its rhythm, yet an undercurrent of unease remained. The scars of their battles, both

177

physical and emotional, were still fresh, and the memory of the Jersey Devil's terror was hard to shake.

John found himself haunted by the faces of those who had perished. Their sacrifices weighed heavily on his conscience, and he often wandered to the forest's edge, contemplating the cost of their victory. The village elders, sensing his turmoil, urged him to take a break and allow himself time to heal.

One morning, while visiting the graves of his fallen comrades, John noticed something peculiar. The ground near the forest's edge was disturbed, as if something—or someone—had recently been there. An uneasy feeling settled in his gut, and he knew he needed to investigate.

Section 2: The Stranger

Word spread quickly that a stranger had been seen near the village. Descriptions were vague—a tall figure, cloaked in

178

shadow, moving silently through the forest. Fear rippled through the villagers, and they looked to John for guidance.

John gathered a small group of trusted allies and set out to find the stranger. The forest, still eerie in its silence, seemed to hold its breath as they moved deeper into its heart. Every rustle of leaves and crack of twigs set them on edge, but they pressed on, determined to uncover the truth.

After hours of searching, they came upon a small clearing. Standing in the center was the stranger—a hooded figure who seemed to blend with the shadows. John approached cautiously, his hand on the hilt of his sword.

"Who are you?" he demanded, his voice firm.

The stranger slowly lowered their hood, revealing a face etched with lines of age and sorrow. "My name is Elara," she said, her voice a soft whisper. "I have

179

come to warn you." **Section 3: A Dire Warning**

Elara's eyes, filled with a haunting wisdom, met John's. "The Jersey Devil was but a harbinger," she said. "A herald of something far more ancient and powerful."

John's heart sank. "What do you mean?" he asked, his voice barely above a whisper.

Elara explained that the Jersey Devil's presence had been a precursor to the awakening of a far greater evil—an entity known as the Shadow King. This ancient being, she revealed, had been imprisoned for centuries, its power sealed away by the same magic that had created the Eye of Shadows.

"But the battle against the Jersey Devil weakened the seal," Elara continued. "The Shadow King stirs, and if he awakens, he will bring ruin to our

180

world."

John felt a chill run down his spine. The Shadow King was a name whispered only in the darkest of legends, a being of unimaginable power and malevolence. He knew they had to act quickly to prevent this catastrophe.

Section 4: Seeking Guidance

John and his companions returned to the village with Elara, her warning weighing heavily on their minds. The elders convened a council, and Elara recounted her tale to them, leaving no detail spared.

The elders debated long into the night, their faces etched with worry. They knew that the Shadow King's awakening would spell doom for them all, and they needed a plan to stop it.

"We must find the original seal," Elara said. "The one created by the ancient mages who imprisoned the Shadow

181

King. Only by restoring it can we hope to keep him contained."

The village elders agreed, and preparations were made for a new expedition. John, ever the leader, volunteered to lead the quest. His companions, loyal and brave, stood by his side, ready to face whatever dangers lay ahead.

Section 5: The Journey Begins

The next morning, John and his team set out on their journey. The path before them was fraught with peril, and they knew that they might not return. But the fate of their village, and perhaps the world, depended on their success.

Elara guided them through the forest, her knowledge of the ancient ways proving invaluable. They traveled for days, encountering treacherous terrain and hostile creatures. Each obstacle they faced tested their resolve, but they pressed on, driven by the gravity of their

182

mission.

As they ventured deeper into the wilderness, the air grew colder, and a sense of foreboding settled over them. They knew they were approaching the source of the Shadow King's power, and their hearts pounded with a mix of fear and determination.

Section 6: The Forgotten Temple

At last, they arrived at their destination —a forgotten temple, hidden deep within the forest. The temple, shrouded in shadows, emanated a palpable sense of ancient power. Its walls were covered in cryptic symbols, and the air was thick with the scent of decay.

John and his companions entered the temple, their footsteps echoing in the silence. As they ventured deeper, they encountered a series of intricate puzzles and traps, designed to deter intruders. With Elara's guidance, they navigated these challenges, their progress slow but

183

steady.

In the heart of the temple, they found what they were looking for—a massive stone door, covered in ancient runes. Elara approached the door, her hands trembling as she traced the symbols with her fingers.

"This is it," she said, her voice filled with awe. "The seal of the Shadow King."

Section 7: The Seal

John stepped forward, his heart pounding. "How do we restore the seal?" he asked.

Elara took a deep breath. "We need to perform a ritual," she explained. "A ritual that requires the Eye of Shadows and the blood of a willing sacrifice."

John's blood ran cold. "A sacrifice?" he repeated, his voice trembling.

Elara nodded solemnly. "The magic that binds the Shadow King is ancient and

184

powerful. It demands a great price."

John looked at his companions, their faces filled with a mix of fear and determination. He knew what he had to do. "I'll do it," he said, his voice steady. "I'll be the sacrifice."

His companions protested, but John was resolute. He had led them this far, and he would see their mission through to the end.

Section 8: The Ritual

With heavy hearts, they began the ritual. Elara recited the incantation, her voice echoing through the temple. The Eye of Shadows pulsed with dark energy, its power resonating with the ancient runes on the door.

John stood in the center of the chamber, his eyes closed, ready to face his fate. As the ritual reached its climax, Elara drew a ceremonial dagger and approached him.

185

"Are you sure about this?" she asked, her voice filled with sorrow.

John nodded. "It's the only way."

With a swift, precise motion, Elara made the cut. John's blood flowed onto the Eye of Shadows, and a blinding light filled the chamber. The runes on the door glowed with an intense, otherworldly light, and the air crackled with energy.

Section 9: The Shadow King's Rage

As the light faded, a deafening roar echoed through the temple. The Shadow King, sensing the restoration of the seal, lashed out with his dark power. The ground trembled, and shadows writhed and twisted around them.

John, weakened by the ritual, struggled to stay on his feet. But he knew that they had succeeded—the seal was restored, and the Shadow King was once again imprisoned.

186

"Hold on, John!" his companions shouted, rushing to his side.

With their help, John managed to stand. He looked at the stone door, now glowing with a faint, reassuring light. The Shadow King was contained, and their world was safe—for now.

Section 10: The Return Home

With the Shadow King sealed away, John and his companions began their journey back to the village. The path was long and arduous, but their spirits were lifted by the knowledge that they had averted a great catastrophe.

When they finally returned, the villagers greeted them with tears of joy and relief. They had saved their village from the darkness once again, and their bravery would be remembered for generations to come.

John, though weakened by his ordeal, felt a sense of peace. He knew that their

187

battle was far from over, but he also knew that they had the strength to face whatever challenges lay ahead.

As the village celebrated their victory, John stood at the edge of the forest, watching the sun set on a new day. The shadows still lingered, but he knew that they would always find a way to banish the darkness.

And as long as they stood together, united in their resolve, they would overcome any obstacle. For in the heart of every shadow, there was a glimmer of light, and that light would always prevail.

Chapter 15: The Whispering Winds

Section 1: A New Threat

The village, still reeling from their recent triumph, basked in a fragile peace. Yet, beneath the surface, a new threat began to stir. The winds carried

188

whispers—faint and eerie—across the Pine Barrens, hinting at an approaching darkness that even the villagers' recent victory could not stave off.

One evening, as the sun dipped below the horizon, John sat by the hearth in his home, trying to rest. His body was still recovering from the ritual, and every movement sent sharp pains through his veins. Despite his exhaustion, sleep eluded him. The whispers on the wind troubled him deeply, gnawing at his subconscious.

As the night deepened, the winds outside grew stronger, rattling the shutters and doors. John's senses were on high alert, a nagging feeling of dread creeping into his bones. He knew better than to ignore such omens.

Section 2: A Mysterious Message

At dawn, John gathered the village elders and his trusted companions to discuss the unsettling events. As they

189

convened, an urgent knock echoed through the hall. A young boy, breathless and wide-eyed, stood at the door, clutching a crumpled piece of parchment.

"This was left at the edge of the forest," the boy stammered, handing the note to John.

John unrolled the parchment, revealing an ancient script he couldn't decipher. He handed it to Elara, who had remained in the village to aid them with her knowledge of the arcane. Her eyes widened as she read the message.

"It's a warning," she said, her voice trembling. "A call for help from a nearby village. They are facing something they call the Wind Walkers—spirits that control the winds and bring death in their wake."

The room fell silent. John felt a surge of determination. Despite their recent ordeal, he knew they couldn't ignore the

190

plight of their neighbors. **Section 3: Gathering the Brave**

John and his companions prepared for the journey. Though still weary, their resolve was unshakable. They armed themselves with weapons and protective charms, each step filled with a sense of foreboding.

As they ventured out, the villagers watched with anxious eyes, hoping their protectors would return unscathed. The path to the neighboring village was fraught with danger, the winds howling as if warning them to turn back.

The forest grew darker and more oppressive with each step. The once familiar trees seemed to twist and contort, casting eerie shadows that danced in the wind. The whispers grew louder, carrying faint cries and ghostly murmurs.

191

Section 4: The Haunted Village

They arrived at the neighboring village to find it in shambles. Homes were destroyed, and the air was thick with fear. The few survivors huddled together, their faces etched with despair. The winds here were even stronger, swirling with a malevolent energy that seemed almost tangible.

An elder of the village approached John, her eyes hollow and filled with tears. "Thank you for coming," she said, her voice barely audible above the wind. "The Wind Walkers have decimated our village. We are all that's left."

John reassured her, though his heart was heavy with the enormity of the task ahead. "We'll do everything we can to help," he promised.

Section 5: Encountering the Wind Walkers

That night, John and his companions set

192

up a watch around the village. The winds grew fiercer, and the whispers turned into wails. Suddenly, shadows began to coalesce in the air, forming ghostly figures with eyes like dark pits and mouths that seemed to suck in the very light around them.

The Wind Walkers had arrived.

John and his companions fought valiantly, but their weapons seemed to have little effect on these ethereal beings. The Wind Walkers moved with the speed of the wind, striking with deadly precision. The villagers joined the battle, armed with makeshift weapons and sheer desperation.

Elara, sensing that conventional means were useless, began to chant an incantation. Her voice rose above the chaos, a beacon of hope in the storm. The Wind Walkers recoiled at the sound, their forms flickering and wavering.

"Keep chanting!" John shouted,

193

realizing that Elara's magic was their only hope.

Section 6: The Heart of the Storm

Elara's incantation grew more powerful, but the Wind Walkers seemed to adapt, pressing their attack with renewed vigor. John knew they needed to find the source of the Wind Walkers' power to truly defeat them.

"Follow me!" he called to his companions, leading them towards the center of the storm. The winds whipped around them, threatening to tear them apart, but they pressed on, driven by a fierce determination.

At the heart of the storm, they found a large, ancient stone altar, covered in runes that pulsed with dark energy. The Wind Walkers seemed to be drawn to it, their forms swirling around it like a vortex.

"This is it," Elara said, her voice barely

194

audible above the howling wind. "We need to destroy the altar."

Section 7: The Final Battle

With renewed purpose, John and his companions attacked the altar. The Wind Walkers, sensing their intent, fought back with ferocity. Elara continued her incantation, directing her magic towards the altar.

The battle raged on, each moment more desperate than the last. John fought with every ounce of strength he had left, his body aching from the strain. His companions stood by his side, their courage unwavering despite the overwhelming odds.

Finally, with a deafening crack, the altar began to crumble. A blinding light erupted from its center, engulfing the Wind Walkers. Their wails filled the air as they were drawn into the light, their forms dissipating into nothingness.

195

As the last of the Wind Walkers vanished, the winds began to die down. The storm dissipated, leaving a calm, eerie silence in its wake.

Section 8: Rebuilding and Reflection

The villagers emerged from their shelters, their faces filled with cautious hope. They had survived the onslaught, thanks to the bravery and sacrifice of John and his companions.

John, exhausted but relieved, looked around at the devastated village. There was much work to be done, but for the first time in days, there was a sense of hope.

"We'll help you rebuild," he promised the elder. "Together, we can make this village strong again."

As they worked side by side, John couldn't help but reflect on the battles they had fought and the darkness they had faced. Each victory had come at a

196

great cost, but it had also brought them closer together, forging unbreakable bonds of friendship and trust.

Section 9: A Glimmer of Light

With the Wind Walkers defeated and the village beginning to recover, John and his companions prepared to return home. The journey back was filled with a sense of accomplishment and relief, though they knew that their fight against the darkness was far from over.

As they approached their village, the sun began to rise, casting a warm, golden light across the land. The shadows that had plagued them seemed to recede, replaced by a glimmer of hope and renewal.

John knew that there would always be new challenges to face, new threats to overcome. But with each victory, they grew stronger, more resilient. And as long as they stood together, they would continue to banish the darkness, one

197

battle at a time.

For in the heart of every shadow, there was a glimmer of light, and that light would always prevail.

Chapter 16: The Forsaken Grove

Section 1: A New Beginning

The village thrived in the aftermath of their victories, with a renewed sense of unity and purpose. John, now a revered leader, continued to guide his people with wisdom and courage. The scars of their past battles were healing, but a sense of vigilance remained, a constant reminder of the lurking dangers in the Pine Barrens.

One evening, as the village gathered to celebrate the harvest festival, a sudden chill swept through the air. The joyous laughter and music faltered as a dense fog rolled in, enveloping the village in an eerie silence. The atmosphere grew

198

heavy, and an uneasy feeling settled over the crowd.

John's instincts kicked in. He knew that such an unnatural phenomenon could only mean one thing: a new threat was approaching.

Section 2: The Stranger in the Fog

As the fog thickened, a figure emerged from the shadows. Clad in tattered robes, the stranger's face was obscured by a hood, and an air of malevolence seemed to surround him. The villagers watched in tense silence as he approached the center of the gathering.

John stepped forward, his hand resting on the hilt of his sword. "Who are you?" he demanded, his voice steady but laced with caution.

The stranger lifted his head, revealing eyes that glowed with an unnatural light. "I am Malachi," he said, his voice a raspy whisper. "I bring a warning."

199

The villagers exchanged nervous glances, the tension palpable. John remained composed, though his mind raced with questions. "What is your warning?" he asked.

Malachi's eyes bore into John's. "The Forsaken Grove has awakened," he said. "A place of ancient evil, long forgotten. It is drawing power from the land, and if left unchecked, it will consume everything in its path."

Section 3: The Legend of the Forsaken Grove

Elara, who had been listening intently, stepped forward. "The Forsaken Grove is a place of legend," she said, her voice trembling. "A cursed forest where no light can penetrate, and where the spirits of the damned are said to dwell."

Malachi nodded. "The grove was sealed by powerful magic centuries ago, but the seal is weakening. The darkness within is growing stronger, feeding on the fear

200

and despair of the living."

John felt a chill run down his spine. The battles they had faced seemed like child's play compared to the threat Malachi described. "What must we do?" he asked, his voice resolute.

Malachi's gaze shifted to Elara. "The seal can be strengthened, but it requires a rare and powerful artifact: the Heart of Shadows. It lies at the center of the grove, guarded by the spirits that dwell there."

Section 4: Preparing for the Journey

The village elders convened an emergency council, and it was decided that a small group would venture into the Forsaken Grove to retrieve the Heart of Shadows. John, Elara, and a few of their most trusted companions volunteered for the perilous mission.

As they prepared for the journey, Malachi provided them with what little

201

knowledge he had about the grove. "The path is treacherous, and the spirits will do everything in their power to stop you," he warned. "But remember, the Heart of Shadows is your only hope. Without it, the grove's darkness will spread, engulfing your village and beyond."

With heavy hearts and steely determination, John and his team set out towards the Forsaken Grove. The villagers watched them go, their prayers and hopes following the brave souls who had once again taken on the mantle of protectors.

Section 5: Into the Darkness

The journey to the Forsaken Grove was arduous. The air grew colder, and the landscape became more desolate with each step. The trees twisted and gnarled, their branches reaching out like skeletal fingers. The fog thickened, and a sense of foreboding settled over the group.

202

As they entered the grove, an oppressive silence enveloped them. The air was heavy with the stench of decay, and the ground was littered with the bones of those who had ventured too far. Shadows flitted at the edge of their vision, and ghostly whispers filled the air.

Elara led the way, her knowledge of ancient magic guiding them through the labyrinthine forest. They moved cautiously, aware that danger lurked in every shadow.

Section 6: The First Encounter

As they ventured deeper into the grove, the whispers grew louder, more insistent. The temperature dropped, and the darkness seemed to close in around them. Suddenly, a wail pierced the silence, and ghostly figures emerged from the shadows.

The spirits of the damned, their faces twisted with agony and rage, attacked

203

with a ferocity that took the group by surprise. John and his companions fought valiantly, their weapons flashing in the dim light. Elara chanted spells of protection, her voice rising above the cacophony.

Despite their efforts, the spirits were relentless. They moved with unnatural speed, their touch draining the life force from those they encountered. John felt his strength waning, but he refused to give in. He knew that they had to reach the center of the grove, no matter the cost.

Section 7: The Heart of Shadows

After what felt like an eternity, they reached the heart of the Forsaken Grove. In the center of a clearing stood a large, ancient tree, its bark blackened and twisted. At its base, pulsating with a dark, otherworldly light, lay the Heart of Shadows.

The air around the heart was thick with

204

malevolent energy, and the spirits converged on them, their wails reaching a fever pitch. Elara stepped forward, her eyes glowing with determination.

"We need to perform the binding ritual," she shouted over the din. "John, keep them off me while I do this."

John nodded, rallying his companions for a final stand. They formed a protective circle around Elara, fighting off the spirits with every ounce of strength they had left. Elara began the ritual, her voice steady and powerful.

The spirits grew more frantic, their attacks more desperate. John felt his limbs growing heavy, his vision blurring. But he fought on, knowing that their only hope lay in Elara's success.

Section 8: The Binding Ritual

Elara's incantation reached its climax, and the Heart of Shadows began to glow brighter. The spirits wailed in agony,

205

their forms flickering and dissipating. The ground trembled, and the ancient tree shuddered.

With a final, deafening roar, the Heart of Shadows unleashed a wave of energy, banishing the spirits and sealing the grove once more. The oppressive darkness lifted, replaced by a strange, serene silence.

Elara collapsed to the ground, exhausted but triumphant. John and his companions, battered and bruised, gathered around her.

"It's done," she said, her voice barely above a whisper. "The grove is sealed."

Section 9: The Return

The journey back to the village was a blur of exhaustion and relief. They moved slowly, their bodies and spirits weary from the ordeal. When they finally emerged from the forest, the sight of their village brought tears to their

206

eyes.

The villagers greeted them with cheers and tears of joy. They had once again faced the darkness and emerged victorious, their bravery and determination a testament to their unbreakable spirit.

John, though exhausted, felt a profound sense of peace. They had faced an ancient evil and won, protecting their village from a fate worse than death. As he looked around at the faces of those he had fought to protect, he knew that their bond was stronger than ever.

Section 10: A New Dawn

As the sun rose, casting its golden light over the village, John stood at the edge of the forest, reflecting on their journey. The shadows had been banished, and a new dawn had begun.

He knew that there would always be challenges to face, but he also knew that

207

they would face them together. The Forsaken Grove was sealed, the darkness contained. And as long as they stood united, they would continue to protect their home, no matter what the future held.

For in the heart of every shadow, there was a glimmer of light, and that light would always prevail.

Chapter 17: The Raven's Warning

Section 1: An Ominous Discovery

The village settled into a period of uneasy peace following the sealing of the Forsaken Grove. Life returned to a semblance of normalcy, yet a lingering sense of vigilance remained. John and his companions continued their duties, ever watchful for signs of new threats.

One crisp morning, as the sun cast its first rays over the Pine Barrens, a raven appeared at the village outskirts. It was

208

an unusual bird, larger than any John had seen before, with feathers that shimmered with an unnatural sheen. It perched on a fence post, its eyes gleaming with an unsettling intelligence.

John approached cautiously, sensing that this was no ordinary bird. As he drew near, the raven cawed loudly, a harsh, echoing sound that sent chills down his spine. The bird tilted its head, as if scrutinizing him, then flapped its wings and took off into the forest, leaving behind a small, rolled-up parchment tied with a black ribbon.

Section 2: The Message

John picked up the parchment, feeling a sense of dread as he unrolled it. The script was elegant but filled with an eerie, otherworldly quality. Elara, drawn by the commotion, joined him and peered over his shoulder.

"The Raven's Warning," she whispered, recognizing the script. "It's an omen of

209

great importance in the arcane world. Let me read it."

The message read:

Beware the gathering storm. The darkness you have faced is but a shadow of what is to come. Seek the Raven's Eye to reveal the truth. Trust in the light, for only it can guide you through the encroaching night.

Elara's face paled as she finished reading. "The Raven's Eye is a powerful artifact, said to have the ability to reveal hidden truths and protect against malevolent forces. It's our only hope to understand and combat this new threat."

Section 3: The Search Begins

Determined to find the Raven's Eye, John gathered his most trusted companions. They set out on a new journey, venturing into the deeper, uncharted parts of the Pine Barrens where few dared to go. The forest was

210

dense and foreboding, filled with ancient trees that seemed to whisper secrets of the past.

The journey was arduous. They faced numerous obstacles: treacherous terrain, wild beasts, and the ever-present sense of being watched. The raven often appeared, guiding them with its eerie cries and leading them deeper into the wilderness.

Section 4: The Hidden Temple

After days of travel, the raven led them to an ancient temple, hidden deep within the forest. The structure was overgrown with vines and moss, its stone walls cracked and weathered by time. The entrance was guarded by two statues of ravens, their eyes seemingly alive with a dark glow.

"This must be it," Elara said, her voice filled with awe and trepidation. "The Temple of the Raven's Eye."

211

They cautiously entered the temple, the air inside cool and damp. The interior was filled with intricate carvings and symbols, all depicting ravens and scenes of prophecy. At the center of the main chamber stood an altar, upon which rested a large, black gemstone—the Raven's Eye.

Section 5: The Guardians Awaken

As they approached the altar, a sense of foreboding filled the air. Suddenly, the ground shook, and the statues at the entrance came to life, their stone forms cracking and shattering to reveal monstrous, raven-like creatures. The guardians screeched, their eyes glowing with malevolent energy.

John and his companions readied themselves for battle. The guardians attacked with swift, deadly precision, their claws and beaks striking with unnatural force. The group fought back fiercely, using all their skills and

212

abilities to fend off the monstrous ravens.

Elara, realizing the importance of securing the Raven's Eye, began to chant an incantation. Her voice rose above the chaos, channeling her magic into a protective barrier around the altar. The guardians screeched in fury, but the barrier held, giving John and the others the chance to strike.

Section 6: The Power of the Raven's Eye

With a final, coordinated effort, they defeated the guardians, their forms crumbling back into stone. Elara completed her incantation, and the barrier around the altar dissipated. John carefully approached the Raven's Eye, feeling its powerful energy pulsing through the air.

As he touched the gemstone, a surge of knowledge and under-standing flooded his mind. Visions of the past and future

213

flashed before his eyes, revealing the true nature of the threats they had faced and those yet to come. The Raven's Eye glowed brightly, illuminating the chamber with a pure, white light.

Elara stepped forward, her eyes wide with awe. "The Raven's Eye has revealed the truth. The darkness we face is part of an ancient prophecy, a cycle of evil that must be broken. We have the power to change our fate, but it will require great sacrifice and unwavering resolve."

Section 7: The Return Home

With the Raven's Eye in their possession, the group made their way back to the village. The journey was filled with a renewed sense of purpose and hope. The visions had shown John not only the dangers that lay ahead but also the strength and unity of their people.

As they neared the village, the raven

214

appeared one last time, its eyes gleaming with approval. It cawed loudly, then disappeared into the forest, leaving them to face the future with newfound determination.

The villagers greeted them with joy and relief, their faces lighting up at the sight of the Raven's Eye. John and Elara shared the knowledge they had gained, preparing everyone for the challenges to come.

Section 8: A New Dawn

The Raven's Warning had brought them together, uniting them in their quest for survival and peace. With the power of the Raven's Eye and the strength of their community, they stood ready to face whatever darkness lay ahead.

As the sun rose, casting its golden light over the village, John felt a renewed sense of hope. The shadows might be ever-present, but with the light of the Raven's Eye to guide them, they would

215

continue to fight, protect, and prevail.

For in the heart of every shadow, there was a glimmer of light, and that light would always prevail.

Chapter 18: The Encroaching Night

Section 1: Shadows on the Horizon

Despite the newfound sense of hope that had settled over the village, the atmosphere remained tense. The Raven's Eye had provided them with crucial knowledge, but the visions had also shown that the true battle was yet to come. The villagers prepared diligently, fortifying their homes and sharpening their weapons. Training sessions became a daily routine, with everyone from the youngest child to the oldest elder participating in some form of defense preparation.

John and Elara spent countless hours studying the Raven's Eye, trying to

216

decipher every fragment of knowledge it held. The more they learned, the more they realized the enormity of the task ahead. The Raven's Eye revealed glimpses of an ancient evil, a darkness that had been growing in strength and influence. The Pine Barrens had always been a place of mystery and danger, but now it seemed as though the very land was conspiring against them.

One evening, as the sun dipped below the horizon and the first stars began to twinkle in the sky, a chilling wind swept through the village. The wind carried a strange, whispering sound, almost like voices murmuring just beyond the edge of hearing. The villagers shivered, feeling an inexplicable sense of dread.

John stood at the edge of the village, staring into the darkening forest. He knew that something was coming, something that would test the limits of their strength and resolve.

217

Section 2: An Unwelcome Visitor

As night fell, the whispers grew louder, and the villagers gathered in the central square, seeking comfort in numbers.

Suddenly, a figure emerged from the shadows. It was Malachi, the mysterious stranger who had first warned them about the Forsaken Grove. He looked even more haggard and haunted than before, his eyes reflecting a deep sorrow.

"Malachi," John called out, stepping forward. "What brings you here?"

Malachi's voice was strained, barely above a whisper. "The darkness is spreading faster than we anticipated. The spirits of the Forsaken Grove were only the beginning. An ancient evil stirs, one that seeks to consume everything in its path."

The villagers murmured in fear, but John raised his hand to silence them. "What do you mean? What are we facing?"

Malachi took a deep breath, his gaze

218

meeting John's. "The visions you saw in the Raven's Eye—they speak of a being known as the Nightbringer, an entity of pure darkness that has been awakened. It feeds on fear and despair, growing stronger with each passing day. It's coming for the Pine Barrens, and it will stop at nothing to claim this land."

Section 3: Preparing for Battle

The news sent a ripple of fear through the village, but John and Elara remained resolute. They knew that they had to act quickly if they were to stand any chance against the Nightbringer. The villagers worked tirelessly, reinforcing their defenses and preparing for the impending battle.

John called a meeting with his most trusted companions, including Elara, Malachi, and the village elders. They gathered around a large table, the Raven's Eye placed at the center, its dark surface pulsing with a faint light.

219

"We need a plan," John said, his voice firm. "We know the Nightbringer is coming, but we don't know when or how. We need to be ready for anything."

Elara nodded, her face etched with determination. "The Raven's Eye has shown us that light is our greatest weapon against the Nightbringer. We need to harness every source of light we can find—torches, lanterns, magical wards. Anything that can keep the darkness at bay."

Malachi added, "The Nightbringer's power is immense, but it's not invincible. If we can weaken it, even for a moment, we might have a chance to strike a decisive blow. We need to find its weakness."

Section 4: The Gathering Storm

As the days passed, the villagers worked relentlessly, their fear transforming into a fierce determination. They built massive bonfires at the village's

220

perimeter, erected magical wards, and created weapons imbued with light. The children helped by gathering firewood and making charms, their innocent laughter a small but vital beacon of hope.

One night, as the preparations continued, John stood watch at the edge of the village. The forest was eerily silent, the usual sounds of nocturnal creatures absent. Suddenly, he heard a rustling in the underbrush. He drew his sword and stepped forward cautiously.

From the shadows, a figure stumbled into view. It was a woman, her clothes torn and muddy, her face pale and gaunt. She collapsed at John's feet, gasping for breath.

"Help... me..." she whispered, her voice barely audible.

John knelt beside her, calling for Elara. The woman's eyes were wide with terror, her body trembling

221

uncontrollably.

Elara arrived quickly, her hands glowing with healing light. "What happened?" she asked, gently touching the woman's forehead.

The woman's eyes flickered open, and she clutched John's arm with surprising strength. "The darkness... it's coming... it took my family... it's coming for us all..."

Section 5: The First Attack

The woman's warning proved to be true. That very night, the first wave of the Nightbringer's minions attacked. Shadows moved through the forest, their forms barely discernible in the dim light. The villagers fought bravely, using their weapons and the light from their bonfires to fend off the attackers.

John led the defense, his sword gleaming as he cut through the shadowy figures. Elara stood at the center of the

222

village, her magic weaving a protective barrier around the most vulnerable.

Despite their efforts, the shadows were relentless. They seemed to rise from the very ground, their numbers growing with each passing moment. The air was filled with the sounds of battle—swords clashing, arrows whistling through the air, and the cries of the wounded.

John felt a surge of anger and determination. He knew they couldn't hold out forever; they needed to find the source of the darkness and destroy it.

Section 6: A Desperate Plan

As dawn approached, the shadows began to retreat, melting back into the forest. The village was left battered and weary, but still standing. John and Elara gathered their companions, knowing that they needed a new strategy.

"We can't keep fighting like this," John said, his voice grim. "We need to take

223

the fight to the Nightbringer. We need to find its lair and destroy it before it can unleash its full power."

Elara nodded, her eyes filled with determination. "The Raven's Eye can guide us. It showed us glimpses of the Nightbringer's lair, hidden deep within the heart of the Pine Barrens. It's a dangerous journey, but it's our only hope."

Malachi stepped forward. "I will go with you. My knowledge of the dark arts might prove useful. Together, we can face the Nightbringer and end this nightmare once and for all."

John looked around at his companions, their faces etched with resolve. They had faced many trials together, and he knew they would face this one with the same courage and determination.

"We leave at first light," he said. "Prepare yourselves. This will be our greatest challenge yet."

224

Section 7: Into the Heart of Darkness

As the sun rose, casting its first light over the village, John, Elara, Malachi, and a select group of warriors set out towards the heart of the Pine Barrens. The air was thick with tension, the forest eerily silent as they made their way deeper into the wilderness.

The Raven's Eye guided them, its light growing brighter as they neared their destination. The journey was fraught with danger, as they encountered more of the Nightbringer's minions along the way. Each battle left them more weary, but their resolve remained unbroken.

Finally, after days of travel, they reached a clearing surrounded by ancient, twisted trees. In the center of the clearing stood a massive stone monolith, its surface covered in dark, pulsating runes. This was the Nightbringer's lair.

225

Section 8: The Final Confrontation

As they approached the monolith, the ground began to tremble, and the air grew thick with darkness. The Nightbringer emerged from the shadows, a towering figure of pure malevolence. Its eyes glowed with an unholy light, and its voice echoed through the clearing, filled with a terrible power.

"You dare to challenge me?" it hissed, its form shifting and writhing. "You are nothing but insects before my might."

John stepped forward, his sword raised. "We will not let you destroy our home. We will fight, and we will prevail."

The battle was fierce and brutal. The Nightbringer wielded dark magic, summoning shadows and blasts of energy to attack them. John and his companions fought with everything they had, using the light of the Raven's Eye to weaken the creature.

226

Elara chanted a powerful incantation, her magic enveloping the Nightbringer in a blinding light. Malachi used his knowledge of the dark arts to counter the creature's spells, creating openings for John and the others to strike.

Despite their efforts, the Nightbringer was incredibly powerful. It fought with a ferocity that seemed unstoppable, its dark energy consuming everything in its path. John felt his strength waning, but he refused to give up.

Section 9: A Sacrifice

As the battle raged on, it became clear that they could not defeat the Nightbringer through sheer force alone. Elara, sensing the desperation of the situation, made a fateful decision.

"John," she called out, her voice filled with resolve. "There is a way to defeat the Nightbringer, but it will require a great sacrifice."

227

John's heart sank as he saw the determination in her eyes. "What do you mean?"

Elara held up the Raven's Eye, its light glowing brightly. "The Raven's Eye can channel the purest light, but it needs a source of immense power. If I channel my life force into it, I can create a burst of light strong enough to destroy the Nightbringer."

John's eyes widened in horror. "No, Elara. There must be another way."

She shook her head, tears in her eyes. "This is the only way. I believe in you, John. You must finish this fight."

Before he could protest further, Elara began to chant, her voice rising in a powerful incantation. The Raven's Eye glowed brighter and brighter, its light filling the clearing. The Nightbringer screamed in rage, sensing the impending threat.

John fought with renewed fury,

228

protecting Elara as she completed the incantation. The light grew blinding, and with a final, heart-wrenching cry, Elara released her magic. A beam of pure, radiant light shot from the Raven's Eye, striking the Nightbringer and enveloping it in a searing brilliance.

The creature shrieked in agony, its form disintegrating under the onslaught of light. The darkness that had consumed the Pine Barrens began to recede, and the forest was bathed in a golden glow.

Section 10: The Aftermath

As the light faded, John collapsed to his knees, grief overwhelming him. Elara lay motionless on the ground, her face peaceful in death. The villagers who had accompanied them gathered around, their faces etched with sorrow and awe.

Malachi placed a hand on John's shoulder. "She saved us all, John. Her sacrifice will be remembered forever."

229

John nodded, tears streaming down his face. "We will honor her memory by rebuilding our village and ensuring that this darkness never returns."

With the Nightbringer defeated, the Pine Barrens began to heal. The villagers returned home, their hearts heavy with loss but filled with hope for the future. They erected a monument in the village square to honor Elara's sacrifice, a symbol of the light that had triumphed over the darkness.

John stood before the monument, his resolve stronger than ever. He knew that the battle against evil was never truly over, but he also knew that as long as they stood together, they could overcome any challenge.

As the sun set, casting its golden light over the village, John felt a renewed sense of purpose. The shadows might still lurk in the corners of the world, but with the light of the Raven's Eye to guide them, they would always find their

230

way through the encroaching night.

Chapter 19: Rebuilding and Reflection

Section 1: The Light After Darkness

The defeat of the Nightbringer brought a renewed sense of peace to the Pine Barrens, but it also left a void that was felt deeply by everyone in the village. Elara's sacrifice had saved them, but the cost was immeasurable. As the days turned into weeks, the villagers worked together to rebuild their homes and lives, always with the memory of Elara's bravery in their hearts.

John took on a new role as the leader of the village, guiding the reconstruction efforts with a steady hand. His grief for Elara was a constant companion, but he channeled it into a fierce determination to honor her memory. The villagers followed his example, each one

231

contributing in their own way to the restoration of their home.

Malachi stayed as well, his knowledge of the arcane arts invaluable in helping to strengthen the village's defenses and ensure that the darkness would never again take root in their land. His presence was a reminder of the broader world beyond the Pine Barrens, a world that still held many mysteries and dangers.

Section 2: New Beginnings

With the physical reconstruction well underway, John and Malachi turned their attention to the spiritual and emotional healing of the community. They organized gatherings where villagers could share their experiences and express their grief. These gatherings became a cornerstone of the village's recovery, allowing people to find solace and strength in each other's company.

Elara's monument became a place of

232

pilgrimage, a symbol of hope and resilience. Villagers left flowers, tokens of remembrance, and offerings of thanks at its base. The monument stood as a testament to the light that had prevailed over the encroaching night, a reminder that even in the darkest times, there is always hope.

The village also welcomed new faces. News of the Nightbringer's defeat spread, drawing people from neighboring regions who sought safety and a new beginning. These newcomers brought with them skills, knowledge, and a fresh perspective that enriched the community. The village grew, not just in numbers, but in spirit and unity.

Section 3: The Wisdom of the Raven's Eye

The Raven's Eye, still pulsing with a faint light, was placed in a sacred chamber within the village's central hall. John and Malachi continued to study it,

233

uncovering more of its secrets and using its wisdom to guide their decisions. The artifact had become a source of immense knowledge and power, its presence a constant reminder of the battle they had fought and the sacrifices they had made.

One evening, as John was examining the Raven's Eye, he was struck by a vision. He saw a figure cloaked in shadows, standing at the edge of a great chasm. The figure turned, revealing Elara's face, her eyes filled with a serene wisdom. She spoke, her voice echoing in his mind.

"John, the journey is not over. There are still many challenges ahead, but you have the strength and the heart to overcome them. Remember, the light within you is the greatest weapon against the darkness. Lead your people with courage and compassion, and you will find your way."

John woke from the vision with a renewed sense of purpose. He shared the

234

vision with Malachi and the village elders, and together they devised a plan to continue protecting and nurturing their home. They established a council to govern the village, ensuring that all voices were heard and that decisions were made with wisdom and foresight.

Section 4: The Path Forward

As the village flourished, John and Malachi began to explore the surrounding regions, seeking out other sources of darkness and threats that might endanger their home. They formed alliances with neighboring communities, sharing knowledge and resources to create a network of support and defense.

Their efforts bore fruit. The Pine Barrens became a beacon of hope and resilience, a place where people could find refuge and strength. The bonds between the villages grew stronger, and together they faced and overcame numerous

235

challenges.

John often thought of Elara, her spirit a guiding force in his life. He felt her presence in the quiet moments, in the laughter of children, and in the strength of his people. Her sacrifice had not only saved their village but had also inspired a new era of unity and hope.

Section 5: A Legacy of Light

Years passed, and the village continued to grow and thrive. The children who had once played in the shadows now trained as protectors of their home, learning the skills and knowledge passed down by John, Malachi, and the elders. The Raven's Eye remained a central part of their lives, its wisdom guiding them through every challenge.

John, now older and wiser, looked upon his village with pride. The legacy of Elara's sacrifice was evident in every smiling face, in every act of kindness, and in the unwavering strength of their

236

community. The darkness that had once threatened to consume them had been pushed back, replaced by a light that shone brightly.

One evening, as the sun set over the Pine Barrens, casting a golden glow over the village, John stood before Elara's monument. He placed a hand on the stone, feeling a deep sense of peace.

"We did it, Elara," he whispered. "We've built something beautiful, something that will endure. Your sacrifice will never be forgotten. Thank you for guiding us, for believing in us. We will continue to honor your memory, now and always."

As the stars began to twinkle in the sky, John felt a warmth in his heart. The journey had been long and arduous, but they had emerged stronger, united, and filled with hope. The light of the Raven's Eye, and the spirit of Elara, would continue to guide them through whatever lay ahead, ensuring that the

237

encroaching night would never again overshadow the light of their lives.

Chapter 20: The Final Darkness

Section 1: A Shroud of Peace

The village of Pine Barrens had become a beacon of hope and resilience. Its people thrived, and the darkness that once overshadowed their lives had been pushed back. John, now an elder, watched over his village with pride, knowing that Elara's sacrifice had led to a prosperous and peaceful future.

The Raven's Eye, though still a powerful artifact, had grown dormant, its light faint but constant. It remained a symbol of their victory and a source of guidance. John and the village council continued to consult it, but its visions had become less frequent, and its warnings less dire.

One evening, as the village prepared for their annual celebration in honor of

238

Elara's sacrifice, a strange unease settled over John. He couldn't shake the feeling that something was amiss, but he dismissed it as a remnant of the countless battles they had fought.

Section 2: The Eclipse

As night fell, the villagers gathered around a large bonfire, their laughter and songs filling the air. The children danced and played, their faces lit by the warm glow of the flames. It was a night of joy and remembrance, a night to honor the light that had saved them.

But as the celebration reached its peak, the sky began to darken unnaturally. The stars winked out one by one, and the moon, full and bright just moments before, was swallowed by an inky blackness. The villagers fell silent, their laughter dying in their throats as a deep, foreboding chill spread through the air.

John's heart raced as he looked up at the sky. This was no ordinary darkness; it

239

felt alive, malevolent. He turned to Malachi, who was already moving towards the Raven's Eye.

"We need to consult the Eye," John said, his voice tense. "Something is terribly wrong."

Section 3: A New Omen

The village council gathered in the central hall, their faces grim and determined. The Raven's Eye sat in its place, its surface dull and lifeless. Malachi placed his hands on the artifact, muttering an incantation. Slowly, the Raven's Eye began to glow, its light flickering like a dying flame.

A vision emerged, but it was unlike any they had seen before. The image was distorted, fragmented, showing glimpses of a vast, consuming darkness. Figures writhed within it, their forms twisted and unnatural. And at the center of the vision, a pair of glowing red eyes stared back at them, filled with an ancient,

240

unrelenting malice.

"It's not over," Malachi whispered, his voice shaking. "The Nightbringer was only a harbinger. There is something else, something even more powerful and ancient. It has been awakened."

John felt a cold dread settle over him. "We need to prepare the village. This darkness is unlike anything we've faced before."

Section 4: The Descent

As the villagers armed themselves and fortified their defenses, the darkness continued to spread. It enveloped the forest, turning familiar paths into shadowy mazes. Strange sounds echoed from the depths of the woods, and an oppressive silence fell over the village, broken only by the whispers of fear.

John and Malachi led a small group into the forest, following the faint light of the Raven's Eye. The journey was fraught

241

with peril, as shadowy figures darted through the trees, watching them with hungry eyes. The air grew colder, and a sense of dread deepened with every step.

They reached a clearing where the darkness seemed to pulse with a life of its own. The ground was scorched, and the trees twisted into grotesque shapes. At the center stood a massive, obsidian obelisk, covered in the same pulsating runes as the Nightbringer's monolith.

"This is it," Malachi said, his voice barely audible. "The source of the darkness."

Section 5: The Final Confrontation

As they approached the obelisk, the ground trembled, and a deep, rumbling growl echoed through the clearing. The air grew thick with shadows, and from the darkness emerged a figure. It was tall and cloaked in a tattered, black shroud, its red eyes burning with an other-worldly fire.

242

"You have come to your doom," it hissed, its voice echoing with a thousand tortured souls. "I am the Eternal Night, the end of all light."

John raised his sword, its blade glowing with the light of the Raven's Eye. "We will not let you destroy our home."

The battle was fierce and chaotic. The Eternal Night wielded dark magic that sapped their strength and filled their minds with terror. John and his companions fought valiantly, their weapons and the light of the Raven's Eye their only defense against the over-whelming darkness.

Malachi chanted powerful spells, his magic clashing with the Eternal Night's. The clearing became a battleground of light and shadow, each side struggling for dominance. But the Eternal Night was relentless, its power seeming to grow with each passing moment.

243

Section 6: A Desperate Gamble

Realizing they could not defeat the Eternal Night through sheer force, John made a desperate decision. "Malachi, we need to use the Raven's Eye. We need to channel all our power into it and strike at the heart of this darkness."

Malachi nodded, understanding the risk. "It may be our only chance."

They gathered around the Raven's Eye, their hands joined, and began to chant. The Eye glowed brighter and brighter, its light pushing back the shadows. The Eternal Night roared in fury, sensing the imminent threat.

With a final, desperate cry, they released the energy of the Raven's Eye. A beam of pure, blinding light shot forth, striking the Eternal Night and the obelisk. The darkness screamed, writhing in agony as the light consumed it.

For a moment, it seemed they had

244

succeeded. The darkness began to dissipate, and the Eternal Night's form wavered. But then, with a final, terrible roar, the obelisk exploded, releasing a shockwave of darkness that engulfed the clearing.

Section 7: The Aftermath

When the dust settled, John and his companions lay on the ground, battered and exhausted. The clearing was silent, the obelisk reduced to rubble. The Eternal Night was gone, but its final act had left a mark. The darkness had not been fully vanquished; it lingered at the edges of their vision, a constant reminder of the threat that still loomed.

They returned to the village, their spirits heavy. The battle had been won, but the war was far from over. The Raven's Eye, now cracked and dim, was a testament to the price they had paid.

As they stood before Elara's monument, John felt a deep sense of unease. The

245

vision of her warning echoed in his mind, a chilling reminder that the darkness was never truly defeated.

"We will continue to fight," he vowed, his voice resolute. "We will protect our home, no matter the cost."

The village of Pine Barrens had faced many trials and had emerged stronger each time. But the final battle had revealed a deeper, more insidious threat. The darkness would always be a part of their world, lurking just beyond the light.

As the villagers gathered to honor their fallen and rebuild once more, a shadow passed over the moon, casting the village into a brief, unsettling twilight. The darkness might have been pushed back, but it had not been destroyed. It waited, biding its time, ready to return when they least expected it.

John looked out over his village, his heart heavy but determined. They had

246

faced the encroaching night and survived, but he knew that the final darkness was still out there, waiting. And when it returned, they would be ready, their light burning brighter than ever.

But in the back of his mind, a chilling thought lingered: would their light be enough next time? Only time would tell, and until then, they would live with the ever-present shadow of fear, knowing that the final darkness was never truly gone.

247

The 13th Child
The Birth Of The Jersey Devil

By

Reece Hensley

Table Of Contents

Chapter 20: Peace Restored

2

Author's Notes

In the heart of New Jersey's Pine Barrens lies a village haunted by a curse born centuries ago. When John, the village leader, and his companions confront the legendary Nightbringer, they believe they've triumphed over darkness. But as shadows stir once more, they face a new, ancient evil—the Eternal Night. With the fate of their home hanging in the balance, they must summon every ounce of courage and light to face this ultimate threat. In a gripping tale of sacrifice, resilience, and the enduring battle between light and darkness, "The Final Darkness" explores the depths of fear and the boundless power of hope in the face of the unknown.

3

Chapter 1: The Unwanted Pregnancy Prologue

The Pine Barrens of New Jersey, 1735. A thick, unsettling fog rolled through the dense forest, cloaking the trees in an eerie shroud. Shadows danced ominously, playing tricks on the eyes of those brave—or foolish—enough to venture into its depths. Whispers of ancient curses and dark legends filled the air, seeping into the minds of the superstitious and the fearful. In the heart of this haunting landscape stood a modest cabin, home to the Leeds family. Little did they know, their lives were about to be forever changed by a night of unparalleled terror.

Section 1: The Leeds Family

The Leeds family was well-known in the Pine Barrens, not for their wealth or

4

status, but for their sheer size. Deborah Leeds, the matriarch, had borne twelve children. Life was hard in the Barrens, and each new child meant another mouth to feed, another body to clothe. John Leeds, Deborah's husband, was a hardworking man, but the endless toil of maintaining their small farm took its toll on his spirit and health.

Deborah was a woman of formidable strength, both physically and mentally. She managed the household with a firm hand, ensuring that her children were disciplined and well-behaved. Yet, as strong as she was, the prospect of another pregnancy weighed heavily on her. She often found herself staring out of the small window of their cabin, watching the shadows of the forest with a growing sense of dread.

Section 2: The Unwelcome News

It was a chilly evening in late autumn when Deborah first suspected she might

5

be pregnant again. She had been feeling unusually tired and nauseous, familiar signs that she had come to recognize all too well. As the realization dawned on her, a deep, bone-chilling fear gripped her heart. She couldn't bear the thought of another child, another burden.

That night, as she lay in bed beside her snoring husband, her mind raced with dark thoughts. She thought about the twelve children already under her care, the relentless work, the sleepless nights. She felt a surge of frustration and despair. In a moment of weakness, she muttered a curse under her breath, condemning the unborn child to a fate worse than death.

Section 3: The Curse

The curse she uttered was not one of mere words. It carried the weight of her anguish, her fear, and her resentment. "Let this child be the devil," she whispered, her voice trembling with a

6

mixture of rage and sorrow. She immediately regretted her words, but it was too late. The curse had been spoken, and the dark forces of the Pine Barrens had heard her plea.

The following days were a blur of dread and denial. Deborah tried to convince herself that the curse was just a momentary lapse, that it held no real power. But deep down, she knew the Barrens were a place of old magic and dark secrets. Whispers of strange creatures and malevolent spirits were woven into the fabric of the land.

Section 4: The Dark Forest

As her pregnancy progressed, Deborah found herself increasingly drawn to the forest. It was as if an invisible force was pulling her into the shadows of the Barrens. She would wander the woods, listening to the rustling leaves and the distant cries of unseen animals. The forest seemed to be alive, pulsating with

7

a sinister energy.

One evening, as the sun dipped below the horizon, Deborah ventured deeper into the woods than she had ever gone before. The trees grew thicker and more twisted, their branches clawing at the sky like skeletal fingers. She stumbled upon an old, abandoned cabin, hidden away in a small clearing. It was a place she had never seen before, a place that seemed to emanate an aura of malevolence.

As she approached the cabin, a sense of foreboding washed over her. The air grew colder, and she felt a chill run down her spine. She hesitated at the threshold, her heart pounding in her chest. Despite her fear, something compelled her to enter.

Section 5: The Witch's Warning

Inside the cabin, the air was thick with the scent of decay. Cobwebs hung from the ceiling, and the floor was covered in

8

dust and debris. In the center of the room stood a figure, cloaked in shadow. As Deborah's eyes adjusted to the dim light, she realized it was an old woman, her face lined with age and her eyes burning with an unnatural fire.

"I've been expecting you," the woman said in a voice that was both ancient and ageless. "You carry a heavy burden, child."

Deborah felt a wave of fear and awe wash over her. She tried to speak, but her voice caught in her throat.

"You have cursed your own flesh and blood," the woman continued, her eyes piercing into Deborah's soul. "The curse you uttered in your moment of weakness has awakened dark forces. The child you carry is marked."

Tears streamed down Deborah's face as the weight of her actions settled upon her. "What can I do?" she whispered, her voice trembling with desperation.

9

The old woman shook her head. "The curse cannot be undone. But there may be a way to protect yourself and your family. You must be strong, for the darkness will come for you."

Section 6: The Descent into Madness

The days and nights that followed were filled with a growing sense of dread. Deborah's pregnancy progressed rapidly, and with it, her fear and anxiety intensified. She began to have vivid nightmares, filled with images of a monstrous creature stalking the woods, its eyes glowing with malevolence.

Her health deteriorated, and she became increasingly isolated from her family. Her children noticed the change in her, but they were too young to understand the depth of her despair. John tried to comfort her, but his efforts were in vain. Deborah was haunted by the knowledge of the curse and the impending birth of her thirteenth child.

10

Section 7: The Storm

As the day of the birth approached, the weather took a turn for the worse. A violent storm swept through the Pine Barrens, lashing the trees with fierce winds and torrential rain. The sky was dark and foreboding, reflecting the turmoil within Deborah's soul.

On the night of the birth, the storm reached its peak. The wind howled like a pack of wolves, and thunder rumbled ominously in the distance. Inside the cabin, the atmosphere was tense and fearful. The midwives arrived, their faces pale and drawn as they prepared for the delivery.

Deborah's labor was long and difficult. She screamed in agony as the storm raged outside, the sound of her cries mingling with the roar of the wind. The midwives worked tirelessly, their hands trembling as they tried to help her through the birth.

11

Section 8: The Birth of the Beast

At last, the child was born. For a brief moment, there was silence. The midwives held their breath, hoping that the baby would be healthy and normal. But their hopes were dashed as the child let out a blood-curdling scream.

The baby, at first glance, appeared to be a normal newborn. But as the minutes passed, a horrifying transformation began. The baby's skin turned a sickly shade of gray, and its eyes glowed with an eerie red light. Wings sprouted from its back, and its fingers elongated into sharp claws. The midwives watched in horror as the child morphed into a monstrous creature, unlike anything they had ever seen.

The creature let out a screech that echoed through the cabin, causing the midwives to recoil in terror. It flapped its wings and flew up the chimney, disappearing into the stormy night. Deborah lay on the bed, exhausted and

12

horrified, her mind reeling from the sight of her transformed child.

Section 9: The Aftermath

The midwives fled the cabin, spreading the tale of the monstrous birth throughout the village. The news spread like wildfire, and soon the entire community was gripped by fear and superstition. The legend of the Jersey Devil was born, and the Pine Barrens were forever changed.

Deborah was left to grapple with the guilt and horror of what she had unleashed. She became a recluse, shunned by the villagers who feared her and the curse she had invoked. John tried to support her, but he too was haunted by the events of that night.

As the weeks passed, reports of strange sightings and eerie occurrences in the Pine Barrens began to surface. Livestock were found mutilated, and strange noises echoed through the woods at night. The

13

villagers lived in constant fear, always looking over their shoulders for the creature that had come to be known as the Jersey Devil.

Section 10: The First Sighting

One cold winter night, a group of hunters ventured into the Pine Barrens in search of game. They were experienced woodsmen, familiar with the dangers of the forest. But nothing could have prepared them for what they encountered.

As they trudged through the snow, they heard a strange, unearthly sound. It was a high-pitched screech, like the cry of a wounded animal, but unlike anything they had ever heard before. They exchanged uneasy glances and pressed on, their guns at the ready.

Suddenly, one of the hunters let out a shout of alarm. The others turned to see a dark figure swooping down from the trees. It moved with incredible speed, its

14

wings beating furiously as it approached. The hunters fired their guns, but the creature was too quick. It let out a terrifying screech and attacked, its claws tearing through their flesh.

The survivors fled in terror, leaving their fallen comrades behind. They ran through the forest, their hearts pounding with fear. When they finally reached the village, they were barely coherent, their minds shattered by the

Chapter 2: The Birth

Section 1: The Storm Approaches

The Pine Barrens were shrouded in an unnatural stillness as the storm approached. The air was thick and heavy, laden with the scent of damp earth and decaying leaves. The animals sensed the impending tempest, their calls falling silent, leaving an eerie quiet.

Inside the Leeds' cabin, Deborah lay in

15

bed, her body racked with pain as labor began. Her twelve children huddled together in a corner, their wide eyes reflecting the flickering light of the fireplace. John paced the room, his face etched with worry and fatigue. The midwives, summoned from the village, prepared for what they hoped would be a normal delivery, but an unspoken dread hung in the air.

Section 2: The Labor Begins

The first contraction hit Deborah like a wave of agony, doubling her over. She gritted her teeth, stifling a scream as she clutched the bed sheets. The midwives moved quickly, their hands steady but their eyes betraying their fear. They had heard the rumors, the whispers of a cursed child, but they pushed those thoughts aside, focusing on their task.

John knelt by Deborah's side, wiping the sweat from her brow. "You're strong, Deborah. You can do this," he

16

murmured, his voice breaking with emotion.

Deborah's eyes met his, filled with a mix of pain and terror. "John, I'm scared. Something's wrong. I can feel it."

John squeezed her hand, trying to mask his own fear. "It's just a difficult labor, that's all. The midwives will help you."

But deep down, he knew there was something unnatural about this birth. The storm outside seemed to mirror the turmoil within their home, growing in intensity as Deborah's labor progressed.

Section 3: The Cabin in Chaos

As the hours dragged on, the storm intensified. Lightning split the sky, followed by deafening cracks of thunder that rattled the cabin's walls. The wind howled like a banshee, and rain lashed against the windows in relentless sheets. Inside, the atmosphere was tense, fraught with fear and anticipation.

17

Deborah's screams grew louder, her pain almost unbearable. The midwives exchanged worried glances, their faces pale in the dim light. "It's taking too long," one of them whispered. "Something's not right."

The children huddled closer together, their small faces contorted with fear. The eldest, a boy of fourteen, tried to comfort his siblings, but his own fear was palpable. "It's going to be okay," he lied, his voice trembling. "Mama's strong. She'll be alright."

John felt helpless, torn between comforting his children and supporting his wife. He prayed silently, begging for strength and protection, but the storm outside seemed to mock his pleas, growing ever more violent.

Section 4: The Moment of Birth

At the height of the storm, a piercing scream filled the cabin, louder and more desperate than any before. Deborah

18

arched her back, her body convulsing as the baby finally began to emerge. The midwives moved swiftly, their hands slick with blood and sweat.

"One more push, Deborah!" one of them urged. "You're almost there!"

Deborah summoned every ounce of strength left in her, pushing with a primal roar. The baby slid into the midwife's waiting hands, and for a brief moment, there was silence. The midwives breathed a collective sigh of relief as they held the newborn, their initial fear giving way to hope.

But their relief was short-lived. **Section 5: The Transformation**

The baby's first cry was unlike any they had ever heard. It started as a normal wail but quickly morphed into a guttural, animalistic screech. The midwives recoiled in horror as the baby began to change before their eyes.

19

The infant's skin darkened to a sickly, mottled gray. Its eyes, once a normal newborn blue, glowed an unnatural red. Small, leathery wings sprouted from its back, and its fingers elongated into sharp, claw-like appendages. The transformation was swift and terrifying, leaving no doubt that this was no ordinary child.

Deborah, weak and exhausted, could only watch in horror as the midwives screamed and backed away from the creature. "No...no, it can't be!" she cried, her voice breaking. "What have I done?"

John stood frozen, his mind struggling to comprehend the nightmare unfolding before him. The creature let out another ear-piercing screech, flapping its wings furiously. The children screamed and huddled closer together, their terror palpable.

Section 6: The Creature Escapes

In a frenzy of motion, the creature flew

20

up the chimney, its claws scraping against the brick. The wind outside howled even louder, as if in response to the creature's escape. John rushed to the fireplace, but it was too late. The monstrous child was gone, lost to the stormy night.

The midwives fled the cabin, their faces ashen with terror. "We must warn the village!" one of them shouted as they disappeared into the darkness. "The devil is loose in the Pine Barrens!"

Deborah collapsed back onto the bed, her body trembling with shock and exhaustion. John wrapped his arms around her, his own heart pounding with fear. "We'll get through this, Deborah," he whispered, though his words felt hollow. "We have to."

Section 7: The Aftermath

The storm began to subside as dawn approached, leaving behind a landscape ravaged by its fury. Inside the cabin, the

21

atmosphere was one of stunned silence and disbelief. The children, exhausted from fear and lack of sleep, had finally dozed off in a huddled mass. Deborah lay in bed, her eyes staring blankly at the ceiling, her mind unable to process the events of the night.

John moved mechanically, cleaning up the remnants of the birth with a heavy heart. He avoided looking at the blood-stained sheets, trying to block out the memory of the creature that had emerged from his wife's womb. His hands trembled as he worked, the full weight of their predicament pressing down on him.

Outside, the Pine Barrens were eerily quiet, the storm having driven away any remaining wildlife. The trees stood like silent sentinels, their branches heavy with rain. The once comforting sounds of nature were replaced by an oppressive stillness, as if the forest itself was holding its breath.

22

Section 8: The Village Reacts

Word of the monstrous birth spread quickly through the village. The midwives, pale and shaken, recounted the horrifying details to anyone who would listen. Fear and superstition took hold of the villagers, who had always harbored a healthy respect for the dark and mysterious Pine Barrens.

The village elders convened an emergency meeting in the town square. People gathered, their faces etched with worry and fear. The atmosphere was tense, whispers of curses and dark magic filling the air.

"We must take action," one elder declared, his voice grave. "This creature cannot be allowed to roam free. It is an abomination, a sign that we have angered the spirits of the forest."

"But what can we do?" another villager

asked, his voice trembling. "We are just

simple folk. How can we fight a creature

23

born of dark magic?"

The elders exchanged uneasy glances. "We must consult the old woman," one of them finally said. "She knows the ways of the forest. Perhaps she can help us."

Section 9: The Old Woman's Guidance

The villagers reluctantly approached the old woman's hut, deep in the heart of the Pine Barrens. She was a reclusive figure, known for her knowledge of herbs and folklore, but also feared for her rumored connections to the supernatural.

The old woman greeted them with a knowing look, as if she had been expecting their visit. "So, the curse has come to pass," she said in a voice that seemed to echo with the weight of centuries. "The creature you speak of is the result of dark forces, awakened by a mother's curse."

24

The villagers listened in stunned silence as she recounted the tale of Deborah Leeds and the curse she had uttered. "There is little that can be done to reverse the curse," she continued. "But there may be a way to protect yourselves and perhaps even banish the creature from these woods."

She handed them a small, leather-bound book filled with ancient symbols and rituals. "This contains the knowledge you seek," she said. "But be warned, the path ahead is fraught with danger. The creature is powerful and will not be easily subdued."

Section 10: A Plan is Formed

Armed with the old woman's guidance, the villagers returned to the town square to formulate a plan. The book detailed a complex ritual that required rare herbs, precise incantations, and the cooperation of the entire village.

"We must prepare," the elder said.

25

"Gather the herbs, memorize the incantations. This is our only chance to rid the Pine Barrens of this curse."

The villagers set to work, each tasked with a specific role. Some ventured into the forest to gather the necessary herbs, while others practiced the incantations. The children were kept indoors, their parents' faces grim with determination and fear.

John and Deborah were asked to participate in the ritual, their presence deemed crucial to its success. Though weak and still in shock, Deborah agreed, driven by a desperate need to right the wrong she had unwittingly caused.

Section 11: The Ritual

As night fell, the villagers gathered in a clearing deep within the Pine Barrens. A large bonfire was lit, casting flickering shadows on the faces of those assembled. The air was thick with tension, the forest silent and watchful.

26

The elder began the ritual, his voice steady but laced with urgency. The villagers chanted the incantations in unison, their voices rising and falling like the wind. Deborah and John stood at the center, their hands clasped tightly together.

The old woman's book guided them through each step, the symbols and words glowing with an eerie light. The atmosphere grew charged with energy, the air crackling with unseen forces. As the ritual reached its climax, the creature appeared, drawn by the power of the incantations.

Section 12: The Creature's Return

The Jersey Devil descended upon the clearing with a ferocious screech, its eyes blazing with fury. The villagers recoiled in fear, but held their ground, their voices unwavering. The creature circled the bonfire, its wings casting monstrous shadows on the trees.

27

John and Deborah faced the creature, their fear overshadowed by a fierce determination. The elder directed them to recite the final incantation, their voices trembling but strong. The air vibrated with power as the words echoed through the clearing.

The creature let out a deafening roar, its body writhing in pain as the ritual took hold. It flapped its wings violently, trying to escape, but the power of the ritual held it in place. The villagers watched in awe and terror as the creature was slowly drawn into the circle of fire.

Section 13: The Final Confrontation

The creature fought against the ritual's power, its claws slashing at the air. The villagers continued to chant, their voices growing louder and more insistent. John and Deborah, their hands still clasped, felt a surge of energy coursing through them.

With one final, desperate effort, the

28

creature broke free from the circle, its wings beating furiously. It let out a spine-chilling screech and lunged at Deborah, its claws outstretched. John stepped in front of her, raising his arm to shield her.

The creature's claws raked across John's arm, drawing blood. He cried out in pain but stood firm, his eyes locked on the creature. "You will not take her!" he shouted, his voice filled with defiance.

The villagers, galvanized by John's bravery, intensified their chanting. The elder raised his arms, calling upon the old woman's guidance to strengthen the ritual. The air shimmered with a blinding light, and the creature was once again pulled towards the circle of fire.

Section 14: The Banishment

The creature's screams grew more desperate as the ritual reached its peak. The villagers' voices rose to a fever pitch, the incantations echoing through

29

the forest. The light around the creature intensified, enveloping it in a blinding glow.

With a final, ear-splitting screech, the creature was consumed by the light. The villagers watched in awe as it was slowly drawn into the fire, its form dissolving into ash. The light dimmed, and the forest fell silent once more.

The villagers collapsed to the ground, exhausted but victorious. The elder approached John and Deborah, his face etched with relief. "It is done," he said, his voice trembling. "The creature is banished."

Section 15: The Aftermath

The village slowly began to recover from the ordeal. The Pine Barrens, once a place of fear and darkness, began to heal. The old woman's guidance had proven true, and the villagers' bravery had driven the Jersey Devil from their midst.

30

Deborah and John returned to their cabin, their bond stronger than ever. The events of that night had left deep scars, but also a renewed sense of hope. They vowed to rebuild their lives, to cherish their children and the peace they had fought so hard to restore.

Section 16: A New Beginning

As the seasons changed, the Pine Barrens began to flourish once more. The village, though still wary of the dark forces that lurked in the forest, found a renewed sense of community and strength. The legend of the Jersey Devil became a cautionary tale, a reminder of the power of curses and the resilience of the human spirit.

John and Deborah welcomed their thirteenth child, a baby boy, into the world. Though their hearts were still heavy with the memory of the curse, they found solace in the love and strength of their family. The boy grew

31

up strong and healthy, a testament to their enduring spirit.

Section 17: The Legend Lives On

The story of the Jersey Devil continued to be told around campfires and in hushed whispers, a reminder of the darkness that had once threatened their lives. But it was also a story of bravery, of a community that had come together to face a terrifying foe and had emerged stronger for it.

The old woman remained a guardian of the forest, her wisdom and knowledge a beacon for those who sought her guidance. The villagers, though respectful of the Pine Barrens, no longer lived in fear. They had faced the darkness and prevailed.

Section 18: The Pine Barrens Watchful Eye

As time passed, the Pine Barrens retained its mysterious allure. The forest,

32

with its ancient trees and hidden secrets, remained a place of wonder and caution. The villagers learned to live in harmony with the land, respecting its power and its beauty.

John and Deborah's family grew, their children learning the ways of the forest and the stories of their ancestors. They taught them to be cautious, but also to be brave, to respect the old magic of the Pine Barrens but not to fear it.

Section 19: The Legacy of the Curse

The legacy of the curse left a lasting impression on the village. It served as a reminder of the consequences of anger and despair, but also of the power of love and community. The villagers learned to face their fears together, to support one another in times of darkness.

The elder, now a respected leader, continued to guide the village with wisdom and compassion. He reminded

33

them of the importance of unity and resilience, of the strength that came from facing their fears together.

Section 20: The Dawn of a New Era

As the years passed, the Pine Barrens remained a place of mystery and wonder. The village thrived, its people living in harmony with the land. The legend of the Jersey Devil became a part of their history, a testament to their bravery and resilience.

John and Deborah, now elders themselves, watched their children and grandchildren grow, their hearts filled with pride and hope. The darkness that had once threatened their lives had been banished, and in its place, a new dawn had risen.

The Pine Barrens, with its watchful trees and whispering winds, remained a place of beauty and mystery. The villagers knew that they had faced the darkness and prevailed, and that their legacy

34

would live on for generations to come.

Chapter 3: The First Night

Section 1: Uneasy Silence

As the sun set over the Pine Barrens, a heavy silence fell upon the Leeds' cabin. The family huddled together, their fear palpable in the dim light of the single flickering candle. Deborah lay in bed, her body still weak from the ordeal, while John kept a watchful eye on the shadows outside.

The forest, usually alive with the sounds of nocturnal creatures, was eerily quiet. The absence of familiar noises only heightened their anxiety. The wind whispered through the trees, carrying with it an unsettling sense of foreboding. The children, wide-eyed and fearful, clung to one another, their hearts pounding in their chests.

35

Section 2: The Creature Returns

In the dead of night, a chilling screech pierced the silence. The sound was otherworldly, sending shivers down the spines of everyone in the cabin. John sprang to his feet, grabbing the hunting rifle he kept by the door. The children whimpered, their eyes wide with terror.

"Stay here," John instructed, his voice trembling. "I'll check outside."

Deborah reached out, her hand trembling. "John, be careful. Please."

John nodded, his jaw set in determination. He stepped out into the night, the cold air biting at his skin. The forest was cloaked in darkness, the moon hidden behind thick clouds. The screech came again, closer this time, and John's heart raced. He moved cautiously, the rifle held tightly in his hands.

Section 3: A Shadow in the Dark

As John ventured deeper into the forest,

36

the screeching grew louder, more insistent. He strained his eyes, searching for any sign of movement in the inky blackness. The trees loomed above him, their branches like skeletal fingers reaching out to ensnare him.

Suddenly, a rustling sound to his left made him whip around. He aimed the rifle, his hands shaking. "Who's there?" he called out, his voice echoing through the silent woods.

There was no response, only the eerie whisper of the wind. John took a cautious step forward, his eyes scanning the darkness. Then, out of the corner of his eye, he saw it – a shadowy figure darting between the trees. He raised the rifle, his finger hovering over the trigger, but the figure was too quick, vanishing into the night.

Section 4: The Creature's Attack

Before John could react, the creature launched itself at him from the darkness.

37

Its eyes glowed with an unholy light, and its wings beat the air with a ferocious intensity. John stumbled back, firing a shot blindly into the night. The sound of the gunshot echoed through the forest, but the creature was unfazed.

It let out a deafening screech, its claws raking across John's chest. He cried out in pain, falling to the ground as the creature circled above him. Blood seeped through his shirt, and his vision blurred as he struggled to stay conscious.

In a desperate attempt to protect his family, John aimed the rifle once more, firing another shot. This time, the bullet found its mark, striking the creature in the wing. It let out a furious cry, retreating into the darkness.

Section 5: The Aftermath

John lay on the ground, his breathing ragged. He clutched his chest, trying to stem the flow of blood. The forest was

38

silent once more, the creature having disappeared into the night. John forced himself to his feet, his vision swimming. He had to get back to his family.

He stumbled through the trees, each step sending waves of pain through his body. By the time he reached the cabin, he was barely conscious. Deborah and the children rushed to his side, their faces etched with fear.

"John! What happened?" Deborah cried, her hands trembling as she pressed a cloth to his wound.

"It... it attacked me," John gasped. "We need to be on our guard. It's still out there."

Section 6: Vigilance

The family spent the rest of the night in a state of heightened alert. John's wound was bandaged as best as they could manage, but the pain was excruciating. Deborah stayed by his side, her eyes

39

never leaving the windows, her ears straining for any sound.

The children, though exhausted, kept watch with their mother. The fear of the creature returning kept them awake, their small bodies trembling with terror. Each creak of the cabin, each rustle of the wind, made their hearts race.

The hours dragged on, each minute feeling like an eternity. The candle flickered, casting eerie shadows on the walls. The family huddled together, finding solace in each other's presence. The night seemed endless, the darkness oppressive.

Section 7: The Elders' Warnings

With the first light of dawn, the family's ordeal was far from over. John's injury needed proper attention, and the threat of the creature loomed large. Deborah made the difficult decision to seek help from the village elders.

40

As the morning sun began to pierce through the trees, Deborah and John's eldest son, Thomas, set out for the village. The journey through the Pine Barrens was fraught with danger, but he moved with determination, driven by the need to protect his family.

The village was in a state of unrest, the rumors of the creature spreading like wildfire. When Thomas arrived, the elders convened an emergency meeting, their faces grim.

"The creature must be dealt with," the head elder declared. "We cannot allow it to terrorize our village."

Thomas relayed the events of the previous night, his voice shaking with fear and anger. The elders listened intently, their faces growing more serious with each word.

"This is no ordinary creature," one of them said. "It is born of dark magic, and it will not be easily defeated."

41

Section 8: Preparing for Battle

The villagers mobilized, gathering weapons and supplies for the hunt. The elders shared ancient knowledge, teaching the villagers how to protect themselves against dark forces. Talismans were crafted, wards were placed around homes, and prayers were recited.

Thomas returned to the cabin with a group of villagers, their faces set with determination. They inspected the scene of the attack, their eyes scanning the forest for any sign of the creature.

John, though weakened by his injuries, insisted on joining the hunt. "This is my fight," he said, his voice firm despite the pain. "I won't let that thing harm my family again."

Deborah, though fearful for her husband, knew there was no dissuading him. She kissed him goodbye, her heart heavy with worry. "Be careful," she whispered,

42

her eyes filled with tears. "Come back to us."

Section 9: The Hunt Begins

The villagers set out into the forest, their torches casting flickering light in the dimness of the Pine Barrens. The air was thick with tension, each step echoing with the weight of their mission. The forest seemed to close in around them, the trees whispering secrets and warnings.

The group moved cautiously, their eyes scanning the shadows for any sign of the creature. The memory of its attack on John was fresh in their minds, and they were determined to end its reign of terror.

Hours passed with no sign of the creature. The forest was eerily quiet, the usual sounds of wildlife conspicuously absent. The villagers' nerves were on edge, each rustle of leaves or snap of a twig sending shivers down their spines.

43

Section 10: The Creature's Lair

As dusk approached, the villagers stumbled upon a clearing deep in the forest. In the center stood an ancient, gnarled tree, its twisted branches reaching out like skeletal fingers. The ground around the tree was littered with bones and remnants of past victims, a testament to the creature's brutality.

"This must be its lair," John said, his voice barely above a whisper. "We need to be ready."

The villagers spread out, forming a perimeter around the clearing. They prepared their weapons, the tension mounting with each passing moment. The air grew colder, and an unnatural silence fell over the forest.

Suddenly, a blood-curdling screech echoed through the trees. The villagers tensed, their eyes darting around the clearing. The creature appeared from the shadows, its eyes glowing with

44

malevolent intent. **Section 11: The Battle**

The creature attacked with a ferocity that took the villagers by surprise. It swooped down, its claws slashing through the air. The villagers fought back with everything they had, their torches and weapons clashing against the creature's dark form.

John, despite his injuries, fought with a renewed determination. He dodged the creature's attacks, using the knowledge the elders had shared to avoid its deadly claws. The villagers worked together, their combined efforts slowly wearing the creature down.

The battle was intense, the clearing filled with the sounds of screams and the clash of metal. The creature fought back viciously, its eyes glowing with unholy fire. The villagers pressed on, their resolve unwavering.

45

Section 12: A Desperate Plan

As the battle raged on, it became clear that the creature was more powerful than they had anticipated. The villagers began to lose hope, their strength waning under the relentless assault. John, his body aching and bleeding, realized they needed a new plan.

"We need to trap it," he shouted over the noise of the battle. "Use the fire to drive it into the tree!"

The villagers quickly regrouped, their torches forming a ring of fire around the clearing. They worked together, driving the creature towards the ancient tree. The creature screeched in fury, its movements growing more frantic as it realized their plan.

With one final push, the villagers managed to corner the creature against the tree. The fire blazed around them, the heat intense. The creature thrashed and screeched, its eyes filled with rage

46

and fear.

Section 13: The Creature's Demise

The villagers held their ground, their torches burning brightly. The creature, now trapped, lashed out in desperation. John stepped forward, his eyes locked on the creature's glowing gaze. He raised his torch, the flames casting a fierce light.

"For my family," he whispered, plunging the torch into the creature's chest.

The creature let out a final, agonizing screech, its body convulsing as the fire consumed it. The villagers watched in awe and terror as the creature writhed in pain, its form dissolving into ash. The fire roared, and then, just as suddenly, it was over. The creature was gone, leaving only a pile of smoldering ashes in its wake.

47

Section 14: The Aftermath

The villagers stood in stunned silence, the reality of their victory slowly sinking in. The forest was quiet once more, the oppressive darkness lifting. The ancient tree stood as a silent witness to their triumph, its twisted branches now holding no menace.

John collapsed to the ground, his body wracked with pain and exhaustion. The villagers rushed to his side, their faces filled with relief and gratitude. They had faced the darkness and emerged victorious, but the cost had been high.

Deborah and the children, waiting anxiously at the cabin, saw the torches returning and ran to meet the villagers. When she saw John, her heart swelled with relief and pride. They embraced, tears streaming down their faces.

Section 15: Healing and Reflection The days that followed were filled with

48

healing and reflection. The village, though scarred by the ordeal, found a renewed sense of community and strength. They mourned their losses but celebrated their victory, knowing they had faced a great evil and prevailed.

John's wounds, though severe, began to heal under Deborah's care. The family grew closer, their bond strengthened by the trials they had endured. The village elders shared their wisdom, helping the community to understand and respect the forces that had been at play.

The legend of the Jersey Devil became a part of their history, a reminder of the darkness that had once threatened their lives. The villagers honored those who had fought and those who had fallen, their bravery a testament to the power of unity and resilience.

Section 16: A New Dawn

As the seasons changed, the Pine Barrens began to flourish once more.

49

The village, though still wary of the dark forces that lurked in the forest, found a renewed sense of peace and hope. The land that had once been shrouded in fear now held the promise of new beginnings.

John and Deborah's thirteenth child grew strong and healthy, a symbol of their family's enduring spirit. The village, though forever changed by their ordeal, emerged stronger and more united. They had faced the darkness and prevailed, their legacy one of bravery and resilience.

Section 17: The Watchful Forest

The Pine Barrens retained its mysterious allure, a place of beauty and caution. The villagers learned to live in harmony with the land, respecting its power and its secrets. The ancient trees, once witnesses to great evil, now stood as guardians of the village's peace.

The forest, though still home to many

50

mysteries, no longer held the same terror. The villagers, guided by the wisdom of the elders and their own experiences, learned to navigate its shadows with respect and care. The Pine Barrens remained a place of wonder, a testament to the enduring spirit of those who called it home.

Section 18: Passing Down the Story

The story of the Jersey Devil was passed down through generations, a cautionary tale and a symbol of hope. The villagers taught their children to respect the old magic of the forest, to understand the power of curses and the strength of community.

John and Deborah, now elders themselves, watched with pride as their children and grandchildren learned the ways of the forest. They shared their experiences, their bravery, and their wisdom, ensuring that the legacy of their victory would never be forgotten.

51

Section 19: A Legacy of Courage

The legacy of the curse left a lasting impression on the village. It served as a reminder of the consequences of anger and despair, but also of the power of love and unity. The villagers learned to face their fears together, to support one another in times of darkness.

The village elder, now a revered leader, continued to guide the community with wisdom and compassion. He reminded them of the importance of unity and resilience, of the strength that came from facing their fears together.

Section 20: The Eternal Vigil

As the years passed, the Pine Barrens remained a place of mystery and wonder. The village thrived, its people living in harmony with the land. The legend of the Jersey Devil became a part of their history, a testament to their bravery and resilience.

52

John and Deborah, having faced unimaginable darkness, found peace in the light of their family and community. Their story, a tale of courage and hope, was a beacon for future generations.

The Pine Barrens, with its watchful trees and whispering winds, remained a place of beauty and mystery. The villagers knew that they had faced the darkness and prevailed, their legacy living on for generations to come. The forest, ever watchful, stood as a silent guardian of their triumph and their enduring spirit.

Chapter 4: The Curse Unveiled

Section 1: Unearthed Secrets

The village had barely begun to recover from the recent encounter with the Jersey Devil. The night had left deep scars, not just on the body but on the minds of those who had faced the creature. As the days passed, John and

53

Deborah found themselves haunted by lingering questions about the origin of the curse that had plagued their family.

One evening, as the sun dipped below the horizon, casting long shadows through the forest, John and Deborah made their way to the village elder's home. The elder, a man of immense wisdom and years, greeted them with a somber expression, as if he had anticipated their visit.

"We need to know more about the curse," John began, his voice filled with a desperate urgency. "Where did it come from? How can we be sure it's truly gone?"

The elder nodded slowly and gestured for them to sit by the fire. "The curse is an old one, rooted in the darkest parts of our history. It is time you learned the full story."

54

Section 2: The Origin of the Curse

The elder began to recount a tale that stretched back centuries, to a time when the Pine Barrens was home to a thriving, if isolated, community. According to legend, a woman named Lydia Leeds had lived in the forest with her husband and twelve children. Stricken with despair over her thirteenth pregnancy, she had cursed the unborn child in a fit of rage and hopelessness.

"That child," the elder said, his voice low and ominous, "was born normal but soon transformed into the creature we now know as the Jersey Devil. It was a manifestation of Lydia's curse, a physical embodiment of her anguish and anger."

John and Deborah listened in silence, the weight of the story sinking in. They had known of the creature's origins in vague terms, but hearing the specifics, and understanding the depth of the curse, was profoundly unsettling.

55

Section 3: Signs of the Curse

As the elder continued, he revealed that the curse did not end with the creature's creation. It had woven itself into the very fabric of the Leeds family line, rearing its head in various forms over the generations. Signs of the curse included strange phenomena and unexplainable events that plagued the family members throughout the years.

"Have you noticed anything unusual?" the elder asked, his gaze piercing.

John and Deborah exchanged worried glances. There had been odd occurrences: objects moving on their own, shadows flitting through the corners of their vision, and a pervasive sense of being watched. They recounted these experiences to the elder, their voices trembling with the memory.

"These are signs that the curse is still active," the elder confirmed. "The creature may be banished, but the curse's

56

influence remains."

Section 4: The Witch's Prophecy

The elder then spoke of a prophecy linked to the curse, one that had been passed down through the generations. According to the prophecy, the curse could only be lifted by confronting the source of Lydia Leeds' anguish and finding a way to atone for her suffering.

"A witch who lived deep within the Pine Barrens foretold this," the elder explained. "She was a seer, able to see into the hearts of men and the threads of fate that bind us all. Her words were cryptic but clear: 'The curse shall break when the anguish of the mother is laid to rest.'"

John and Deborah felt a chill run down their spines. They realized that their battle was far from over. To truly rid themselves of the curse, they would need to delve deeper into the past and uncover the truth of Lydia Leeds'

57

suffering.

Section 5: The Journey Begins

Determined to free their family from the curse once and for all, John and Deborah set out on a journey to find the witch's hut, deep within the Pine Barrens. They prepared for the expedition with the help of the villagers, gathering supplies and weapons to defend themselves against any lingering dark forces.

Their children, though young, understood the gravity of their parents' mission. The village rallied around the Leeds family, offering support and protection while John and Deborah embarked on their perilous quest.

The forest seemed more menacing than ever as they ventured deeper into its heart. The trees, twisted and gnarled, appeared to watch their every move. The air was thick with an eerie stillness, broken only by the occasional rustle of unseen creatures.

58

Section 6: Night Terrors

On the first night of their journey, John and Deborah set up camp in a small clearing. The flickering firelight cast long, dancing shadows on the trees. Despite their exhaustion, sleep did not come easily. The darkness seemed alive, pressing in on them from all sides.

In the middle of the night, Deborah awoke with a start, a cold sweat dripping down her back. She had dreamt of Lydia Leeds, her face twisted with rage and sorrow, her eyes burning with a desperate plea for help. Deborah could still hear the echoes of Lydia's cries ringing in her ears.

John, too, was plagued by nightmares. He saw visions of the Jersey Devil, its eyes glowing with malevolent intent, its claws reaching out for him and his family. He woke with a start, his heart pounding in his chest.

The forest around them was silent, save

59

for the occasional rustle of leaves. The night seemed endless, each minute stretching into an eternity. The darkness felt oppressive, as if it were closing in on them, smothering their hope.

Section 7: The Witch's Hut

After days of treacherous travel, John and Deborah finally reached the witch's hut. It was a dilapidated structure, half-hidden by the encroaching forest. Vines and moss covered the weathered wood, and an eerie silence hung in the air.

They approached cautiously, their senses on high alert. The hut exuded a sense of foreboding, as if it were a living entity that did not welcome their presence. Taking a deep breath, John pushed open the creaking door, and they stepped inside.

The interior was dark and musty, filled with the remnants of a life long gone. Cobwebs draped the corners, and the air was thick with the smell of decay. In the

60

center of the room stood a weathered table, covered in dust and old, crumbling books.

As they explored the hut, they found a small, intricately carved box hidden under a loose floorboard. Inside the box was a collection of old letters, their ink faded but still legible. They realized these letters were from Lydia Leeds herself, written in the days leading up to the birth of her thirteenth child.

Section 8: Lydia's Anguish

Reading through the letters, John and Deborah discovered the depth of Lydia's despair. She had been isolated, living in fear of her husband's wrath and the judgment of the villagers. Each letter was a cry for help, a desperate plea for someone to understand her pain and suffering.

One letter, in particular, stood out. In it, Lydia wrote about the moment she cursed her unborn child, her words filled

61

with regret and sorrow. "I did not mean for this to happen," she wrote. "I was lost in my own anguish, and now my child suffers for it."

The letters painted a picture of a woman pushed to the brink, her spirit broken by years of hardship and neglect. John and Deborah felt a deep sense of sorrow and empathy for Lydia, understanding for the first time the true extent of her suffering.

Section 9: The Ritual of Atonement

As they continued to search the hut, they found an old, leather-bound book that seemed to contain instructions for a ritual of atonement. The ritual, according to the book, could lift the curse by addressing Lydia's anguish and offering a means of reconciliation.

The ritual required several rare ingredients, many of which could only be found deep within the Pine Barrens. John and Deborah knew that obtaining these ingredients would be no easy task,

62

but they were determined to see it through.

They left the hut with a renewed sense of purpose, ready to face whatever challenges lay ahead. The forest seemed to come alive around them, the shadows deepening and the air growing colder. They pressed on, their resolve unwavering.

Section 10: Gathering the Ingredients

The first ingredient on their list was a rare herb known as "Witch's Heart," said to grow only in the darkest, most secluded parts of the forest. John and Deborah navigated through treacherous terrain, the forest becoming increasingly hostile the deeper they ventured.

They encountered numerous obstacles, from treacherous bogs to dense thickets that seemed to close in around them. The air was filled with the sounds of unseen creatures, and the oppressive darkness made it difficult to see.

63

After hours of searching, they finally found a small patch of Witch's Heart growing at the base of a twisted tree.

The herb glowed faintly in the dim light, its leaves a deep, blood-red color. They carefully harvested the herb, their hands trembling with a mix of fear and excitement.

Section 11: The Guardian

Their next task was to find a rare crystal known as the "Tear of the Forest." According to the book, the crystal was guarded by an ancient spirit that resided in a hidden cave deep within the Pine Barrens. John and Deborah followed the directions, their journey fraught with danger.

As they neared the cave, the forest grew eerily quiet. The entrance was obscured by thick vines and moss, and an overwhelming sense of dread washed over them. Taking a deep breath, they pushed through the undergrowth and

64

entered the cave.

Inside, the air was cold and damp, the walls covered in strange, glowing symbols. They ventured deeper, the light from their torches casting eerie shadows. Suddenly, a low growl echoed through the cave, and they realized they were not alone.

A figure emerged from the darkness, its eyes glowing with an otherworldly light. The guardian of the crystal was a towering, spectral figure, its form shifting and changing as it moved. It let out a bone-chilling wail, sending shivers down their spines.

Section 12: The Battle for the Tear

John and Deborah knew they had to confront the guardian to obtain the Tear of the Forest. The spectral figure lunged at them, its form passing through the walls of the cave as if it were made of smoke. They fought back with all their might, using the knowledge they had

65

gained from the village elders.

The battle was intense, the cave echoing with the sounds of their struggle. The guardian's attacks were swift and relentless, its ethereal form difficult to combat. John and Deborah worked together, their movements synchronized as they dodged and struck back.

Finally, with a desperate lunge, John managed to strike the guardian with a silver dagger blessed by the village elders. The guardian let out a final, haunting wail before dissolving into mist, leaving behind a small, glowing crystal.

The Tear of the Forest pulsed with a soft, blue light. John and Deborah carefully picked it up, their bodies trembling with exhaustion and relief. They had succeeded, but the cost had been high.

Section 13: The Final Ingredient The last ingredient they needed was the

66

"Blood of the Innocent," a euphemism for the essence of purity and hope. According to the book, this ingredient could only be obtained from the heart of the forest, where the ancient spirits of the land resided.

John and Deborah made their way to the heart of the Pine Barrens, the journey growing increasingly perilous. The forest seemed to sense their purpose, the shadows growing darker and the air colder. They pressed on, driven by their determination to lift the curse.

In the heart of the forest, they found a clearing bathed in an ethereal light. In the center of the clearing stood an ancient tree, its branches reaching towards the sky. The air was filled with a sense of peace and tranquility, a stark contrast to the rest of the forest.

As they approached the tree, they felt a presence watching them. The spirits of the land, ancient and wise, revealed themselves in the form of shimmering

67

lights. John and Deborah explained their quest, their voices filled with reverence and humility.

Section 14: The Blessing of the Spirits

The spirits listened to their plea, their forms shifting and swirling around the ancient tree. After a moment of silence, they granted their blessing, offering a vial of pure, glowing liquid – the essence of purity and hope.

John and Deborah accepted the vial with gratitude, their hearts filled with hope. They had obtained all the ingredients needed for the ritual of atonement. Now, they had to return to the witch's hut and perform the ritual.

Section 15: The Ritual Begins

Returning to the witch's hut, John and Deborah prepared for the ritual with a mix of anticipation and dread. The air was thick with tension as they laid out the ingredients on the weathered table.

68

The ancient book lay open, its pages filled with instructions written in an archaic script.

They began the ritual, following the steps meticulously. They combined the Witch's Heart, the Tear of the Forest, and the essence of purity, chanting the incantations written in the book. The air around them crackled with energy, the light in the hut growing dim.

As they performed the ritual, they felt a presence growing stronger. The spirit of Lydia Leeds seemed to materialize before them, her form faint but unmistakable. Her eyes were filled with sorrow, her expression one of anguish and regret.

Section 16: Confronting the Past

Lydia's spirit spoke, her voice echoing through the hut. "Why have you summoned me?"

John and Deborah explained their

69

purpose, their voices trembling with emotion. They spoke of their desire to lift the curse, to bring peace to Lydia's tormented soul and free their family from the darkness that had plagued them for generations.

Lydia listened, her eyes softening with understanding. She revealed the true depth of her suffering, the years of isolation and fear that had driven her to curse her unborn child. Her regret was palpable, her desire for redemption clear.

Section 17: The Moment of Atonement

As the ritual reached its climax, John and Deborah felt a surge of energy. The air around them shimmered, and the spirit of Lydia Leeds began to fade, her form dissolving into the light. The hut was filled with a sense of peace, the oppressive darkness lifting.

The curse, bound by Lydia's anguish and regret, began to unravel. The shadows

70

that had haunted the Leeds family for generations dissipated, replaced by a sense of hope and renewal. The forest, once menacing and dark, seemed to breathe a sigh of relief.

Section 18: The Aftermath

With the ritual complete, John and Deborah returned to their village, their hearts lighter. The villagers greeted them with relief and joy, their faces filled with gratitude. The curse had been lifted, and the village could finally begin to heal.

John's injuries, though severe, began to mend more quickly. The oppressive weight that had hung over the Leeds family was gone, replaced by a sense of peace. The village, though still wary of the dark forces that lurked in the forest, found a renewed sense of unity and hope.

Section 19: Healing and Reflection The days that followed were filled with

71

healing and reflection. The villagers, having faced a great evil, emerged stronger and more united. They honored those who had fought and those who had fallen, their bravery a testament to the power of community and resilience.

John and Deborah shared their experiences with the villagers, their story serving as a reminder of the importance of understanding and compassion. The legend of the Jersey Devil became a part of their history, a symbol of the darkness they had overcome.

Section 20: A New Beginning

As the seasons changed, the Pine Barrens began to flourish once more. The village, though forever changed by their ordeal, found a renewed sense of peace and hope. The land that had once been shrouded in fear now held the promise of new beginnings.

John and Deborah's thirteenth child

72

grew strong and healthy, a symbol of their family's enduring spirit. The village, guided by the wisdom of the elders and the lessons of the past, embraced the future with open hearts.

The Pine Barrens, with its watchful trees and whispering winds, remained a place of beauty and mystery. The villagers, now wiser and more united, lived in harmony with the land, respecting its power and its secrets.

The legacy of the curse, a tale of sorrow and redemption, lived on in the hearts and minds of the villagers. The story of the Jersey Devil, once a source of fear, became a testament to their courage and resilience. The forest, ever watchful, stood as a silent guardian of their triumph and their enduring spirit.

73

Chapter 5: Echoes of the Past

Section 1: The Silent Return

John and Deborah returned to their cabin, their faces lined with exhaustion and relief. The villagers greeted them with a mixture of awe and respect, knowing the sacrifices they had made to lift the curse. The forest seemed calmer, as if acknowledging their victory. However, an unsettling feeling lingered in the air, like the echo of a scream that refused to fade away.

As they settled back into their routine, John couldn't shake the feeling that something still lurked in the shadows. The nights were eerily silent, the usual sounds of the forest replaced by an oppressive stillness. It was as if the Pine Barrens itself was holding its breath, waiting for something to happen.

Section 2: Strange Happenings The first signs of trouble came in the

74

form of small, inexplicable events. Objects in the cabin would move on their own, shifting positions overnight. Strange symbols appeared in the dirt outside their home, symbols that John recognized from the witch's hut. The air grew colder, and the shadows seemed to deepen, even in the daylight.

Deborah found herself plagued by nightmares. In her dreams, she saw the forest alive with shadows, the trees whispering in a language she couldn't understand. Lydia Leeds' spirit appeared to her, not as the tormented soul seeking redemption, but as a vengeful specter, her eyes burning with anger.

John, too, felt the weight of an unseen presence. He often found himself staring into the forest, feeling as if he was being watched. The sense of unease grew stronger with each passing day, making it difficult for him to focus on his work or sleep soundly at night.

75

Section 3: The First Attack

One night, the peaceful quiet of the village was shattered by a blood-curdling scream. John and Deborah rushed outside to find a villager, one of their closest friends, lying in the dirt, his body covered in deep, ragged wounds. He was barely alive, his eyes wide with terror.

"It was the Devil," he gasped, his voice barely a whisper. "It's not gone. It's still here."

The village was thrown into chaos. Fear spread like wildfire, and whispers of the Jersey Devil's return filled the air. The elder, who had guided John and Deborah through the ritual, looked more troubled than ever. He called a meeting, urging the villagers to remain calm and to stay indoors at night.

John and Deborah were devastated. They had risked everything to lift the curse, and now it seemed as though their

76

efforts had been in vain. The Jersey Devil was back, and it was more vengeful than ever.

Section 4: The Elders' Warning

The village elder pulled John and Deborah aside after the meeting. His eyes were dark with worry, and his voice was filled with a grave urgency. "The curse was never truly lifted," he said. "The ritual appeased Lydia's spirit, but it did not banish the creature itself. The Devil is a manifestation of pure rage and darkness. It cannot be destroyed so easily."

John felt a cold chill settle over him. "What do we do now?" he asked, his voice hoarse with fear.

"The creature feeds on fear and despair," the elder explained. "We must find a way to weaken it, to drive it back into the darkness from which it came. The forest holds many secrets, and there may be other ways to fight it. We need to

77

seek out the oldest and most hidden knowledge."

Section 5: The Forbidden Knowledge

The elder led them to a hidden section of the village archives, a place few knew existed. The air was thick with dust, and the shelves were lined with ancient tomes and scrolls. These were the records of the village's darkest times, accounts of battles with the supernatural and the unknown.

They pored over the texts, searching for anything that could help them. They found references to an ancient artifact, a relic that was said to have the power to banish dark spirits. The artifact, known as the "Heart of the Forest," was hidden somewhere within the Pine Barrens, protected by powerful enchantments.

"The Heart of the Forest," the elder said, his voice trembling with a mix of hope and fear. "If we can find it, we may have a chance to banish the Jersey Devil for

78

good."

Section 6: The Search Begins

Armed with this new knowledge, John and Deborah prepared to venture back into the forest. They knew the journey would be dangerous, but they had no choice. The Jersey Devil was growing bolder, its attacks becoming more frequent and violent. The village could not withstand its wrath for much longer.

The villagers rallied around them, providing supplies and weapons. Their faces were etched with determination and fear, knowing that their fate rested on John and Deborah's shoulders. The couple bid their children a tearful goodbye, promising to return and end the nightmare once and for all.

As they entered the forest, the trees seemed to close in around them, their branches twisting like skeletal fingers. The air was thick with an oppressive darkness, and the sounds of the forest

79

were unnaturally muted. They pressed on, their hearts heavy with the weight of their mission.

Section 7: The Trials of the Forest

The Pine Barrens was a labyrinth of twisting paths and hidden dangers. John and Deborah encountered numerous obstacles, from treacherous swamps to tangled thickets that seemed to have a life of their own. They fought off wild animals and avoided deadly traps set by the forest itself.

Each night, they were plagued by nightmares. The Jersey Devil haunted their dreams, its eyes glowing with malevolence. They woke up in cold sweats, their bodies trembling with fear. The forest seemed to mock them, its whispers growing louder and more insistent.

Despite the hardships, they pressed on, driven by the desperate need to save their village and their family. They

80

followed the clues in the ancient texts, navigating the forest with a mix of caution and determination. The further they went, the more they felt the presence of something powerful and ancient watching over them.

Section 8: The Guardian of the Heart

After days of grueling travel, they finally reached a hidden glade, bathed in an eerie, otherworldly light. In the center of the glade stood a massive tree, its trunk twisted and gnarled. At the base of the tree lay a stone altar, and upon it rested the Heart of the Forest.

The artifact was a small, intricately carved wooden heart, glowing with a soft, pulsating light. As they approached, a figure emerged from the shadows. The guardian of the Heart was a spectral being, its form shifting and ethereal. Its eyes glowed with a piercing blue light, and its voice echoed through the glade.

"Who dares to seek the Heart of the

81

Forest?" the guardian intoned, its voice filled with an ancient power.

John and Deborah explained their mission, their voices trembling with a mix of fear and determination. The guardian listened, its eyes narrowing as it considered their words.

"The Heart is a powerful artifact," the guardian said. "It can banish the darkness, but it requires a great sacrifice. Are you willing to pay the price?"

Section 9: The Price of Power

John and Deborah hesitated, knowing that the guardian's words were not to be taken lightly. The price of power was often steep, and they feared what it might entail. But they had come too far to turn back now.

"We are willing," John said, his voice resolute. "Whatever it takes, we will do it."

The guardian nodded, its eyes glowing

82

with approval. "Very well. The Heart requires a life force to activate its power. One of you must offer your essence to the artifact. It is the only way."

John and Deborah exchanged a pained look. They knew the choice was inevitable, but it didn't make it any easier. Deborah stepped forward, her eyes filled with determination and love.

"I will do it," she said, her voice steady. "For our family, for our village. I will give my essence to the Heart."

Section 10: The Ritual of Sacrifice

The guardian led them to the altar, its movements graceful and fluid. Deborah lay down on the stone, her heart pounding with fear and resolve. John stood beside her, his hand gripping hers tightly. The guardian began the ritual, chanting in an ancient language that resonated through the glade.

As the chant grew louder, the Heart of

83

the Forest began to glow brighter. Tendrils of light reached out from the artifact, wrapping around Deborah's body. She felt a searing pain as her essence was drawn into the Heart, her life force merging with its power.

John watched in horror and awe as the ritual continued. Deborah's body glowed with an ethereal light, her face serene despite the pain. The guardian's chant reached a crescendo, and the Heart pulsed with a blinding light.

In that moment, Deborah's essence fused with the Heart, imbuing it with the power to banish the Jersey Devil. Her body went limp, and John caught her in his arms, his heart breaking with grief and love.

Section 11: The Power of the Heart

With the ritual complete, the Heart of the Forest glowed with a newfound intensity. The guardian nodded, its eyes filled with a mixture of sadness and

84

respect. "The power of the Heart is now yours," it said. "Use it wisely, and you may banish the darkness that plagues your land."

John, his heart heavy with sorrow, took the Heart and vowed to fulfill Deborah's sacrifice. He left the glade, the guardian's eyes following him as he disappeared into the forest. The journey back to the village was long and arduous, the weight of his loss pressing down on him with each step.

Section 12: The Final Confrontation

When John returned to the village, the air was thick with fear and anticipation. The villagers gathered around him, their faces filled with hope and dread. John held up the Heart of the Forest, its glow a beacon of hope in the darkness.

"The Jersey Devil will come for us," John said, his voice strong despite his grief. "But we have the power to banish it. We must stand together and face it as

85

one."

The villagers, inspired by John's determination, prepared for the final confrontation. They fortified the village, setting traps and gathering weapons. As night fell, they waited with bated breath, knowing that the Jersey Devil would soon make its move.

The creature's arrival was heralded by an eerie silence, the air growing colder and the shadows deepening. The villagers stood their ground, their hearts pounding with fear and resolve. The Jersey Devil emerged from the darkness, its eyes glowing with malevolence.

John stepped forward, holding the Heart of the Forest high. The artifact pulsed with light, its power radiating through the village. The Jersey Devil let out a roar of rage, its form shifting and writhing as it approached.

86

Section 13: The Battle for the Village

The battle was fierce and terrifying. The Jersey Devil attacked with relentless fury, its claws slashing through the air and its eyes burning with hatred. The villagers fought back with all their might, their weapons gleaming in the light of the Heart.

John focused on the artifact, channeling its power to drive back the creature. The Heart's light grew brighter, casting out the shadows and weakening the Jersey Devil's form. The creature howled in pain, its body flickering as it struggled against the Heart's power.

Despite their fear, the villagers fought bravely, their determination unwavering. They knew that this was their only chance to banish the creature and save their village. They struck at the Jersey Devil with a ferocity born of desperation and hope.

87

Section 14: The Sacrifice Fulfilled

As the battle raged on, John felt Deborah's presence beside him, her essence guiding him and lending him strength. He knew that her sacrifice had given them the power to banish the darkness, and he was determined to see it through.

With a final, desperate effort, John channeled the full power of the Heart of the Forest. The artifact blazed with light, its energy enveloping the Jersey Devil and forcing it back. The creature let out a final, ear-piercing scream as it was consumed by the light, its form dissolving into nothingness.

The village fell silent, the air thick with the aftermath of the battle. The Jersey Devil was gone, banished by the power of the Heart and Deborah's sacrifice. The villagers stood in stunned silence, their hearts filled with a mixture of relief and sorrow.

88

Section 15: The Aftermath

With the Jersey Devil banished, the village began to heal. The oppressive darkness that had hung over the Pine Barrens lifted, replaced by a sense of peace and renewal. The villagers honored Deborah's sacrifice, her bravery and love a testament to the strength of their community.

John, though heartbroken by his loss, found solace in the knowledge that Deborah's sacrifice had saved their family and their village. He dedicated himself to preserving her memory and ensuring that the village remained safe from the darkness that had once plagued them.

The Heart of the Forest was returned to its sacred glade, its power a guardian against future threats. The villagers continued to honor the ancient knowledge and traditions, knowing that they held the key to their survival and prosperity.

89

Section 16: Healing and Reflection

In the months that followed, the village thrived. The land, once shrouded in fear, began to flourish, its beauty and vitality restored. The villagers worked together to rebuild and strengthen their community, their bonds forged in the fires of their shared ordeal.

John and his children found a new sense of peace, their hearts filled with the love and memory of Deborah. They knew that her spirit would always be with them, guiding and protecting them. The village, though forever changed by their experiences, emerged stronger and more united.

Section 17: The Legacy of the Curse

The story of the Jersey Devil and the curse of the Leeds family became a part of the village's history, a reminder of the darkness they had overcome. The legend was passed down through generations, a tale of bravery, sacrifice, and

90

redemption.

The villagers, now wiser and more vigilant, remained ever watchful of the forest and its secrets. They knew that the Pine Barrens held both beauty and danger, and they respected its power and mystery.

Section 18: A New Dawn

As time passed, the village continued to thrive, its people living in harmony with the land. The Pine Barrens, once a place of fear and darkness, became a symbol of resilience and hope. The villagers embraced their history, knowing that their strength and unity had saved them from the brink of despair.

John, now an elder himself, shared the story of Deborah and the Heart of the Forest with the younger generations. He taught them the importance of courage, sacrifice, and the power of love. The village, guided by these values, faced the future with hope and determination.

91

Section 19: The Spirit of the Forest

The Pine Barrens, ever watchful, stood as a silent guardian of the village's triumph. The forest, with its ancient trees and whispering winds, held the memories of the past and the promise of the future. The villagers, now attuned to the forest's rhythms, lived in harmony with its natural beauty and power.

The spirit of Deborah, ever present, watched over her family and village. Her sacrifice had brought peace and light to the Pine Barrens, and her legacy would endure through the ages. The villagers, guided by her memory, honored the land and its secrets, knowing that they held the key to their survival and prosperity.

Section 20: The Eternal Watch

As the years passed, the village continued to thrive, its people living in harmony with the land and each other. The story of the Jersey Devil and the curse of the Leeds family became a

92

cherished part of their history, a testament to their courage and resilience.

The Pine Barrens, with its ancient trees and whispering winds, remained a place of beauty and mystery. The villagers, now wiser and more united, lived in peace and harmony, their hearts filled with hope and gratitude.

The legacy of the curse, a tale of sorrow and redemption, lived on in the hearts and minds of the villagers. The story of the Jersey Devil, once a source of fear, became a symbol of their strength and unity. The forest, ever watchful, stood as a silent guardian of their triumph and their enduring spirit.

Chapter 6: The Whispers of Darkness

Section 1: Lingering Shadows

In the aftermath of the battle with the Jersey Devil, the village was shrouded in an uneasy calm. The air was thick with

93

the scent of smoke and fear, and the villagers moved about with a wary tension. Despite the creature's banishment, a sense of unease lingered in the air, like the echo of a nightmare that refused to fade away.

John felt the weight of Deborah's absence like a physical ache in his chest. Every corner of their cabin seemed haunted by memories of her, and he struggled to find solace in the quiet moments of solitude. The nights were the hardest, filled with restless dreams and whispered voices that seemed to echo from the darkness outside.

Section 2: The Return of the Shadows

As the days passed, strange occurrences began to plague the village once more. Animals went missing, their tracks leading into the forest but never returning. Villagers reported seeing shadowy figures lurking in the trees, their eyes glowing with an otherworldly

94

light. The air grew colder, and the once-familiar sounds of the forest were replaced by an eerie silence.

Whispers spread among the villagers, fueled by fear and uncertainty. Some believed that the Jersey Devil had returned, its banishment only temporary. Others whispered of darker forces at work, ancient spirits awakened by the battle and seeking vengeance upon the living.

John knew that something was terribly wrong. The peace they had fought so hard to achieve was unraveling before his eyes, and he feared that the darkness they had faced was far from defeated. He resolved to uncover the truth, no matter the cost.

Section 3: A Desperate Search

John sought out the village elder, hoping to find answers to the growing darkness that threatened to engulf them once more. The elder's face was drawn with

95

worry, his eyes clouded with a sense of foreboding.

"The Jersey Devil may be gone," the elder said, his voice grave, "but its presence has awakened something far more ancient and sinister. The forest holds many secrets, and I fear that we have only scratched the surface of its true power."

John listened intently, his heart heavy with dread. He knew that they were facing a threat unlike anything they had encountered before, and he vowed to do whatever it took to protect his family and his village.

"We must find the source of this darkness," John said, his voice firm. "We cannot allow it to consume us."

The elder nodded in agreement, his expression grim. "We will need to venture into the heart of the forest, to confront the darkness at its source. But be warned, John. The journey will be

96

perilous, and the dangers we face may be greater than anything we have ever known."

Section 4: Into the Abyss

Armed with determination and desperation, John and a small group of villagers set out into the heart of the Pine Barrens. The forest seemed to close in around them, its branches reaching out like grasping fingers. The air was thick with an oppressive darkness, and the ground seemed to tremble beneath their feet.

They pressed on, their hearts pounding with fear and anticipation. The forest seemed to come alive around them, its shadows twisting and shifting with unnatural movements. Strange symbols appeared on the trees, glowing with an eerie light that sent shivers down their spines.

As they ventured deeper into the forest, the air grew colder, and the darkness

97

seemed to deepen. They heard strange whispers echoing through the trees, voices that spoke in a language they could not understand. The ground beneath them seemed to shift and writhe, as if the very earth itself was alive with malevolent intent.

Section 5: The Ancient Ruins

After days of grueling travel, they stumbled upon a clearing in the forest, bathed in an ethereal light. In the center of the clearing stood a circle of ancient stone ruins, their weathered faces covered in strange symbols and carvings.

The air was thick with a sense of ancient power, and the hairs on the back of John's neck stood on end. He could feel the weight of centuries pressing down upon him, as if the very fabric of reality was unraveling before his eyes.

"This place reeks of dark magic," one of the villagers whispered, his voice

98

trembling with fear. "We should turn back while we still can."

But John knew that they had come too far to turn back now. Whatever darkness lurked within these ruins, they had to confront it head-on if they were to have any hope of saving their village.

Chapter 7

Section 6: The Guardian of the Ruins

As they approached the ruins, a figure emerged from the shadows, its form shrouded in darkness. Its eyes gleamed with a malevolent light, and its voice echoed through the clearing like a whisper on the wind.

"Who dares to disturb the ancient guardians of this forest?" the figure intoned, its voice dripping with malice.

John stepped forward, his heart pounding with fear and resolve. "We seek answers," he said, his voice steady

99

despite the tremble in his limbs. "We seek to understand the darkness that plagues our village, and to put an end to it once and for all."

The figure regarded him with a mix of amusement and contempt. "You are fools to think that you can challenge the darkness that lurks within these ruins," it said, its voice echoing with a chilling finality. "But if you are determined to proceed, know that the price of your folly may be greater than you can imagine."

Section 7: The Trial of Shadows

The figure vanished into the darkness, leaving John and the villagers to confront the ancient ruins alone. They entered cautiously, their senses on high alert for any sign of danger. The air was thick with an oppressive stillness, and the silence seemed to press down upon them like a weight.

As they ventured deeper into the ruins,

100

they encountered strange traps and obstacles, designed to test their resolve and their strength. They fought off swarms of shadowy creatures that seemed to materialize out of thin air, their claws and fangs glinting in the dim light.

With each passing moment, the darkness seemed to close in around them, threatening to swallow them whole. But they pressed on, driven by the desperate need to uncover the truth and to save their village from the growing menace.

Section 8: The Chamber of Shadows

At last, they reached the heart of the ruins, a chamber bathed in an otherworldly glow. In the center of the chamber stood a pedestal, upon which rested a small, glowing orb. The orb pulsed with a faint light, its surface swirling with shadows and whispers.

"This must be the source of the darkness," one of the villagers said, his

101

voice hushed with awe.

John approached the pedestal cautiously, his heart pounding with anticipation. He reached out to touch the orb, his fingers trembling with fear and uncertainty.

But before he could make contact, a voice echoed through the chamber, freezing him in his tracks.

"Who dares to disturb the ancient guardians of this forest?"

Section 9: The Guardian's Challenge

A figure emerged from the shadows, its form shrouded in darkness. Its eyes gleamed with a malevolent light, and its voice echoed through the chamber like a whisper on the wind.

"We are the guardians of this forest," the figure intoned, its voice dripping with malice. "And we will own you.

John stood his ground, his heart pounding with fear and determination. "We mean no harm," he said, his voice

102

steady despite the tremble in his limbs. "We seek to understand the darkness that plagues our village, and to put an end to it once and for all."

The figure regarded him with a mix of amusement and contempt. "You are foolish to think that you can challenge the darkness that lurks within these ruins," it said, its voice echoing with a chilling finality. "But if you are determined to proceed, know that the price of your folly may be greater than you can imagine."

John exchanged a glance with the villagers, their faces pale with fear but their resolve unwavering. They knew that they had come too far to turn back now, and they were prepared to face whatever darkness awaited them within the ruins.

"We understand the risks," John said, his voice firm. "But we cannot allow the darkness to consume our village. We will do whatever it takes to protect our

103

home and our loved ones."

The figure regarded them for a moment, its eyes narrowing with suspicion. Then, with a gesture of its hand, it vanished into the shadows, leaving John and the villagers to confront the darkness alone.

Section 10: The Trials of the Ruins

As they ventured deeper into the chamber, they encountered strange traps and obstacles, designed to test their resolve and their strength. They fought off swarms of shadowy creatures that seemed to materialize out of thin air, their claws and fangs glinting in the dim light.

With each passing moment, the darkness seemed to close in around them, threatening to swallow them whole. But they pressed on, driven by the desperate need to uncover the truth and to save their village from the growing menace.

They encountered puzzles and riddles,

104

each more fiendish than the last, designed to challenge their minds and their wits. They faced illusions and hallucinations, their senses assaulted by visions of their deepest fears and darkest desires.

But through it all, they remained steadfast, their determination unwavering in the face of overwhelming darkness. They knew that they were fighting for more than just their own lives—they were fighting for the future of their village, and for the light that still flickered within their hearts.

Section 11: Confronting the Darkness

At last, they reached the heart of the ruins, a chamber bathed in an otherworldly glow. In the center of the chamber stood a pedestal, upon which rested a small, glowing orb. The orb pulsed with a faint light, its surface swirling with shadows and whispers.

"This must be the source of the

105

darkness," one of the villagers said, his voice hushed with awe.

John approached the pedestal cautiously, his heart pounding with anticipation. He reached out to touch the orb, his fingers trembling with fear and uncertainty.

But before he could make contact, a voice echoed through the chamber, freezing him in his tracks.

"Who dares to disturb the ancient guardians of this forest?"

Section 12: The Guardian's Challenge

A figure emerged from the shadows, its form shrouded in darkness. Its eyes gleamed with a malevolent light, and its voice echoed through the chamber like a whisper on the wind.

"We are the guardians of this forest," the figure intoned, its voice dripping with malice. "And we will not allow you to defile our sacred sanctuary."

John stood his ground, his heart

106

pounding with fear and determination. "We mean no harm," he said, his voice steady despite the tremble in his limbs.

"We seek to understand the darkness that plagues our village, and to put an end to it once and for all."

The figure regarded him with a mix of amusement and contempt. "You are foolish to think that you can challenge the darkness that lurks within these ruins," it said, its voice echoing with a chilling finality. "But if you are determined to proceed, know that the price of your folly may be greater than you can imagine."

John exchanged a glance with the villagers, their faces pale with fear but their resolve unwavering. They knew that they had come too far to turn back now, and they were prepared to face whatever darkness awaited them within the ruins.

"We understand the risks," John said, his voice firm. "But we cannot allow the

107

darkness to consume our village. We will do whatever it takes to protect our home and our loved ones."

The figure regarded them for a moment, its eyes narrowing with suspicion. Then, with a gesture of its hand, it vanished into the shadows, leaving John and the villagers to confront the darkness alone.

Section 13: The Heart of Darkness

As they approached the pedestal, the orb seemed to pulse with a dark energy, its light flickering and wavering like a dying flame. John reached out to touch it, his fingers trembling with fear and uncertainty.

But as soon as his hand made contact with the orb, a wave of darkness washed over him, engulfing him in its suffocating embrace. Visions flashed before his eyes—images of death and destruction, of despair and madness.

He heard the voices of the ancient

108

guardians, whispering in his mind like a serpent's hiss. They spoke of power and corruption, of the temptations of darkness and the folly of mortals who dared to challenge their authority.

John felt himself being pulled deeper into the abyss, his mind and soul consumed by the darkness that surrounded him. He fought against it with all his strength, clinging to the light that still burned within him like a flickering candle in the night.

Section 14: The Battle Within

With a desperate effort, John summoned all his courage and will-power, pushing back against the darkness that threatened to overwhelm him. He called upon the memories of his loved ones, of Deborah and their children, of the village that he had sworn to protect.

Slowly, agonizingly, he felt the darkness begin to recede, like a tide retreating from the shore. He reached out with his

109

mind and heart, reaching for the light that still burned within him, drawing strength from its warmth and purity.

At last, with a final surge of determination, John broke free from the darkness that had ensnared him, his spirit soaring like a bird released from its cage. He stood before the pedestal, his eyes blazing with defiance and resolve.

Section 15: The Power Within

With a steady hand, John reached out and touched the orb once more, his fingers tingling with a strange energy. As soon as his hand made contact, the orb began to glow with a brilliant light, its surface shimmering with a kaleidoscope

The Dance of Shadows Section 1: A Fractured Reality

As John touched the orb, a surge of power coursed through him, sending

110

shockwaves of energy rippling through the chamber. The air crackled with electricity, and the shadows seemed to twist and contort as if alive. With a blinding flash, the darkness was expelled, replaced by a blinding light that filled the chamber.

When John's vision cleared, he found himself standing in a realm unlike any he had ever seen before. The world around him seemed to flicker and shift, as if caught between dimensions. Strange symbols danced in the air, their meaning incomprehensible to mortal eyes.

Beside him, the villagers stood in awe and terror, their faces pale with fear. They clung to each other, seeking comfort in the face of the unknown. John knew that they had entered a realm of ancient magic and dark power, and that they would need all their strength and courage to survive.

111

Section 2: The Guardians' Trial

As they ventured deeper into the realm, they encountered strange trials and challenges, each more fiendish than the last. They faced illusions and hallucinations, their senses assaulted by visions of their deepest fears and darkest desires. They battled creatures of shadow and flame, their forms shifting and changing with each blow.

But through it all, they remained steadfast, their determination unwavering in the face of overwhelming darkness. They knew that they were fighting for more than just their own lives—they were fighting for the future of their village, and for the light that still flickered within their hearts.

Section 3: The Chamber of Echoes

At last, they reached the heart of the realm, a chamber bathed in an otherworldly glow. In the center of the chamber stood a pedestal, upon which

112

rested a small, glowing orb. The orb pulsed with a faint light, its surface swirling with shadows and whispers.

"This must be the source of the darkness," one of the villagers said, his voice hushed with awe.

John approached the pedestal cautiously, his heart pounding with anticipation. He reached out to touch the orb, his fingers trembling with fear and uncertainty.

But before he could make contact, a voice echoed through the chamber, freezing him in his tracks.

"Who dares to disturb the ancient guardians of this realm?"

Section 4: The Guardians' Challenge

A figure emerged from the shadows, its form shrouded in darkness. Its eyes gleamed with a malevolent light, and its voice echoed through the chamber like a whisper on the wind.

"We are the guardians of this realm," the

113

figure intoned, its voice dripping with malice. "And we will not allow you to defile our sacred sanctuary."

John stood his ground, his heart pounding with fear and determination. "We mean no harm," he said, his voice steady despite the tremble in his limbs. "We seek to understand the darkness that plagues our village, and to put an end to it once and for all."

The figure regarded him with a mix of amusement and contempt. "You are foolish to think that you can challenge the darkness that lurks within these ruins," it said, its voice echoing with a chilling finality. "But if you are determined to proceed, know that the price of your folly may be greater than you can imagine."

John exchanged a glance with the villagers, their faces pale with fear but their resolve unwavering. They knew that they had come too far to turn back now, and they were prepared to face

114

whatever darkness awaited them within the ruins.

"We understand the risks," John said, his voice firm. "But we cannot allow the darkness to consume our village. We will do whatever it takes to protect our home and our loved ones."

The figure regarded them for a moment, its eyes narrowing with suspicion. Then, with a gesture of its hand, it vanished into the shadows, leaving John and the villagers to confront the darkness alone.

Section 5: The Trials of the Ruins

As they ventured deeper into the chamber, they encountered strange traps and obstacles, designed to test their resolve and their strength.

They fought off swarms of shadowy creatures that seemed to materialize out of thin air, their claws and fangs glinting in the dim light.

With each passing moment, the darkness

115

seemed to close in around them, threatening to swallow them
whole. But they pressed on, driven by the desperate need to uncover
the truth and to save their village from the growing menace.

They encountered puzzles and riddles, each more fiendish than
the last, designed to challenge their minds and their wits. They faced
illusions and hallucinations, their senses assaulted by visions of their
deepest fears and darkest desires.

But through it all, they remained steadfast, their determination unwavering in the face of overwhelming darkness. They knew that they
were fighting for more than just their own lives—they were fighting for
the future of their village, and for the light that still flickered within
their hearts.

Section 6: Confronting the Darkness

At last, they reached the heart of the ruins, a chamber bathed
in an

116

otherworldly glow. In the center of the chamber stood a pedestal,
upon which rested a small, glowing orb. The orb pulsed with a faint
light, its surface swirling with shadows and whispers.

"This must be the source of the darkness," one of the villagers said,
his voice hushed with awe.

John approached the pedestal cautiously, his heart pounding with
anticipation. He reached out to touch the orb, his fingers trembling
with fear and uncertainty.

But before he could make contact, a voice echoed through the
chamber, freezing him in his tracks.

"Who dares to disturb the ancient guardians of this forest?"

Section 7: The Guardian's Challenge

A figure emerged from the shadows, its form shrouded in darkness. Its eyes gleamed with a malevolent light, and its voice echoed through the chamber like a

117

whisper on the wind.

"We are the guardians of this forest," the figure intoned, its voice dripping with malice. "And we will not allow you to defile our sacred sanctuary."

John stood his ground, his heart pounding with fear and determination. "We mean no harm," he said, his voice steady despite the tremble in his limbs. "We seek to understand the darkness that plagues our village, and to put an end to it once and for all."

The figure regarded him with a mix of amusement and contempt. "You are foolish to think that you can challenge the darkness that lurks within these ruins," it said, its voice echoing with a chilling finality. "But if you are determined to proceed, know that the price of your folly may be greater than you can imagine."

John exchanged a glance with the villagers, their faces pale with fear but

118

their resolve unwavering. They knew that they had come too far to turn back now, and they were prepared to face whatever darkness awaited them within the ruins.

Chapter 8: The Labyrinth of Nightmares

Section 1: Echoes of Despair

As the figure's words faded into the darkness, John and the villagers stood frozen in apprehension. The air seemed to thicken around them, suffused with an oppressive weight that pressed down upon their chests. The chamber pulsed with an eerie glow, casting long shadows that danced across the ancient ruins.

John's mind raced with uncertainty, his thoughts consumed by the gravity of their situation. He knew that they had ventured into the heart of darkness, where the line between reality and

119

nightmare blurred into obscurity. With a deep breath, he steeled himself for the trials that lay ahead.

"We cannot falter," John declared, his voice resonating with determination. "Whatever lies within these ruins, we face it together, as one."

The villagers nodded in agreement, their expressions a mixture of fear and resolve. With a shared sense of purpose, they stepped forward, prepared to confront the shadows that lurked within the labyrinth of nightmares.

Section 2: The Veil of Illusions

As they ventured deeper into the ruins, they found themselves ensnared in a labyrinth of illusions and deceptions. The walls seemed to shift and warp, twisting their perceptions of reality with each passing moment. Familiar landmarks vanished into the darkness, replaced by mirages that taunted their senses.

120

John's heart raced as he struggled to discern truth from falsehood, his mind assailed by visions of his deepest fears and regrets. He saw Deborah's face in the shadows, her eyes filled with reproach and sorrow. He heard the laughter of their children echoing through the darkness, a cruel reminder of the life he had lost.

But through the haze of illusions, John clung to the light that burned within him, a beacon of hope amidst the encroaching darkness. With each step, he pushed forward, determined to unravel the mysteries of the ruins and banish the shadows that threatened to consume them all.

Section 3: The Whispers of Madness

As they pressed on, the air grew thick with the whispers of unseen voices, their words a cacophony of madness and despair. John felt the weight of their words pressing down upon him,

121

threatening to drown him in a sea of doubt and uncertainty.

"Weakness," the voices taunted, their words like daggers in his mind. "Failure. Despair."

But John refused to succumb to the darkness, his willpower a shield against the onslaught of madness. With each whispered insult, he pushed back, his determination unwavering in the face of adversity.

"We are stronger than you know," John declared, his voice ringing out with defiance. "We will not be swayed by your lies."

The villagers rallied behind him, their voices joining in a chorus of determination and defiance. Together, they pushed forward, their spirits unbroken despite the darkness that surrounded them.

122

Section 4: The Trial of Shadows

At last, they reached the heart of the ruins, a chamber bathed in an otherworldly glow. In the center of the chamber stood a pedestal, upon which rested a small, glowing orb. The orb pulsed with a faint light, its surface swirling with shadows and whispers.

"This must be the source of the darkness," one of the villagers said, his voice hushed with awe.

John approached the pedestal cautiously, his heart pounding with anticipation. He reached out to touch the orb, his fingers trembling with fear and uncertainty.

But before he could make contact, a voice echoed through the chamber, freezing him in his tracks.

"Who dares to disturb the ancient guardians of this forest?"

Section 5: The Guardian's Challenge

A figure emerged from the shadows, its

123

form shrouded in darkness. Its eyes gleamed with a malevolent light, and its voice echoed through the chamber like a whisper on the wind.

"We are the guardians of this forest," the figure intoned, its voice dripping with malice. "And we will not allow you to defile our sacred sanctuary."

John stood his ground, his heart pounding with fear and determination. "We mean no harm," he said, his voice steady despite the tremble in his limbs. "We seek to understand the darkness that plagues our village, and to put an end to it once and for all."

The figure regarded him with a mix of amusement and contempt. "You are foolish to think that you can challenge the darkness that lurks within these ruins," it said, its voice echoing with a chilling finality. "But if you are determined to proceed, know that the price of your folly may be greater than you can imagine."

124

John exchanged a glance with the villagers, their faces pale with fear but their resolve unwavering. They knew that they had come too far to turn back now, and they were prepared to face whatever darkness awaited them within the ruins.

"We understand the risks," John said, his voice firm. "But we cannot allow the darkness to consume our village. We will do whatever it takes to protect our home and our loved ones."

The figure regarded them for a moment, its eyes narrowing with suspicion. Then, with a gesture of its hand, it vanished into the shadows, leaving John and the villagers to confront the darkness alone.

Section 6: The Trials of the Ruins

As they ventured deeper into the chamber, they encountered strange traps and obstacles, designed to test their resolve and their strength. They fought off swarms of shadowy creatures that

125

seemed to materialize out of thin air, their claws and fangs glinting in the dim light.

With each passing moment, the darkness seemed to close in around them, threatening to swallow them whole. But they pressed on, driven by the desperate need to uncover the truth and to save their village from the growing menace.

They encountered puzzles and riddles, each more fiendish than the last, designed to challenge their minds and their wits. They faced illusions and hallucinations, their senses assaulted by visions of their deepest fears and darkest desires.

But through it all, they remained steadfast, their determination unwavering in the face of overwhelming darkness. They knew that they were fighting for more than just their own lives—they were fighting for the future of their village, and for the light that still flickered within their hearts.

126

Section 7: Confronting the Darkness

At last, they reached the heart of the ruins, a chamber bathed in an otherworldly glow. In the center of the chamber stood a pedestal, upon which rested a small, glowing orb. The orb pulsed with a faint light, its surface swirling with shadows and whispers.

"This must be the source of the darkness," one of the villagers said, his voice hushed with awe.

John approached the pedestal cautiously, his heart pounding with anticipation. He reached out to touch the orb, his fingers trembling with fear and uncertainty.

But before he could make contact, a voice echoed through the chamber, freezing him in his tracks.

"Who dares to disturb the ancient guardians of this forest?"

Section 8: The Guardian's Challenge

A figure emerged from the shadows, its

127

form shrouded in darkness. Its eyes gleamed with a malevolent light, and its voice echoed through the chamber like a whisper on the wind.

"We are the guardians of this forest," the figure intoned, its voice dripping with malice. "And we will not allow you to defile our sacred sanctuary."

John stood his ground, his heart pounding with fear and determination. "We mean no harm," he said, his voice steady despite the tremble in his limbs. "We seek to understand the darkness that plagues our village, and to put an end to it once and for all."

The figure regarded him with a mix of amusement and contempt. "You are foolish to think that you can challenge the darkness that lurks within these ruins," it said, its voice echoing with a chilling finality. "But if you are determined to proceed, know that the price of your folly may be greater than you can imagine."

128

John exchanged a glance with the villagers, their faces pale with fear but their resolve unwavering. They knew that they had come too far to turn back now, and they were prepared to face whatever darkness awaited them within the ruins.

"We understand the risks," John said, his voice firm. "But we cannot allow the darkness to consume our village. We will do whatever it takes to protect our home and our loved ones."

The figure regarded them for a moment, its eyes narrowing with suspicion. Then, with a gesture of its hand, it vanished into the shadows, leaving John and the villagers to confront the darkness alone.

Section 9: The Labyrinth's Trials

As they ventured deeper into the ruins, they encountered a series of trials designed to test their courage and resilience. They traversed treacherous pathways that seemed to shift and

129

change with each step, leading them deeper into the heart of darkness. They faced monstrous creatures that lurked in the shadows, their eyes gleaming with hunger and malice.

With each trial they faced, the darkness seemed to grow stronger, its presence looming over them like a suffocating fog. But John and the villagers refused to yield, their determination unyielding in the face of adversity. They pressed on, driven by the desperate need to uncover the truth and to save their village from the growing menace.

Section 10: The Chamber of Shadows

At last, they reached the heart of the ruins, a chamber bathed in an otherworldly glow. In the center of the chamber stood a pedestal, upon which rested a small, glowing orb. The orb pulsed with a faint light, its surface swirling with shadows and whispers.

"This must be the source of the

130

darkness," one of the villagers said, his voice hushed with awe.

John approached the pedestal cautiously, his heart pounding with anticipation. He reached out to touch the orb, his fingers trembling with fear and uncertainty.

But before he could make contact, a voice echoed through the chamber, freezing him in his tracks.

"Who dares to disturb the ancient guardians of this forest?"

Section 11: The Guardian's Challenge

A figure emerged from the shadows, its form shrouded in darkness. Its eyes gleamed with a malevolent light, and its voice echoed through the chamber like a whisper on the wind.

"We are the guardians of this forest," the figure intoned, its voice dripping with malice. "And we will not allow you to defile our sacred sanctuary."

John stood his ground, his heart

131

pounding with fear and determination. "We mean no harm," he said, his voice steady despite the tremble in his limbs.

"We seek to understand the darkness that plagues our village, and to put an end to it once and for all."

The figure regarded him with a mix of amusement and contempt. "You are foolish to think that you can challenge the darkness that lurks within these ruins," it said, its voice echoing with a chilling finality. "But if you are determined to proceed, know that the price of your folly may be greater than you can imagine."

John exchanged a glance with the villagers, their faces pale with fear but their resolve unwavering. They knew that they had come too far to turn back now, and they were prepared to face whatever darkness awaited them within the ruins.

"We understand the risks," John said, his voice firm. "But we cannot allow the

132

darkness to consume our village. We will do whatever it takes to protect our home and our loved ones."

The figure regarded them for a moment, its eyes narrowing with suspicion. Then, with a gesture of its hand, it vanished into the shadows, leaving John and the villagers to confront the darkness alone.

Section 12: The Trials of the Ruins

As they ventured deeper into the chamber, they encountered strange traps and obstacles, designed to test their resolve and their strength. They fought off swarms of shadowy creatures that seemed to materialize out of thin air, their claws and fangs glinting in the dim light.

With each passing moment, the darkness seemed to close in around them, threatening to swallow them whole. But they pressed on, driven by the desperate need to uncover the truth and to save their village from the growing menace.

133

They encountered puzzles and riddles, each more fiendish than the last, designed to challenge their minds and their wits. They faced illusions and hallucinations, their senses assaulted by visions of their deepest fears and darkest desires.

But through it all, they remained steadfast, their determination unwavering in the face of overwhelming darkness. They knew that they were fighting for more than just their own lives—they were fighting for the future of their village, and for the light that still flickered within their hearts.

Section 13: Confronting the Darkness

At last, they reached the heart of the ruins, a chamber bathed in an otherworldly glow. In the center of the chamber stood a pedestal, upon which rested a small, glowing orb. The orb pulsed with a faint light, its surface swirling with shadows and whispers.

134

"This must be the source of the darkness," one of the villagers said, his voice hushed with awe.

John approached the pedestal cautiously, his heart pounding with anticipation. He reached out to touch the orb, his fingers trembling with fear and uncertainty.

But before he could make contact, a voice echoed through the chamber, freezing him in his tracks.

"Who dares to disturb the ancient guardians of this forest?"

Chapter 9: The Abyss of Torment

Section 1: The Veil of Shadows

As John's fingers hovered inches away from the pulsating orb, the air around them seemed to thicken, suffused with a palpable sense of malevolence. The whispers of unseen entities echoed through the chamber, their words a

135

sinister chorus of doubt and despair.

"You are not worthy," they hissed, their voices like daggers in John's mind. "You will fail. Surrender to the darkness."

But John refused to yield, his resolve unshaken by the onslaught of darkness. With a determined grit, he pushed forward, his hand trembling as it reached out to make contact with the orb.

Suddenly, the chamber erupted into chaos, shadows writhing and twisting as if alive. The ground beneath them trembled, cracks spider-webbing across the stone floor like veins of darkness.

Section 2: The Guardian's Wrath

From the depths of the shadows, the figure emerged once more, its form contorted with rage. Its eyes blazed with an otherworldly fire, and its voice boomed through the chamber like thunder.

"Your defiance will not go unpunished,"

136

it roared, its words reverberating off the walls of the ruins. "You dare to challenge the darkness that has consumed this realm? Then prepare to face the consequences."

With a wave of its hand, the figure unleashed a torrent of dark energy, sending John and the villagers tumbling backward. They struggled to regain their footing as the darkness closed in around them, threatening to engulf them in its suffocating embrace.

But John refused to surrender, his spirit unyielding in the face of adversity. With a fierce cry, he raised his sword high, ready to face whatever horrors awaited them in the depths of the abyss.

Section 3: The Descent into Madness

With a collective resolve, John and the villagers plunged deeper into the ruins, their path shrouded in darkness. The air grew thick with the stench of decay, and the walls seemed to pulse with a

137

sickening energy.

They traversed treacherous passageways lined with jagged spikes and gaping chasms, each step bringing them closer to the heart of the abyss. Shadows danced on the walls, twisting and contorting into grotesque shapes that seemed to leer at them with malevolent intent.

But John pressed on, his determination unwavering in the face of the horrors that surrounded them. He knew that they were close to uncovering the truth behind the darkness that plagued their village, and he would not rest until they had banished it from their midst.

Section 4: The Chamber of Torment

At last, they reached the heart of the abyss, a chamber bathed in an eerie crimson light. In the center of the chamber stood a towering monolith, its surface etched with ancient runes and symbols. Dark energy crackled around

138

it, casting long shadows that seemed to reach out with grasping hands.

"This must be the source of the darkness," one of the villagers whispered, his voice trembling with fear.

John nodded grimly, his eyes fixed on the monolith before them. He knew that they had come too far to turn back now, and he would not allow the darkness to consume them.

With a determined stride, he approached the monolith, his sword at the ready. He could feel the energy pulsing from it, a malevolent force that threatened to overwhelm him.

But he would not falter. He raised his sword high and struck the monolith with all his might, unleashing a wave of light that banished the darkness from the chamber.

Section 5: The Guardian's Last Stand As the darkness receded, the figure

139

emerged from the shadows once more, its form twisted and contorted with rage. It bellowed with fury, its voice a cacophony of hatred and despair.

"You dare to defy me?" it roared, its eyes blazing with otherworldly fire. "You will pay for your insolence with your lives."

But John stood firm, his sword raised high in defiance. He would not allow the guardian to harm his village, no matter the cost.

With a mighty roar, he charged forward, his sword slicing through the darkness with ease. The guardian recoiled, its form flickering and fading as if unable to withstand the onslaught of light.

With a final blow, John struck the guardian down, banishing it from the realm once and for all. The chamber trembled with the force of the blow, and then fell silent, the darkness dissipating like morning mist.

140

Section 6: The Return to Light

As the darkness receded, John and the villagers emerged from the ruins, their hearts lightened by their victory. The sun shone brightly overhead, its warmth a welcome reprieve from the chill of the abyss.

They returned to their village, their spirits lifted by the knowledge that they had vanquished the darkness that had plagued them for so long. The townsfolk greeted them with cheers and applause, their faces alight with hope and gratitude.

John smiled as he looked out at the village he had sworn to protect. Though the scars of their ordeal would linger, he knew that they would rebuild, stronger than ever before.

And as he watched the sun set on the horizon, casting its golden light across the land, John knew that the darkness had been banished, and that light would

141

always prevail in the end.

Chapter 10: The Haunting Whispers

Section 1: Lingering Shadows

Despite the apparent victory over the darkness in the ruins, an eerie sense of unease settled over the village like a shroud. The air seemed heavier, laden with a palpable tension that refused to dissipate. Whispers of unseen specters and lingering shadows haunted the minds of the villagers, casting doubt on their newfound sense of security.

John, ever vigilant, sensed that their ordeal was far from over. He could feel the lingering presence of malevolent forces, their whispers echoing in the depths of his mind like a sinister melody. Determined to uncover the truth behind the lingering darkness, he gathered a group of brave volunteers to delve deeper into the mysteries that plagued

142

their village.

Section 2: The Withering Fields

Their investigation led them to the outskirts of the village, where the once lush fields now lay barren and desolate. The crops withered and died, their twisted forms a grim testament to the encroaching darkness that threatened to consume everything in its path.

As they ventured further into the fields, they encountered strange phenomena that defied explanation. Unearthly wails echoed through the air, sending shivers down their spines. Shadows danced on the horizon, their forms shifting and contorting with unnatural fluidity.

John's heart sank as he surveyed the devastation before him. It was clear that the darkness had not been vanquished— it had merely retreated, biding its time until it could strike once more.

143

Section 3: The Specter's Call

Suddenly, a piercing cry split the air, freezing John and his companions in their tracks. They turned as one, their eyes widening in horror as a figure emerged from the shadows. Its form was hazy and indistinct, its features obscured by a veil of darkness.

"Who dares to trespass in my domain?" the figure intoned, its voice a chilling whisper that sent shivers down their spines.

John stepped forward, his voice steady despite the tremble in his limbs. "We mean no harm," he said, his words ringing out with conviction. "We seek to understand the darkness that plagues our village, and to put an end to it once and for all."

The figure regarded him with a mix of amusement and contempt. "You think you can defeat me?" it said, its voice dripping with malice. "You are but ants

144

crawling in the shadows, powerless to stop the inevitable."

But John refused to be cowed by the specter's taunts. With a defiant glare, he raised his sword high, ready to face whatever horrors awaited them in the depths of the fields.

Section 4: The Haunted Grove

Their journey led them deeper into the heart of the fields, where a dense grove of gnarled trees loomed on the horizon. The air grew thick with an oppressive weight, and the trees seemed to leer down at them with twisted branches and grasping roots.

As they ventured further into the grove, they encountered strange apparitions that flitted through the shadows like wraiths. Their eyes gleamed with an otherworldly light, and their whispers filled the air with a cacophony of madness and despair.

145

John and his companions pressed on, their resolve unyielding in the face of the horrors that surrounded them. They knew that they were close to uncovering the truth behind the darkness that plagued their village, and they would not rest until they had banished it from their midst.

Section 5: The Guardian's Curse

At last, they reached the heart of the grove, where a towering figure stood silhouetted against the moonlit sky. Its form was twisted and contorted, its eyes burning with a malevolent light.

"We are the guardians of this land," the figure intoned, its voice echoing through the grove like a funeral dirge. "And we will not allow you to defile our sacred sanctuary."

John stepped forward, his sword raised high in defiance. "We seek only to rid our village of the darkness that plagues it," he said, his voice ringing out with

146

determination. "We mean no harm to you or your domain."

But the guardian would not be swayed. With a gesture of its hand, it unleashed a wave of dark energy, sending John and his companions tumbling backward.

Section 6: The Curse of the Guardian

As they struggled to regain their footing, the guardian advanced, its form wreathed in shadows. With each step, its presence seemed to grow stronger, its malevolent aura suffusing the grove with an oppressive darkness.

John knew that they were outmatched, their weapons powerless against the guardian's otherworldly strength. But he refused to surrender, his spirit unyielding in the face of adversity.

With a mighty roar, he charged forward, his sword flashing in the moonlight. But the guardian was ready, its form shifting and twisting to evade his blows.

147

As the battle raged on, John felt a creeping sense of dread wash over him. The guardian seemed invincible, its power beyond comprehension. And with each passing moment, the darkness seemed to close in around them, threatening to consume them all.

Section 7: The Guardian's Revelation

But just as all hope seemed lost, a voice echoed through the grove, cutting through the darkness like a ray of light. It was the voice of the guardian, its tone tinged with sadness and regret.

"We are not your enemy," the guardian said, its words a whisper on the wind. "We are but prisoners of the darkness that consumes us, cursed to wander these lands for eternity."

John's heart ached with sympathy as he looked upon the guardian's twisted form. He knew that they had been wrong to judge it so harshly, that it was not the enemy they had believed it to be.

148

"We seek to free you from your curse," John said, his voice filled with determination. "To banish the darkness that binds you and your brethren to this realm."

The guardian regarded him with a mix of surprise and gratitude. "You would do this for us?" it asked, its voice filled with disbelief.

John nodded solemnly. "We seek only to bring peace to our village," he said. "And if that means facing the darkness head-on, then so be it."

With a wave of its hand, the guardian released a burst of light that enveloped the grove, banishing the darkness and freeing the guardians from their cursed prison.

Section 8: The Return of Light

As the darkness receded, John and his companions emerged from the grove, their hearts lightened by their victory.

149

The fields began to flourish once more, their crops sprouting anew from the fertile soil.

The villagers greeted them with cheers and applause, their faces alight with hope and gratitude. John smiled as he looked out at the village he had sworn to protect. Though the scars of their ordeal would linger, he knew that they would rebuild, stronger than ever before.

And as he watched the sun rise on the horizon, casting its golden light across the land, John knew that the darkness had been banished once and for all, and that light would always prevail in the end.

Chapter 11: The Cursed Woods

Section 1: Whispering Shadows

Despite the recent victories against the darkness, a new sense of unease settled upon the village like a heavy fog.

150

Strange occurrences began to plague the outskirts of the settlement, rumors spreading of a malevolent force lurking within the nearby woods.

John, ever vigilant, could not ignore the whispers of fear that echoed through the village. Gathering a group of brave volunteers, he resolved to confront the darkness that threatened to engulf their home once more.

Section 2: The Forbidden Forest

Their journey led them deep into the heart of the forest, where ancient trees loomed overhead like silent sentinels. The air grew thick with an oppressive weight, and the shadows seemed to dance with a sinister life of their own.

As they ventured further into the forest, they encountered strange phenomena that defied explanation. Unearthly wails echoed through the trees, sending shivers down their spines. Eyes gleamed in the darkness, watching their every

151

move with a malevolent intent.

John's heart sank as he surveyed the twisted landscape before him. It was clear that they had entered a realm of darkness unlike anything they had encountered before, and he knew that they were in grave danger.

Section 3: The Haunted Clearing

Their journey led them to a clearing bathed in an eerie moonlight, where a sense of foreboding hung heavy in the air. Strange symbols adorned the trees, their meaning lost to the ages. A chill wind whispered through the undergrowth, carrying with it the faint scent of decay.

As they approached the center of the clearing, they encountered a figure cloaked in shadows. Its eyes gleamed with an otherworldly light, and its voice echoed through the night like a mournful lament.

152

"Who dares to disturb the peace of the forest?" the figure intoned, its voice filled with a sense of ancient sorrow.

John stepped forward, his voice steady despite the tremble in his limbs. "We seek only to understand the darkness that plagues our village," he said, his words ringing out with conviction. "We mean no harm to you or your domain."

But the figure would not be swayed. With a gesture of its hand, it unleashed a wave of dark energy, sending John and his companions tumbling backward.

Section 4: The Curse of the Forest

As they struggled to regain their footing, the figure advanced, its form wreathed in shadows. With each step, its presence seemed to grow stronger, its malevolent aura suffusing the clearing with an oppressive darkness.

John knew that they were outmatched, their weapons powerless against the

153

figure's otherworldly strength. But he refused to surrender, his spirit unyielding in the face of adversity.

With a mighty roar, he charged forward, his sword flashing in the moonlight. But the figure was ready, its form shifting and twisting to evade his blows.

As the battle raged on, John felt a creeping sense of dread wash over him. The figure seemed invincible, its power beyond comprehension.

And with each passing moment, the darkness seemed to close in around them, threatening to consume them all.

Section 5: The Guardian's Revelation

But just as all hope seemed lost, a voice echoed through the clearing, cutting through the darkness like a ray of light. It was the voice of the figure, its tone tinged with sadness and regret.

"We are not your enemy," the figure said, its words a whisper on the wind.

154

"We are but prisoners of the darkness that consumes us, cursed to wander these lands for eternity."

John's heart ached with sympathy as he looked upon the figure's twisted form. He knew that they had been wrong to judge it so harshly, that it was not the enemy they had believed it to be.

"We seek to free you from your curse," John said, his voice filled with determination. "To banish the darkness that binds you and your brethren to this realm."

The figure regarded him with a mix of surprise and gratitude. "You would do this for us?" it asked, its voice filled with disbelief.

John nodded solemnly. "We seek only to bring peace to our village," he said. "And if that means facing the darkness head-on, then so be it."

With a wave of its hand, the figure released a burst of light that enveloped

155

the clearing, banishing the darkness and freeing the guardians from their cursed prison.

Chapter 12: The Cursed Crypts

Section 1: Foreboding Silence

Despite the recent victories against the darkness, an ominous pall hung over the village like a shroud. Strange omens began to appear, unsettling the villagers and sowing seeds of fear and doubt. John, undeterred by the encroaching dread, resolved to uncover the source of the lingering malevolence.

Gathering a group of stalwart volunteers, he embarked on a perilous journey into the depths of the nearby crypts, where ancient secrets lay buried beneath layers of stone and shadow.

156

Section 2: Into the Abyss

The entrance to the crypts loomed before them, a gaping maw of darkness that seemed to swallow the feeble light that dared to penetrate its depths. As they ventured deeper into the earth, the air grew thick with a suffocating weight, and the darkness pressed in on them from all sides.

John led the way, his heart heavy with the weight of responsibility. He knew that they were treading on treacherous ground, where unseen dangers lurked in the shadows, waiting to ensnare the unwary.

But he refused to falter, his resolve unyielding in the face of adversity. With each step, he pushed forward, determined to uncover the truth hidden beneath the surface of the earth.

Section 3: Echoes of the Past

As they delved deeper into the crypts,

157

the air grew colder, and the darkness seemed to deepen. Strange whispers echoed through the corridors, their voices indistinct but filled with a sense of malevolence. Shadows danced on the walls, twisting and contorting into grotesque shapes that seemed to leer at them with malicious intent.

John and his companions pressed on, their spirits undaunted by the encroaching darkness. They knew that they were on the brink of discovering something terrible, something that threatened to tear their world apart.

But they would not be deterred. They had come too far to turn back now.

Section 4: The Chamber of Torment

At last, they reached the heart of the crypts, where a vast chamber stretched out before them. Ancient sarcophagi lined the walls, their stone lids adorned with intricate carvings depicting scenes of death and decay. A chill wind

158

whispered through the air, carrying with it the faint scent of decay and ancient malevolence.

In the center of the chamber stood a pedestal, upon which rested a small, glowing orb. The orb pulsed with a faint light, its surface swirling with shadows and whispers.

"This must be the source of the darkness," one of the volunteers said, his voice hushed with awe.

John approached the pedestal cautiously, his heart pounding with anticipation. He reached out to touch the orb, his fingers trembling with fear and uncertainty.

But before he could make contact, a deep, guttural growl reverberated through the chamber, freezing John and his companions in their tracks.

Section 5: The Guardian's Challenge

Out of the shadows emerged a towering figure, its form twisted and contorted

159

into a grotesque mockery of humanity. Its eyes burned with a malevolent fire, and its lips curled into a sinister grin.

"You dare to disturb the sanctity of this place?" the figure hissed, its voice echoing with the weight of centuries. "You trespass upon sacred ground, ignorant of the darkness that dwells within."

John squared his shoulders, his resolve unwavering despite the fear that gnawed at his insides. "We seek only to rid our village of the darkness that plagues it," he declared, his voice steady with determination. "We mean no harm to you or your domain."

The figure laughed, a sound that sent shivers down the spines of all who heard it. "You are but insects, scurrying in the shadows," it sneered. "You cannot hope to comprehend the true nature of the darkness that lurks within these crypts."

With a wave of its hand, the figure

160

unleashed a wave of dark energy, sending John and his companions sprawling to the ground. Shadows writhed and twisted around them, threatening to engulf them in their suffocating embrace.

But John refused to yield. With a fierce cry, he raised his sword high, ready to face whatever horrors awaited them in the depths of the crypts.

Section 6: The Abyssal Confrontation

As the battle raged on, John and his companions fought with a desperation born of necessity. They clashed with shadowy apparitions and twisted abominations, their weapons flashing in the dim light of the crypts.

But the darkness seemed endless, its depths unfathomable to mortal minds. With each passing moment, it seemed to grow stronger, its malevolent presence threatening to overwhelm them.

161

John gritted his teeth, his muscles straining with the effort of each blow. He knew that they were facing an enemy unlike any they had encountered before, and that their very souls were at stake.

But still, he fought on, driven by the desperate need to protect his village and his loved ones. He would not allow the darkness to consume them, not while he still drew breath.

Section 7: The Revelation of the Ancients

As the battle reached its crescendo, a voice echoed through the chamber, cutting through the darkness like a ray of light. It was the voice of the figure, its tone tinged with sorrow and regret.

"We are not your enemy," the figure said, its words a whisper on the wind. "We are but guardians of this realm, cursed to wander these crypts for all eternity."

162

John's heart ached with sympathy as he looked upon the figure's twisted form. He knew that they had been wrong to judge it so harshly, that it was not the enemy they had believed it to be.

"We seek to free you from your curse," John said, his voice filled with determination. "To banish the darkness that binds you and your brethren to this realm."

The figure regarded him with a mix of surprise and gratitude. "You would do this for us?" it asked, its voice filled with disbelief.

John nodded solemnly. "We seek only to bring peace to our village," he said. "And if that means facing the darkness head-on, then so be it."

With a wave of its hand, the figure released a burst of light that enveloped the chamber, banishing the darkness and freeing the guardians from their cursed prison.

163

Section 8: The Return of Light

As the darkness receded, John and his companions emerged from the crypts, their hearts lightened by their victory. The village greeted them with cheers and applause, their faces alight with hope and gratitude.

John smiled as he looked out at the village he had sworn to protect. Though the scars of their ordeal would linger, he knew that they would rebuild, stronger than ever before.

And as he watched the sun rise on the horizon, casting its golden light across the land, John knew that the darkness had been banished once and for all, and that light would always prevail in the end.

Chapter 13: The Return of the Devil

Section 1: Unsettling Calm

Despite the recent triumph over the

164

darkness in the crypts, an uneasy calm settled over the village. The air felt heavy, charged with a sense of foreboding that set the villagers on edge. They whispered among themselves, fearing that their victory was but a temporary reprieve from the malevolent forces that haunted their lives.

John, ever vigilant, sensed the lingering tension. He had learned to trust his instincts, and they told him that something dark and powerful still lurked in the shadows. Determined to protect his village, he gathered his closest allies to discuss the unsettling calm.

"We can't ignore the signs," John said, his voice grave. "There's something else out there, something worse than what we've faced before."

His companions nodded in agreement, their expressions grim. They knew that their battle was far from over.

165

Section 2: The Omen

As the villagers went about their daily routines, a series of strange and inexplicable events began to unfold. Animals went missing, their frantic cries echoing through the night. The once clear skies turned dark and stormy, casting an ominous shadow over the village. And then, one fateful evening, a blood-curdling scream pierced the air.

John and his companions rushed to the source of the scream, their hearts pounding with fear and anticipation. They found a young woman, her face pale and eyes wide with terror, standing at the edge of the forest.

"It's back," she whispered, her voice trembling. "The Devil... it's back."

A chill ran down John's spine as he looked into the depths of the forest. He knew that they were dealing with something far more sinister than they had ever encountered before.

166

Section 3: The Hunt Begins

Determined to confront the threat head-on, John and his companions prepared for a perilous journey into the heart of the forest. They armed themselves with weapons and provisions, knowing that they would need all the strength and courage they could muster.

The forest was a place of darkness and dread, its twisted trees and overgrown underbrush casting eerie shadows in the dim light. As they ventured deeper, the air grew colder, and the silence was broken only by the rustling of leaves and the distant howl of a wolf.

John led the way, his senses alert to every sound and movement. He knew that they were being watched, and he could feel the malevolent presence growing stronger with each step they took.

167

Section 4: The Abandoned Cabin

After hours of trekking through the dense forest, they stumbled upon an old, abandoned cabin. Its wooden walls were weathered and covered in moss, and the windows were shattered, giving it an eerie, haunted appearance.

"This place gives me the creeps," one of John's companions muttered, his voice barely above a whisper.

John nodded, his eyes scanning the area for any signs of danger. "Stay alert," he warned. "We don't know what we're dealing with yet."

As they cautiously approached the cabin, they noticed strange symbols carved into the door and walls. The symbols were unlike anything they had seen before, their meaning shrouded in mystery.

Pushing the door open, they entered the cabin, their weapons at the ready. Inside, they found remnants of a long-forgotten past—old furniture, dusty books, and the

168

remains of what appeared to be a ritualistic altar.

"What is this place?" another companion asked, his voice filled with unease.

John's eyes were drawn to a large, leather-bound book on the altar. He carefully opened it, revealing pages filled with cryptic writings and drawings of grotesque creatures.

"It's a journal," he said, his voice hushed. "A record of someone who lived here... someone who knew about the darkness in these woods."

Section 5: The Journal

As John read through the journal, a chilling story began to unfold. The journal belonged to a man named Ezekiel, who had once lived in the cabin and dedicated his life to studying the dark forces that inhabited the forest.

Ezekiel's writings spoke of a creature known as the Jersey Devil, a monstrous

169

being born of a curse and bound to the forest. He described its horrifying appearance—bat-like wings, a horse's head, and glowing red eyes that burned with a malevolent fire.

"The Jersey Devil is no mere legend," Ezekiel wrote. "It is a creature of pure evil, a harbinger of death and destruction. It feeds on fear and despair, and it will stop at nothing to claim its victims."

John's heart sank as he realized the gravity of their situation. The Jersey Devil was real, and it was hunting them.

Section 6: The First Attack

As they continued to read through the journal, a sudden noise outside the cabin made them freeze in their tracks. The sound of heavy footsteps and the rustling of leaves grew louder, and an overwhelming sense of dread filled the air.

170

"Prepare yourselves," John said, his voice steady but filled with urgency.

The door to the cabin burst open, and the Jersey Devil emerged from the shadows, its terrifying form illuminated by the moonlight. Its eyes glowed with a malevolent fire, and its mouth opened in a chilling roar.

John and his companions fought valiantly, their weapons clashing against the creature's hide. But the Jersey Devil was unlike any foe they had faced before —its strength was immense, and its movements were swift and deadly.

One by one, John's companions fell, their screams echoing through the night. John fought with all his might, but he knew that they were outmatched.

With a final, desperate cry, he plunged his sword into the creature's side, and the Jersey Devil let out a deafening roar of pain. But instead of retreating, it lashed out with renewed fury, sending

171

John crashing to the ground.

Section 7: The Aftermath

When John awoke, he found himself alone in the cabin, his body bruised and battered. The Jersey Devil was gone, leaving behind a trail of destruction and death.

With a heavy heart, he gathered the bodies of his fallen companions and carried them back to the village. The villagers watched in silence as he returned, their faces filled with grief and fear.

"We've lost too many," John said, his voice breaking. "But we can't give up. We have to find a way to stop this creature once and for all."

The village elders convened a council, and John shared what he had learned from Ezekiel's journal. They discussed possible strategies and sought the wisdom of ancient texts, hoping to find a

172

way to defeat the Jersey Devil.

Section 8: The Ritual

As they delved deeper into their research, they discovered an ancient ritual that could potentially banish the Jersey Devil from their world. The ritual required a rare and powerful artifact, known as the Eye of Shadows, which was said to be hidden deep within the forest.

John and a select group of volunteers prepared for their final journey. They knew that this would be their last chance to rid their village of the Jersey Devil, and they steeled themselves for the dangerous path ahead.

With the knowledge of the ritual and the determination to save their village, they set out into the forest once more, ready to face whatever horrors awaited them.

173

Section 9: The Eye of Shadows

Their journey led them to a hidden cave, its entrance concealed by overgrown vines and ancient stone. Inside, they found a series of treacherous passages and traps, designed to protect the Eye of Shadows from those who would misuse its power.

With careful precision, they navigated the cave's dangers, their hearts pounding with each step. At last, they reached a chamber bathed in an eerie light, where the Eye of Shadows rested upon a pedestal.

The artifact was a large, crystalline orb, its surface swirling with dark energy. As John approached it, he felt a surge of power, and he knew that this was the key to their salvation.

Carefully, he retrieved the Eye of Shadows, and they made their way back to the village, their spirits bolstered by the hope of victory.

174

Section 10: The Final Battle

With the Eye of Shadows in their possession, they prepared for the final battle against the Jersey Devil. The villagers gathered in the town square, their faces filled with determination and resolve.

As night fell, the air grew thick with tension, and a sense of impending doom settled over the village. They knew that the Jersey Devil would come for them, and they were ready.

The creature emerged from the shadows, its eyes burning with hatred and fury. It let out a chilling roar, and the villagers stood their ground, ready to face their fears.

John held the Eye of Shadows aloft, its dark energy pulsing with power. He began to recite the ancient incantation, his voice steady and strong.

The Jersey Devil lunged at them, its claws outstretched, but a barrier of light

175

surrounded the villagers, repelling the creature's attack. As John continued the ritual, the light grew brighter, and the Jersey Devil let out a howl of pain.

With a final, desperate effort, John completed the incantation, and the Eye of Shadows released a burst of energy that engulfed the Jersey Devil. The creature writhed in agony, its form disintegrating into shadows and smoke.

The villagers watched in awe as the Jersey Devil was banished, its malevolent presence eradicated from their world. A sense of peace and relief washed over them, and they knew that they had triumphed.

Section 11: A New Dawn

As the first light of dawn broke over the horizon, the villagers gathered to celebrate their victory. They mourned the loss of those who had fallen, but they knew that their sacrifice had not been in vain.

176

John stood at the edge of the forest, his heart filled with a mix of sorrow and hope. He knew that the darkness would always be a part of their world, but he also knew that they had the strength to face it.

With the Jersey Devil defeated and the Eye of Shadows safely hidden away, the village could finally begin to heal. They would rebuild, stronger and more united than ever before.

And as they watched the sun rise, casting its golden light across the land, they knew that they had emerged from the darkness, victorious and unbroken.

Chapter 14: Shadows of the Past

Section 1: Echoes of the Fallen

The village began its slow recovery from the horrors of the past. Life resumed its rhythm, yet an undercurrent of unease remained. The scars of their battles, both

177

physical and emotional, were still fresh, and the memory of the Jersey Devil's terror was hard to shake.

John found himself haunted by the faces of those who had perished. Their sacrifices weighed heavily on his conscience, and he often wandered to the forest's edge, contemplating the cost of their victory. The village elders, sensing his turmoil, urged him to take a break and allow himself time to heal.

One morning, while visiting the graves of his fallen comrades, John noticed something peculiar. The ground near the forest's edge was disturbed, as if something—or someone—had recently been there. An uneasy feeling settled in his gut, and he knew he needed to investigate.

Section 2: The Stranger

Word spread quickly that a stranger had been seen near the village. Descriptions were vague—a tall figure, cloaked in

178

shadow, moving silently through the forest. Fear rippled through the villagers, and they looked to John for guidance.

John gathered a small group of trusted allies and set out to find the stranger. The forest, still eerie in its silence, seemed to hold its breath as they moved deeper into its heart. Every rustle of leaves and crack of twigs set them on edge, but they pressed on, determined to uncover the truth.

After hours of searching, they came upon a small clearing. Standing in the center was the stranger—a hooded figure who seemed to blend with the shadows. John approached cautiously, his hand on the hilt of his sword.

"Who are you?" he demanded, his voice firm.

The stranger slowly lowered their hood, revealing a face etched with lines of age and sorrow. "My name is Elara," she said, her voice a soft whisper. "I have

179

come to warn you." **Section 3: A Dire Warning**

Elara's eyes, filled with a haunting wisdom, met John's. "The Jersey Devil was but a harbinger," she said. "A herald of something far more ancient and powerful."

John's heart sank. "What do you mean?" he asked, his voice barely above a whisper.

Elara explained that the Jersey Devil's presence had been a precursor to the awakening of a far greater evil—an entity known as the Shadow King. This ancient being, she revealed, had been imprisoned for centuries, its power sealed away by the same magic that had created the Eye of Shadows.

"But the battle against the Jersey Devil weakened the seal," Elara continued. "The Shadow King stirs, and if he awakens, he will bring ruin to our

180

world."

John felt a chill run down his spine. The Shadow King was a name whispered only in the darkest of legends, a being of unimaginable power and malevolence. He knew they had to act quickly to prevent this catastrophe.

Section 4: Seeking Guidance

John and his companions returned to the village with Elara, her warning weighing heavily on their minds. The elders convened a council, and Elara recounted her tale to them, leaving no detail spared.

The elders debated long into the night, their faces etched with worry. They knew that the Shadow King's awakening would spell doom for them all, and they needed a plan to stop it.

"We must find the original seal," Elara said. "The one created by the ancient mages who imprisoned the Shadow

181

King. Only by restoring it can we hope to keep him contained."

The village elders agreed, and preparations were made for a new expedition. John, ever the leader, volunteered to lead the quest. His companions, loyal and brave, stood by his side, ready to face whatever dangers lay ahead.

Section 5: The Journey Begins

The next morning, John and his team set out on their journey. The path before them was fraught with peril, and they knew that they might not return. But the fate of their village, and perhaps the world, depended on their success.

Elara guided them through the forest, her knowledge of the ancient ways proving invaluable. They traveled for days, encountering treacherous terrain and hostile creatures. Each obstacle they faced tested their resolve, but they pressed on, driven by the gravity of their

182

mission.

As they ventured deeper into the wilderness, the air grew colder, and a sense of foreboding settled over them. They knew they were approaching the source of the Shadow King's power, and their hearts pounded with a mix of fear and determination.

Section 6: The Forgotten Temple

At last, they arrived at their destination —a forgotten temple, hidden deep within the forest. The temple, shrouded in shadows, emanated a palpable sense of ancient power. Its walls were covered in cryptic symbols, and the air was thick with the scent of decay.

John and his companions entered the temple, their footsteps echoing in the silence. As they ventured deeper, they encountered a series of intricate puzzles and traps, designed to deter intruders. With Elara's guidance, they navigated these challenges, their progress slow but

183

steady.

In the heart of the temple, they found what they were looking for—a massive stone door, covered in ancient runes. Elara approached the door, her hands trembling as she traced the symbols with her fingers.

"This is it," she said, her voice filled with awe. "The seal of the Shadow King."

Section 7: The Seal

John stepped forward, his heart pounding. "How do we restore the seal?" he asked.

Elara took a deep breath. "We need to perform a ritual," she explained. "A ritual that requires the Eye of Shadows and the blood of a willing sacrifice."

John's blood ran cold. "A sacrifice?" he repeated, his voice trembling.

Elara nodded solemnly. "The magic that binds the Shadow King is ancient and

184

powerful. It demands a great price."

John looked at his companions, their faces filled with a mix of fear and determination. He knew what he had to do. "I'll do it," he said, his voice steady. "I'll be the sacrifice."

His companions protested, but John was resolute. He had led them this far, and he would see their mission through to the end.

Section 8: The Ritual

With heavy hearts, they began the ritual. Elara recited the incantation, her voice echoing through the temple. The Eye of Shadows pulsed with dark energy, its power resonating with the ancient runes on the door.

John stood in the center of the chamber, his eyes closed, ready to face his fate. As the ritual reached its climax, Elara drew a ceremonial dagger and approached him.

185

"Are you sure about this?" she asked, her voice filled with sorrow.

John nodded. "It's the only way."

With a swift, precise motion, Elara made the cut. John's blood flowed onto the Eye of Shadows, and a blinding light filled the chamber. The runes on the door glowed with an intense, otherworldly light, and the air crackled with energy.

Section 9: The Shadow King's Rage

As the light faded, a deafening roar echoed through the temple. The Shadow King, sensing the restoration of the seal, lashed out with his dark power. The ground trembled, and shadows writhed and twisted around them.

John, weakened by the ritual, struggled to stay on his feet. But he knew that they had succeeded—the seal was restored, and the Shadow King was once again imprisoned.

186

"Hold on, John!" his companions shouted, rushing to his side.

With their help, John managed to stand. He looked at the stone door, now glowing with a faint, reassuring light. The Shadow King was contained, and their world was safe—for now.

Section 10: The Return Home

With the Shadow King sealed away, John and his companions began their journey back to the village. The path was long and arduous, but their spirits were lifted by the knowledge that they had averted a great catastrophe.

When they finally returned, the villagers greeted them with tears of joy and relief. They had saved their village from the darkness once again, and their bravery would be remembered for generations to come.

John, though weakened by his ordeal, felt a sense of peace. He knew that their

187

battle was far from over, but he also knew that they had the strength to face whatever challenges lay ahead.

As the village celebrated their victory, John stood at the edge of the forest, watching the sun set on a new day. The shadows still lingered, but he knew that they would always find a way to banish the darkness.

And as long as they stood together, united in their resolve, they would overcome any obstacle. For in the heart of every shadow, there was a glimmer of light, and that light would always prevail.

Chapter 15: The Whispering Winds

Section 1: A New Threat

The village, still reeling from their recent triumph, basked in a fragile peace. Yet, beneath the surface, a new threat began to stir. The winds carried

188

whispers—faint and eerie—across the Pine Barrens, hinting at an approaching darkness that even the villagers' recent victory could not stave off.

One evening, as the sun dipped below the horizon, John sat by the hearth in his home, trying to rest. His body was still recovering from the ritual, and every movement sent sharp pains through his veins. Despite his exhaustion, sleep eluded him. The whispers on the wind troubled him deeply, gnawing at his subconscious.

As the night deepened, the winds outside grew stronger, rattling the shutters and doors. John's senses were on high alert, a nagging feeling of dread creeping into his bones. He knew better than to ignore such omens.

Section 2: A Mysterious Message

At dawn, John gathered the village elders and his trusted companions to discuss the unsettling events. As they

189

convened, an urgent knock echoed through the hall. A young boy, breathless and wide-eyed, stood at the door, clutching a crumpled piece of parchment.

"This was left at the edge of the forest," the boy stammered, handing the note to John.

John unrolled the parchment, revealing an ancient script he couldn't decipher. He handed it to Elara, who had remained in the village to aid them with her knowledge of the arcane. Her eyes widened as she read the message.

"It's a warning," she said, her voice trembling. "A call for help from a nearby village. They are facing something they call the Wind Walkers—spirits that control the winds and bring death in their wake."

The room fell silent. John felt a surge of determination. Despite their recent ordeal, he knew they couldn't ignore the

190

plight of their neighbors. **Section 3: Gathering the Brave**

John and his companions prepared for the journey. Though still weary, their resolve was unshakable. They armed themselves with weapons and protective charms, each step filled with a sense of foreboding.

As they ventured out, the villagers watched with anxious eyes, hoping their protectors would return unscathed. The path to the neighboring village was fraught with danger, the winds howling as if warning them to turn back.

The forest grew darker and more oppressive with each step. The once familiar trees seemed to twist and contort, casting eerie shadows that danced in the wind. The whispers grew louder, carrying faint cries and ghostly murmurs.

191

Section 4: The Haunted Village

They arrived at the neighboring village to find it in shambles. Homes were destroyed, and the air was thick with fear. The few survivors huddled together, their faces etched with despair. The winds here were even stronger, swirling with a malevolent energy that seemed almost tangible.

An elder of the village approached John, her eyes hollow and filled with tears. "Thank you for coming," she said, her voice barely audible above the wind. "The Wind Walkers have decimated our village. We are all that's left."

John reassured her, though his heart was heavy with the enormity of the task ahead. "We'll do everything we can to help," he promised.

Section 5: Encountering the Wind Walkers

That night, John and his companions set

192

up a watch around the village. The winds grew fiercer, and the whispers turned into wails. Suddenly, shadows began to coalesce in the air, forming ghostly figures with eyes like dark pits and mouths that seemed to suck in the very light around them.

The Wind Walkers had arrived.

John and his companions fought valiantly, but their weapons seemed to have little effect on these ethereal beings. The Wind Walkers moved with the speed of the wind, striking with deadly precision. The villagers joined the battle, armed with makeshift weapons and sheer desperation.

Elara, sensing that conventional means were useless, began to chant an incantation. Her voice rose above the chaos, a beacon of hope in the storm. The Wind Walkers recoiled at the sound, their forms flickering and wavering.

"Keep chanting!" John shouted,

193

realizing that Elara's magic was their only hope.

Section 6: The Heart of the Storm

Elara's incantation grew more powerful, but the Wind Walkers seemed to adapt, pressing their attack with renewed vigor. John knew they needed to find the source of the Wind Walkers' power to truly defeat them.

"Follow me!" he called to his companions, leading them towards the center of the storm. The winds whipped around them, threatening to tear them apart, but they pressed on, driven by a fierce determination.

At the heart of the storm, they found a large, ancient stone altar, covered in runes that pulsed with dark energy. The Wind Walkers seemed to be drawn to it, their forms swirling around it like a vortex.

"This is it," Elara said, her voice barely

194

audible above the howling wind. "We need to destroy the altar."

Section 7: The Final Battle

With renewed purpose, John and his companions attacked the altar. The Wind Walkers, sensing their intent, fought back with ferocity. Elara continued her incantation, directing her magic towards the altar.

The battle raged on, each moment more desperate than the last. John fought with every ounce of strength he had left, his body aching from the strain. His companions stood by his side, their courage unwavering despite the overwhelming odds.

Finally, with a deafening crack, the altar began to crumble. A blinding light erupted from its center, engulfing the Wind Walkers. Their wails filled the air as they were drawn into the light, their forms dissipating into nothingness.

195

As the last of the Wind Walkers vanished, the winds began to die down. The storm dissipated, leaving a calm, eerie silence in its wake.

Section 8: Rebuilding and Reflection

The villagers emerged from their shelters, their faces filled with cautious hope. They had survived the onslaught, thanks to the bravery and sacrifice of John and his companions.

John, exhausted but relieved, looked around at the devastated village. There was much work to be done, but for the first time in days, there was a sense of hope.

"We'll help you rebuild," he promised the elder. "Together, we can make this village strong again."

As they worked side by side, John couldn't help but reflect on the battles they had fought and the darkness they had faced. Each victory had come at a

196

great cost, but it had also brought them closer together, forging unbreakable bonds of friendship and trust.

Section 9: A Glimmer of Light

With the Wind Walkers defeated and the village beginning to recover, John and his companions prepared to return home. The journey back was filled with a sense of accomplishment and relief, though they knew that their fight against the darkness was far from over.

As they approached their village, the sun began to rise, casting a warm, golden light across the land. The shadows that had plagued them seemed to recede, replaced by a glimmer of hope and renewal.

John knew that there would always be new challenges to face, new threats to overcome. But with each victory, they grew stronger, more resilient. And as long as they stood together, they would continue to banish the darkness, one

197

battle at a time.

For in the heart of every shadow, there was a glimmer of light, and that light would always prevail.

Chapter 16: The Forsaken Grove

Section 1: A New Beginning

The village thrived in the aftermath of their victories, with a renewed sense of unity and purpose. John, now a revered leader, continued to guide his people with wisdom and courage. The scars of their past battles were healing, but a sense of vigilance remained, a constant reminder of the lurking dangers in the Pine Barrens.

One evening, as the village gathered to celebrate the harvest festival, a sudden chill swept through the air. The joyous laughter and music faltered as a dense fog rolled in, enveloping the village in an eerie silence. The atmosphere grew

198

heavy, and an uneasy feeling settled over the crowd.

John's instincts kicked in. He knew that such an unnatural phenomenon could only mean one thing: a new threat was approaching.

Section 2: The Stranger in the Fog

As the fog thickened, a figure emerged from the shadows. Clad in tattered robes, the stranger's face was obscured by a hood, and an air of malevolence seemed to surround him. The villagers watched in tense silence as he approached the center of the gathering.

John stepped forward, his hand resting on the hilt of his sword. "Who are you?" he demanded, his voice steady but laced with caution.

The stranger lifted his head, revealing eyes that glowed with an unnatural light. "I am Malachi," he said, his voice a raspy whisper. "I bring a warning."

199

The villagers exchanged nervous glances, the tension palpable. John remained composed, though his mind raced with questions. "What is your warning?" he asked.

Malachi's eyes bore into John's. "The Forsaken Grove has awakened," he said. "A place of ancient evil, long forgotten. It is drawing power from the land, and if left unchecked, it will consume everything in its path."

Section 3: The Legend of the Forsaken Grove

Elara, who had been listening intently, stepped forward. "The Forsaken Grove is a place of legend," she said, her voice trembling. "A cursed forest where no light can penetrate, and where the spirits of the damned are said to dwell."

Malachi nodded. "The grove was sealed by powerful magic centuries ago, but the seal is weakening. The darkness within is growing stronger, feeding on the fear

200

and despair of the living."

John felt a chill run down his spine. The battles they had faced seemed like child's play compared to the threat Malachi described. "What must we do?" he asked, his voice resolute.

Malachi's gaze shifted to Elara. "The seal can be strengthened, but it requires a rare and powerful artifact: the Heart of Shadows. It lies at the center of the grove, guarded by the spirits that dwell there."

Section 4: Preparing for the Journey

The village elders convened an emergency council, and it was decided that a small group would venture into the Forsaken Grove to retrieve the Heart of Shadows. John, Elara, and a few of their most trusted companions volunteered for the perilous mission.

As they prepared for the journey, Malachi provided them with what little

201

knowledge he had about the grove. "The path is treacherous, and the spirits will do everything in their power to stop you," he warned. "But remember, the Heart of Shadows is your only hope. Without it, the grove's darkness will spread, engulfing your village and beyond."

With heavy hearts and steely determination, John and his team set out towards the Forsaken Grove. The villagers watched them go, their prayers and hopes following the brave souls who had once again taken on the mantle of protectors.

Section 5: Into the Darkness

The journey to the Forsaken Grove was arduous. The air grew colder, and the landscape became more desolate with each step. The trees twisted and gnarled, their branches reaching out like skeletal fingers. The fog thickened, and a sense of foreboding settled over the group.

202

As they entered the grove, an oppressive silence enveloped them. The air was heavy with the stench of decay, and the ground was littered with the bones of those who had ventured too far. Shadows flitted at the edge of their vision, and ghostly whispers filled the air.

Elara led the way, her knowledge of ancient magic guiding them through the labyrinthine forest. They moved cautiously, aware that danger lurked in every shadow.

Section 6: The First Encounter

As they ventured deeper into the grove, the whispers grew louder, more insistent. The temperature dropped, and the darkness seemed to close in around them. Suddenly, a wail pierced the silence, and ghostly figures emerged from the shadows.

The spirits of the damned, their faces twisted with agony and rage, attacked

203

with a ferocity that took the group by surprise. John and his companions fought valiantly, their weapons flashing in the dim light. Elara chanted spells of protection, her voice rising above the cacophony.

Despite their efforts, the spirits were relentless. They moved with unnatural speed, their touch draining the life force from those they encountered. John felt his strength waning, but he refused to give in. He knew that they had to reach the center of the grove, no matter the cost.

Section 7: The Heart of Shadows

After what felt like an eternity, they reached the heart of the Forsaken Grove. In the center of a clearing stood a large, ancient tree, its bark blackened and twisted. At its base, pulsating with a dark, otherworldly light, lay the Heart of Shadows.

The air around the heart was thick with

204

malevolent energy, and the spirits converged on them, their wails reaching a fever pitch. Elara stepped forward, her eyes glowing with determination.

"We need to perform the binding ritual," she shouted over the din. "John, keep them off me while I do this."

John nodded, rallying his companions for a final stand. They formed a protective circle around Elara, fighting off the spirits with every ounce of strength they had left. Elara began the ritual, her voice steady and powerful.

The spirits grew more frantic, their attacks more desperate. John felt his limbs growing heavy, his vision blurring. But he fought on, knowing that their only hope lay in Elara's success.

Section 8: The Binding Ritual

Elara's incantation reached its climax, and the Heart of Shadows began to glow brighter. The spirits wailed in agony,

205

their forms flickering and dissipating. The ground trembled, and the ancient tree shuddered.

With a final, deafening roar, the Heart of Shadows unleashed a wave of energy, banishing the spirits and sealing the grove once more. The oppressive darkness lifted, replaced by a strange, serene silence.

Elara collapsed to the ground, exhausted but triumphant. John and his companions, battered and bruised, gathered around her.

"It's done," she said, her voice barely above a whisper. "The grove is sealed."

Section 9: The Return

The journey back to the village was a blur of exhaustion and relief. They moved slowly, their bodies and spirits weary from the ordeal. When they finally emerged from the forest, the sight of their village brought tears to their

206

eyes.

The villagers greeted them with cheers and tears of joy. They had once again faced the darkness and emerged victorious, their bravery and determination a testament to their unbreakable spirit.

John, though exhausted, felt a profound sense of peace. They had faced an ancient evil and won, protecting their village from a fate worse than death. As he looked around at the faces of those he had fought to protect, he knew that their bond was stronger than ever.

Section 10: A New Dawn

As the sun rose, casting its golden light over the village, John stood at the edge of the forest, reflecting on their journey. The shadows had been banished, and a new dawn had begun.

He knew that there would always be challenges to face, but he also knew that

207

they would face them together. The Forsaken Grove was sealed, the darkness contained. And as long as they stood united, they would continue to protect their home, no matter what the future held.

For in the heart of every shadow, there was a glimmer of light, and that light would always prevail.

Chapter 17: The Raven's Warning
Section 1: An Ominous Discovery

The village settled into a period of uneasy peace following the sealing of the Forsaken Grove. Life returned to a semblance of normalcy, yet a lingering sense of vigilance remained. John and his companions continued their duties, ever watchful for signs of new threats.

One crisp morning, as the sun cast its first rays over the Pine Barrens, a raven appeared at the village outskirts. It was

208

an unusual bird, larger than any John had seen before, with feathers that shimmered with an unnatural sheen. It perched on a fence post, its eyes gleaming with an unsettling intelligence.

John approached cautiously, sensing that this was no ordinary bird. As he drew near, the raven cawed loudly, a harsh, echoing sound that sent chills down his spine. The bird tilted its head, as if scrutinizing him, then flapped its wings and took off into the forest, leaving behind a small, rolled-up parchment tied with a black ribbon.

Section 2: The Message

John picked up the parchment, feeling a sense of dread as he unrolled it. The script was elegant but filled with an eerie, otherworldly quality. Elara, drawn by the commotion, joined him and peered over his shoulder.

"The Raven's Warning," she whispered, recognizing the script. "It's an omen of

209

great importance in the arcane world. Let me read it."

The message read:

Beware the gathering storm. The darkness you have faced is but a shadow of what is to come. Seek the Raven's Eye to reveal the truth. Trust in the light, for only it can guide you through the encroaching night.

Elara's face paled as she finished reading. "The Raven's Eye is a powerful artifact, said to have the ability to reveal hidden truths and protect against malevolent forces. It's our only hope to understand and combat this new threat."

Section 3: The Search Begins

Determined to find the Raven's Eye, John gathered his most trusted companions. They set out on a new journey, venturing into the deeper, uncharted parts of the Pine Barrens where few dared to go. The forest was

210

dense and foreboding, filled with ancient trees that seemed to whisper secrets of the past.

The journey was arduous. They faced numerous obstacles: treacherous terrain, wild beasts, and the ever-present sense of being watched. The raven often appeared, guiding them with its eerie cries and leading them deeper into the wilderness.

Section 4: The Hidden Temple

After days of travel, the raven led them to an ancient temple, hidden deep within the forest. The structure was overgrown with vines and moss, its stone walls cracked and weathered by time. The entrance was guarded by two statues of ravens, their eyes seemingly alive with a dark glow.

"This must be it," Elara said, her voice filled with awe and trepidation. "The Temple of the Raven's Eye."

211

They cautiously entered the temple, the air inside cool and damp. The interior was filled with intricate carvings and symbols, all depicting ravens and scenes of prophecy. At the center of the main chamber stood an altar, upon which rested a large, black gemstone—the Raven's Eye.

Section 5: The Guardians Awaken

As they approached the altar, a sense of foreboding filled the air. Suddenly, the ground shook, and the statues at the entrance came to life, their stone forms cracking and shattering to reveal monstrous, raven-like creatures. The guardians screeched, their eyes glowing with malevolent energy.

John and his companions readied themselves for battle. The guardians attacked with swift, deadly precision, their claws and beaks striking with unnatural force. The group fought back fiercely, using all their skills and

212

abilities to fend off the monstrous ravens.

Elara, realizing the importance of securing the Raven's Eye, began to chant an incantation. Her voice rose above the chaos, channeling her magic into a protective barrier around the altar. The guardians screeched in fury, but the barrier held, giving John and the others the chance to strike.

Section 6: The Power of the Raven's Eye

With a final, coordinated effort, they defeated the guardians, their forms crumbling back into stone. Elara completed her incantation, and the barrier around the altar dissipated. John carefully approached the Raven's Eye, feeling its powerful energy pulsing through the air.

As he touched the gemstone, a surge of knowledge and under-standing flooded his mind. Visions of the past and future

213

flashed before his eyes, revealing the true nature of the threats they had faced and those yet to come. The Raven's Eye glowed brightly, illuminating the chamber with a pure, white light.

Elara stepped forward, her eyes wide with awe. "The Raven's Eye has revealed the truth. The darkness we face is part of an ancient prophecy, a cycle of evil that must be broken. We have the power to change our fate, but it will require great sacrifice and unwavering resolve."

Section 7: The Return Home

With the Raven's Eye in their possession, the group made their way back to the village. The journey was filled with a renewed sense of purpose and hope. The visions had shown John not only the dangers that lay ahead but also the strength and unity of their people.

As they neared the village, the raven

214

appeared one last time, its eyes gleaming with approval. It cawed loudly, then disappeared into the forest, leaving them to face the future with newfound determination.

The villagers greeted them with joy and relief, their faces lighting up at the sight of the Raven's Eye. John and Elara shared the knowledge they had gained, preparing everyone for the challenges to come.

Section 8: A New Dawn

The Raven's Warning had brought them together, uniting them in their quest for survival and peace. With the power of the Raven's Eye and the strength of their community, they stood ready to face whatever darkness lay ahead.

As the sun rose, casting its golden light over the village, John felt a renewed sense of hope. The shadows might be ever-present, but with the light of the Raven's Eye to guide them, they would

215

continue to fight, protect, and prevail.

For in the heart of every shadow, there was a glimmer of light, and that light would always prevail.

Chapter 18: The Encroaching Night

Section 1: Shadows on the Horizon

Despite the newfound sense of hope that had settled over the village, the atmosphere remained tense. The Raven's Eye had provided them with crucial knowledge, but the visions had also shown that the true battle was yet to come. The villagers prepared diligently, fortifying their homes and sharpening their weapons. Training sessions became a daily routine, with everyone from the youngest child to the oldest elder participating in some form of defense preparation.

John and Elara spent countless hours studying the Raven's Eye, trying to

216

decipher every fragment of knowledge it held. The more they learned, the more they realized the enormity of the task ahead. The Raven's Eye revealed glimpses of an ancient evil, a darkness that had been growing in strength and influence. The Pine Barrens had always been a place of mystery and danger, but now it seemed as though the very land was conspiring against them.

One evening, as the sun dipped below the horizon and the first stars began to twinkle in the sky, a chilling wind swept through the village. The wind carried a strange, whispering sound, almost like voices murmuring just beyond the edge of hearing. The villagers shivered, feeling an inexplicable sense of dread.

John stood at the edge of the village, staring into the darkening forest. He knew that something was coming, something that would test the limits of their strength and resolve.

217

Section 2: An Unwelcome Visitor

As night fell, the whispers grew louder, and the villagers gathered in the central square, seeking comfort in numbers.

Suddenly, a figure emerged from the shadows. It was Malachi, the mysterious stranger who had first warned them about the Forsaken Grove. He looked even more haggard and haunted than before, his eyes reflecting a deep sorrow.

"Malachi," John called out, stepping forward. "What brings you here?"

Malachi's voice was strained, barely above a whisper. "The darkness is spreading faster than we anticipated. The spirits of the Forsaken Grove were only the beginning. An ancient evil stirs, one that seeks to consume everything in its path."

The villagers murmured in fear, but John raised his hand to silence them. "What do you mean? What are we facing?"

Malachi took a deep breath, his gaze

218

meeting John's. "The visions you saw in the Raven's Eye—they speak of a being known as the Nightbringer, an entity of pure darkness that has been awakened. It feeds on fear and despair, growing stronger with each passing day. It's coming for the Pine Barrens, and it will stop at nothing to claim this land."

Section 3: Preparing for Battle

The news sent a ripple of fear through the village, but John and Elara remained resolute. They knew that they had to act quickly if they were to stand any chance against the Nightbringer. The villagers worked tirelessly, reinforcing their defenses and preparing for the impending battle.

John called a meeting with his most trusted companions, including Elara, Malachi, and the village elders. They gathered around a large table, the Raven's Eye placed at the center, its dark surface pulsing with a faint light.

219

"We need a plan," John said, his voice firm. "We know the Nightbringer is coming, but we don't know when or how. We need to be ready for anything."

Elara nodded, her face etched with determination. "The Raven's Eye has shown us that light is our greatest weapon against the Nightbringer. We need to harness every source of light we can find—torches, lanterns, magical wards. Anything that can keep the darkness at bay."

Malachi added, "The Nightbringer's power is immense, but it's not invincible. If we can weaken it, even for a moment, we might have a chance to strike a decisive blow. We need to find its weakness."

Section 4: The Gathering Storm

As the days passed, the villagers worked relentlessly, their fear transforming into a fierce determination. They built massive bonfires at the village's

220

perimeter, erected magical wards, and created weapons imbued with light. The children helped by gathering firewood and making charms, their innocent laughter a small but vital beacon of hope.

One night, as the preparations continued, John stood watch at the edge of the village. The forest was eerily silent, the usual sounds of nocturnal creatures absent. Suddenly, he heard a rustling in the under-brush. He drew his sword and stepped forward cautiously.

From the shadows, a figure stumbled into view. It was a woman, her clothes torn and muddy, her face pale and gaunt. She collapsed at John's feet, gasping for breath.

"Help... me..." she whispered, her voice barely audible.

John knelt beside her, calling for Elara. The woman's eyes were wide with terror, her body trembling

221

uncontrollably.

Elara arrived quickly, her hands glowing with healing light. "What happened?" she asked, gently touching the woman's forehead.

The woman's eyes flickered open, and she clutched John's arm with surprising strength. "The darkness... it's coming... it took my family... it's coming for us all..."

Section 5: The First Attack

The woman's warning proved to be true. That very night, the first wave of the Nightbringer's minions attacked. Shadows moved through the forest, their forms barely discernible in the dim light. The villagers fought bravely, using their weapons and the light from their bonfires to fend off the attackers.

John led the defense, his sword gleaming as he cut through the shadowy figures. Elara stood at the center of the

222

village, her magic weaving a protective barrier around the most vulnerable.

Despite their efforts, the shadows were relentless. They seemed to rise from the very ground, their numbers growing with each passing moment. The air was filled with the sounds of battle—swords clashing, arrows whistling through the air, and the cries of the wounded.

John felt a surge of anger and determination. He knew they couldn't hold out forever; they needed to find the source of the darkness and destroy it.

Section 6: A Desperate Plan

As dawn approached, the shadows began to retreat, melting back into the forest. The village was left battered and weary, but still standing. John and Elara gathered their companions, knowing that they needed a new strategy.

"We can't keep fighting like this," John said, his voice grim. "We need to take

223

the fight to the Nightbringer. We need to find its lair and destroy it before it can unleash its full power."

Elara nodded, her eyes filled with determination. "The Raven's Eye can guide us. It showed us glimpses of the Nightbringer's lair, hidden deep within the heart of the Pine Barrens. It's a dangerous journey, but it's our only hope."

Malachi stepped forward. "I will go with you. My knowledge of the dark arts might prove useful. Together, we can face the Nightbringer and end this nightmare once and for all."

John looked around at his companions, their faces etched with resolve. They had faced many trials together, and he knew they would face this one with the same courage and determination.

"We leave at first light," he said. "Prepare yourselves. This will be our greatest challenge yet."

224

Section 7: Into the Heart of Darkness

As the sun rose, casting its first light over the village, John, Elara, Malachi, and a select group of warriors set out towards the heart of the Pine Barrens. The air was thick with tension, the forest eerily silent as they made their way deeper into the wilderness.

The Raven's Eye guided them, its light growing brighter as they neared their destination. The journey was fraught with danger, as they encountered more of the Nightbringer's minions along the way. Each battle left them more weary, but their resolve remained unbroken.

Finally, after days of travel, they reached a clearing surrounded by ancient, twisted trees. In the center of the clearing stood a massive stone monolith, its surface covered in dark, pulsating runes. This was the Nightbringer's lair.

225

Section 8: The Final Confrontation

As they approached the monolith, the ground began to tremble, and the air grew thick with darkness. The Nightbringer emerged from the shadows, a towering figure of pure malevolence. Its eyes glowed with an unholy light, and its voice echoed through the clearing, filled with a terrible power.

"You dare to challenge me?" it hissed, its form shifting and writhing. "You are nothing but insects before my might."

John stepped forward, his sword raised. "We will not let you destroy our home. We will fight, and we will prevail."

The battle was fierce and brutal. The Nightbringer wielded dark magic, summoning shadows and blasts of energy to attack them. John and his companions fought with everything they had, using the light of the Raven's Eye to weaken the creature.

226

Elara chanted a powerful incantation, her magic enveloping the Nightbringer in a blinding light. Malachi used his knowledge of the dark arts to counter the creature's spells, creating openings for John and the others to strike.

Despite their efforts, the Nightbringer was incredibly powerful. It fought with a ferocity that seemed unstoppable, its dark energy consuming everything in its path. John felt his strength waning, but he refused to give up.

Section 9: A Sacrifice

As the battle raged on, it became clear that they could not defeat the Nightbringer through sheer force alone. Elara, sensing the desperation of the situation, made a fateful decision.

"John," she called out, her voice filled with resolve. "There is a way to defeat the Nightbringer, but it will require a great sacrifice."

227

John's heart sank as he saw the determination in her eyes. "What do you mean?"

Elara held up the Raven's Eye, its light glowing brightly. "The Raven's Eye can channel the purest light, but it needs a source of immense power. If I channel my life force into it, I can create a burst of light strong enough to destroy the Nightbringer."

John's eyes widened in horror. "No, Elara. There must be another way."

She shook her head, tears in her eyes. "This is the only way. I believe in you, John. You must finish this fight."

Before he could protest further, Elara began to chant, her voice rising in a powerful incantation. The Raven's Eye glowed brighter and brighter, its light filling the clearing. The Nightbringer screamed in rage, sensing the impending threat.

John fought with renewed fury,

228

protecting Elara as she completed the incantation. The light grew blinding, and with a final, heart-wrenching cry, Elara released her magic. A beam of pure, radiant light shot from the Raven's Eye, striking the Nightbringer and enveloping it in a searing brilliance.

The creature shrieked in agony, its form disintegrating under the onslaught of light. The darkness that had consumed the Pine Barrens began to recede, and the forest was bathed in a golden glow.

Section 10: The Aftermath

As the light faded, John collapsed to his knees, grief overwhelming him. Elara lay motionless on the ground, her face peaceful in death. The villagers who had accompanied them gathered around, their faces etched with sorrow and awe.

Malachi placed a hand on John's shoulder. "She saved us all, John. Her sacrifice will be remembered forever."

229

John nodded, tears streaming down his face. "We will honor her memory by rebuilding our village and ensuring that this darkness never returns."

With the Nightbringer defeated, the Pine Barrens began to heal. The villagers returned home, their hearts heavy with loss but filled with hope for the future. They erected a monument in the village square to honor Elara's sacrifice, a symbol of the light that had triumphed over the darkness.

John stood before the monument, his resolve stronger than ever. He knew that the battle against evil was never truly over, but he also knew that as long as they stood together, they could overcome any challenge.

As the sun set, casting its golden light over the village, John felt a renewed sense of purpose. The shadows might still lurk in the corners of the world, but with the light of the Raven's Eye to guide them, they would always find their

230

way through the encroaching night.

Chapter 19: Rebuilding and Reflection

Section 1: The Light After Darkness

The defeat of the Nightbringer brought a renewed sense of peace to the Pine Barrens, but it also left a void that was felt deeply by everyone in the village. Elara's sacrifice had saved them, but the cost was immeasurable. As the days turned into weeks, the villagers worked together to rebuild their homes and lives, always with the memory of Elara's bravery in their hearts.

John took on a new role as the leader of the village, guiding the reconstruction efforts with a steady hand. His grief for Elara was a constant companion, but he channeled it into a fierce determination to honor her memory. The villagers followed his example, each one

231

contributing in their own way to the restoration of their home.

Malachi stayed as well, his knowledge of the arcane arts invaluable in helping to strengthen the village's defenses and ensure that the darkness would never again take root in their land. His presence was a reminder of the broader world beyond the Pine Barrens, a world that still held many mysteries and dangers.

Section 2: New Beginnings

With the physical reconstruction well underway, John and Malachi turned their attention to the spiritual and emotional healing of the community. They organized gatherings where villagers could share their experiences and express their grief. These gatherings became a cornerstone of the village's recovery, allowing people to find solace and strength in each other's company.

Elara's monument became a place of

232

pilgrimage, a symbol of hope and resilience. Villagers left flowers, tokens of remembrance, and offerings of thanks at its base. The monument stood as a testament to the light that had prevailed over the encroaching night, a reminder that even in the darkest times, there is always hope.

The village also welcomed new faces. News of the Nightbringer's defeat spread, drawing people from neighboring regions who sought safety and a new beginning. These newcomers brought with them skills, knowledge, and a fresh perspective that enriched the community. The village grew, not just in numbers, but in spirit and unity.

Section 3: The Wisdom of the Raven's Eye

The Raven's Eye, still pulsing with a faint light, was placed in a sacred chamber within the village's central hall. John and Malachi continued to study it,

233

uncovering more of its secrets and using its wisdom to guide their decisions. The artifact had become a source of immense knowledge and power, its presence a constant reminder of the battle they had fought and the sacrifices they had made.

One evening, as John was examining the Raven's Eye, he was struck by a vision. He saw a figure cloaked in shadows, standing at the edge of a great chasm. The figure turned, revealing Elara's face, her eyes filled with a serene wisdom. She spoke, her voice echoing in his mind.

"John, the journey is not over. There are still many challenges ahead, but you have the strength and the heart to overcome them. Remember, the light within you is the greatest weapon against the darkness. Lead your people with courage and compassion, and you will find your way."

John woke from the vision with a renewed sense of purpose. He shared the

234

vision with Malachi and the village elders, and together they devised a plan to continue protecting and nurturing their home. They established a council to govern the village, ensuring that all voices were heard and that decisions were made with wisdom and foresight.

Section 4: The Path Forward

As the village flourished, John and Malachi began to explore the surrounding regions, seeking out other sources of darkness and threats that might endanger their home. They formed alliances with neighboring communities, sharing knowledge and resources to create a network of support and defense.

Their efforts bore fruit. The Pine Barrens became a beacon of hope and resilience, a place where people could find refuge and strength. The bonds between the villages grew stronger, and together they faced and overcame numerous

235

challenges.

John often thought of Elara, her spirit a guiding force in his life. He felt her presence in the quiet moments, in the laughter of children, and in the strength of his people. Her sacrifice had not only saved their village but had also inspired a new era of unity and hope.

Section 5: A Legacy of Light

Years passed, and the village continued to grow and thrive. The children who had once played in the shadows now trained as protectors of their home, learning the skills and knowledge passed down by John, Malachi, and the elders. The Raven's Eye remained a central part of their lives, its wisdom guiding them through every challenge.

John, now older and wiser, looked upon his village with pride. The legacy of Elara's sacrifice was evident in every smiling face, in every act of kindness, and in the unwavering strength of their

236

community. The darkness that had once threatened to consume them had been pushed back, replaced by a light that shone brightly.

One evening, as the sun set over the Pine Barrens, casting a golden glow over the village, John stood before Elara's monument. He placed a hand on the stone, feeling a deep sense of peace.

"We did it, Elara," he whispered. "We've built something beautiful, something that will endure. Your sacrifice will never be forgotten. Thank you for guiding us, for believing in us. We will continue to honor your memory, now and always."

As the stars began to twinkle in the sky, John felt a warmth in his heart. The journey had been long and arduous, but they had emerged stronger, united, and filled with hope. The light of the Raven's Eye, and the spirit of Elara, would continue to guide them through whatever lay ahead, ensuring that the

237

encroaching night would never again overshadow the light of their lives.

Chapter 20: The Final Darkness

Section 1: A Shroud of Peace

The village of Pine Barrens had become a beacon of hope and resilience. Its people thrived, and the darkness that once overshadowed their lives had been pushed back. John, now an elder, watched over his village with pride, knowing that Elara's sacrifice had led to a prosperous and peaceful future.

The Raven's Eye, though still a powerful artifact, had grown dormant, its light faint but constant. It remained a symbol of their victory and a source of guidance. John and the village council continued to consult it, but its visions had become less frequent, and its warnings less dire.

One evening, as the village prepared for their annual celebration in honor of

238

Elara's sacrifice, a strange unease settled over John. He couldn't shake the feeling that something was amiss, but he dismissed it as a remnant of the countless battles they had fought.

Section 2: The Eclipse

As night fell, the villagers gathered around a large bonfire, their laughter and songs filling the air. The children danced and played, their faces lit by the warm glow of the flames. It was a night of joy and remembrance, a night to honor the light that had saved them.

But as the celebration reached its peak, the sky began to darken unnaturally. The stars winked out one by one, and the moon, full and bright just moments before, was swallowed by an inky blackness. The villagers fell silent, their laughter dying in their throats as a deep, foreboding chill spread through the air.

John's heart raced as he looked up at the sky. This was no ordinary darkness; it

239

felt alive, malevolent. He turned to Malachi, who was already moving towards the Raven's Eye.

"We need to consult the Eye," John said, his voice tense. "Something is terribly wrong."

Section 3: A New Omen

The village council gathered in the central hall, their faces grim and determined. The Raven's Eye sat in its place, its surface dull and lifeless. Malachi placed his hands on the artifact, muttering an incantation. Slowly, the Raven's Eye began to glow, its light flickering like a dying flame.

A vision emerged, but it was unlike any they had seen before. The image was distorted, fragmented, showing glimpses of a vast, consuming darkness. Figures writhed within it, their forms twisted and unnatural. And at the center of the vision, a pair of glowing red eyes stared back at them, filled with an ancient,

240

unrelenting malice.

"It's not over," Malachi whispered, his voice shaking. "The Nightbringer was only a harbinger. There is something else, something even more powerful and ancient. It has been awakened."

John felt a cold dread settle over him. "We need to prepare the village. This darkness is unlike anything we've faced before."

Section 4: The Descent

As the villagers armed themselves and fortified their defenses, the darkness continued to spread. It enveloped the forest, turning familiar paths into shadowy mazes. Strange sounds echoed from the depths of the woods, and an oppressive silence fell over the village, broken only by the whispers of fear.

John and Malachi led a small group into the forest, following the faint light of the Raven's Eye. The journey was fraught

241

with peril, as shadowy figures darted through the trees, watching them with hungry eyes. The air grew colder, and a sense of dread deepened with every step.

They reached a clearing where the darkness seemed to pulse with a life of its own. The ground was scorched, and the trees twisted into grotesque shapes. At the center stood a massive, obsidian obelisk, covered in the same pulsating runes as the Nightbringer's monolith.

"This is it," Malachi said, his voice barely audible. "The source of the darkness."

Section 5: The Final Confrontation

As they approached the obelisk, the ground trembled, and a deep, rumbling growl echoed through the clearing. The air grew thick with shadows, and from the darkness emerged a figure. It was tall and cloaked in a tattered, black shroud, its red eyes burning with an other-worldly fire.

242

"You have come to your doom," it hissed, its voice echoing with a thousand tortured souls. "I am the Eternal Night, the end of all light."

John raised his sword, its blade glowing with the light of the Raven's Eye. "We will not let you destroy our home."

The battle was fierce and chaotic. The Eternal Night wielded dark magic that sapped their strength and filled their minds with terror. John and his companions fought valiantly, their weapons and the light of the Raven's Eye their only defense against the over-whelming darkness.

Malachi chanted powerful spells, his magic clashing with the Eternal Night's. The clearing became a battleground of light and shadow, each side struggling for dominance. But the Eternal Night was relentless, its power seeming to grow with each passing moment.

243

Section 6: A Desperate Gamble

Realizing they could not defeat the Eternal Night through sheer force, John made a desperate decision. "Malachi, we need to use the Raven's Eye. We need to channel all our power into it and strike at the heart of this darkness."

Malachi nodded, understanding the risk. "It may be our only chance."

They gathered around the Raven's Eye, their hands joined, and began to chant. The Eye glowed brighter and brighter, its light pushing back the shadows. The Eternal Night roared in fury, sensing the imminent threat.

With a final, desperate cry, they released the energy of the Raven's Eye. A beam of pure, blinding light shot forth, striking the Eternal Night and the obelisk. The darkness screamed, writhing in agony as the light consumed it.

For a moment, it seemed they had

244

succeeded. The darkness began to dissipate, and the Eternal Night's form wavered. But then, with a final, terrible roar, the obelisk exploded, releasing a shockwave of darkness that engulfed the clearing.

Section 7: The Aftermath

When the dust settled, John and his companions lay on the ground, battered and exhausted. The clearing was silent, the obelisk reduced to rubble. The Eternal Night was gone, but its final act had left a mark. The darkness had not been fully vanquished; it lingered at the edges of their vision, a constant reminder of the threat that still loomed.

They returned to the village, their spirits heavy. The battle had been won, but the war was far from over. The Raven's Eye, now cracked and dim, was a testament to the price they had paid.

As they stood before Elara's monument, John felt a deep sense of unease. The

245

vision of her warning echoed in his mind, a chilling reminder that the darkness was never truly defeated.

"We will continue to fight," he vowed, his voice resolute. "We will protect our home, no matter the cost."

The village of Pine Barrens had faced many trials and had emerged stronger each time. But the final battle had revealed a deeper, more insidious threat. The darkness would always be a part of their world, lurking just beyond the light.

As the villagers gathered to honor their fallen and rebuild once more, a shadow passed over the moon, casting the village into a brief, unsettling twilight. The darkness might have been pushed back, but it had not been destroyed. It waited, biding its time, ready to return when they least expected it.

John looked out over his village, his heart heavy but determined. They had

246

faced the encroaching night and survived, but he knew that the final darkness was still out there, waiting. And when it returned, they would be ready, their light burning brighter than ever.

But in the back of his mind, a chilling thought lingered: would their light be enough next time? Only time would tell, and until then, they would live with the ever-present shadow of fear, knowing that the final darkness was never truly gone.

247